Christmas Wishes
and
New Year's Kisses

The characters in this book are fictitious. Any similarity to real persons, living or dead, places, or events is coincidental and not intended by author.

The Mistletoe Mistake
Copyright © 2020 by Scarlett Kol

A Christmas Mulligan
Copyright © 2020 by Stella Brecht

Snowmen and Shenanigans
Copyright © 2020 by Ivy Fernwood

That Big Romantic Moment
Copyright © 2020 by Celia Mulder

All rights reserved.

Cover Design by EVE Graphic Design LLC

No part of this book may be reproduced in any form or by any electronic or mechanical means, including information storage and retrieval systems, without written permission from the author, except for the use of brief quotations in a book review.

CHRISTMAS WISHES AND NEW
YEAR'S KISSES

The Mistletoe Mistake **by Scarlett Kol**

When Holly Brighton kisses a handsome stranger under the mistletoe, she never expected that he would turn out to be her new boss. Now with changes happening at her office she struggles to keep from losing her job, but with this new guy in town, she might lose her heart first.

A Christmas Mulligan **by Stella Brecht**

Ginny Wellner never expected a trip to a golf course to change her life. Greg Hix always expected it would change his. Neither of them expected each other. When fate places them in the same small mountain town at Christmas, they just might get the mulligan they both deserve.

Snowmen and Shenanigans **by Ivy Fernwood**

Emery's sole focus this Christmas is beating her nemesis at the annual Jack Frost Festival. After a run-in with Finn, the handsome carpenter, she's in danger of losing more than just the trophy.

That Big Romantic Moment **by Celia Mulder**
Mio's one wish has always been to get a big, romantic, midnight kiss on New Year's Eve. When his former best friend and unrequited crush Elliot comes back to town, Mio might just get his wish.

The Mistletoe Mistake

by

Scarlett Kol

CHAPTER 1

"To amazing friends and even better drinks."

I raised my shot glass and clinked it against Claire's matching one, already hoisted in the air. Bits of the sugar rim flaked off and drifted to the bar top like glittering flakes of snow.

"Here, here." Claire jerked her head back and downed the shooter with a cringe and a smile.

My stomach clenched. I'd never been able to handle shots. I'd had too many terrible nights that started with a few innocent drinks. But tonight would be different. Just one shooter. No more. Besides, after the last few days, I needed a little something to numb my brain. I licked the sweet sugared rim and took a deep breath. The liquor burned down my throat, but in a more pleasant minty way than the burn of straight tequila, or worse, whiskey. I wiped my mouth with the back of my hand as I forced myself to swallow.

Claire slammed her glass down on the bar. "Pretty good, huh? Another round?"

"Nope. I'm good." I put my glass beside hers and waved off Danny, the all-too-anxious bartender already waiting with a bottle of peppermint schnapps. "It tastes like I forgot to spit out my mouthwash."

"It's called Candy Cane Storm, what did you expect?"

"Of course it is." I swiveled on my stool and rested my back against the bar. Just another reminder of Christmas and how fast it kept creeping up, no matter how much I tried to deny it. I couldn't handle it this year. Everything was just too festive for my sour mood and nothing I did seemed to get me in the spirit. Why couldn't everyone skip it for one year?

I sighed at the lazy swoops of red and green lights strung around the room. They twined around the jukebox on the far wall as a melancholy version of "Have Yourself a Merry Little Christmas" drifted from its speakers. Bah humbug. I'd figured Danny's Tavern would be the safest place in Havenbrook to get away from all this obligatory celebrating, but for an Irish tavern it held no luck. Just happy smiles and happier couples shining under the tacky holiday lights.

"It will be okay. It was a lousy month for this to happen, but at least now you know. He could have strung you along until January, and then you would've wasted all that time on the slime ball." Claire passed me a red cocktail in a hurricane glass and nudged her shoulder into mine.

"Thanks." I nudged her back and yanked out the candy cane garnish, discretely sneaking it onto the bar behind me. "And at least I can return that camera I bought him. It cost a fortune."

"See, there is a bright side. Forget about Fletcher Hollingwood." She cast me a wary grin, then shifted on her barstool. "Besides, Holly Hollingwood completely sounds like a fake name. You dodged a bullet, my friend."

"Maybe." I laughed. Hearing her say it sounded odd now, but there had been so many times I'd dreamed about it being true. I'd pictured the white dress and the cake, and, until last week, I expected to see a ring under the tree this year. The way Fletch had been acting shifty around me lately. The calls from the jewelry store he tried to hide from me. Never once did I think it might be because he'd moved on with the girl who worked there. Dierdre. Ugh. Even the way it rolled off my tongue seemed wrong, dirty even. "But it's not just that. It's all this." I waved my arm in the air, trying not to upend my drink on my dress.

"Danny's. What's wrong with it? We come here all the time."

"No, it's the happy Christmas stuff. It's everywhere. I can't get away from it. Even at work, all I get are letters from people trying to make their Christmas romance come true. All those card companies and the movie industry have told everyone that you have to have the perfect Christmas. It's always 'Dear Holly, how can I make my next-door neighbor notice me' 'Dear Holly, I want to tell the woman on my bowling team that I love her during the holidays, what is the perfect present?' 'Dear Holly, how can I make sure I have the most magical holiday if my boyfriend doesn't celebrate Christmas?' It's exhausting."

Claire scanned me over as she sipped her drink. Her eyes narrowed, processing like a supercomputer. "Really? Because if I remember correctly, you told me you loved giving relationship advice. That it gave you purpose or some higher calling or whatever."

"I think I used to. But…" I tried to come up with a better excuse, but what was the point? Claire had stuck with me since high school and lying to her, let alone getting away with it, would be next to impossible. "How are people going to react when they find out I'm a fraud? If I can't keep a relationship together, how am I supposed to give them advice on what to do in their lives?"

She shook her head and laughed. "Are you kidding me? You're awesome at your job. Fletcher being a cheating loser isn't on you, honey. Besides, you've been doing this for over, what, three years now? People trust you, they aren't going to quit because of this."

I took a sip and squirmed on my stool, the cocktail pleasantly much fruiter than the awful shooter.

"That's not all, is it?" She leaned back against the bar, swirling her straw in her drink as she scrutinized my lousy posture.

I pushed my shoulders back and sat up. "What about your trip to Huatulco for New Year's? You and Austin must be getting pretty excited. Only a few more weeks, then nothing but beaches, sun—"

"Nice try, Holls. You've always sucked at deflection, so just spill it."

"Alright. I'm tired of being 'Ask Holly' all the time," I said, with a loud sigh. "When I started this job, Jenkins promised it would only be temporary until a reporting job opened up and then I could work on being a proper journalist. Build my portfolio and move on to something bigger. But there have been five people who've been promoted to reporter jobs and I never get my chance."

"Have you asked though?"

"Every time. Jenkins just tells me I'm so good at my job and if I could hang on for a little while longer they will find the right person to fill my column and any position I want is mine. He keeps telling me that the corporation who owns the paper doesn't want to mess with what's working."

"Then tell him. Tomorrow morning, march into the office of Mr. Peter Jenkins III and tell him you're done putting up with his corporate mandate." She shook a defiant fist in the air, the momentum nearly knocking her off her stool. She straightened herself. "And if he doesn't give you a timeline on a reporter job, you're quitting."

"Quitting?" I choked. I loved the paper. I didn't want to quit.

"Of course, what else do you have to lose? You said you wanted to move on to bigger and better things. Fletcher isn't keeping you in this town anymore. It's time to get what you want."

The seeds of regret washed away with Claire's encouragement. I'd come back to Havenbrook only to sit on the advice column for way too long. My college friends had bylines in major papers. They did the nightly news updates in towns much bigger than here. But I gave that all up so long ago, I couldn't possibly go back. Besides, I couldn't leave my home again. Could I?

"But what about you, Claire? I couldn't leave you."

"Of course, you could. We went to schools across the country and still found our way back to each other. Moving onward and upward is not going to change that. Besides, it would give me a place to go when my mother-in-law decides to come visit."

I slid from my stool and wrapped my arms around her. "You're the best, you know that?"

"Oh, I know." She patted me on the back, her soft auburn curls tickling my nose. "Just don't forget about me when you're super famous."

I laughed as the strains of Elvis' "Blue Christmas" whined through the air. "I don't think I'm quite done with Havenbrook yet, but I've had enough of this. How about some vintage Bon Jovi or something?"

"'Please Come Home for Christmas'?" She clamped her lips around her straw and winked.

Shaking my head, I turned away and shimmied through the bodies toward the far side of the bar. A typical Sunday night. Not enough time before the magic of the weekend ended to venture just over the border to a Kansas City pub, so Danny's packed up tight from dinner to closing time.

The air seemed heavier the farther I strayed from the safety of the bar into the crowd. Loud, sweaty patrons filled every available space and pulled extra chairs to overfilled tables making it nearly impossible to pass. I held my drink over my head, regretting that I hadn't left it with Claire, but still in the habit of carrying it from clubbing in college.

Finally, I reached the electronic jukebox. They replaced the classic one a few years ago, and a pang of nostalgia stung in my chest. Why did everything need to change? Couldn't people appreciate the comfort in the familiar?

I flipped through the menus, trying to find anything that wouldn't make me want to rip my ears off, but the jukebox had clearly been programmed to force Christmas cheer down everyone's throats, like it or not. Near the end I found a tolerable mid-90's throwback album, and clicked every track to keep the place holiday free until at least closing time, even though I'd already be long gone.

The guitar riff whined from the speakers and I inhaled deeply, my shoulders finally relaxing. I closed my eyes for a moment, letting the gritty rock music ease my mind. I whirled around.

Smack!

A wall of muscle slammed into me. My glass wedged between us as the colorful cocktail poured down the front of my dress before smashing into shards on the floor.

I jumped back from the mess and rammed my hip into the side of the jukebox. *Ow!* "What the hell?"

"I'm so, so sorry." Hands waved in front of me as I retreated from my assailant.

"Watch where you're going next time." I swiped the liquid from my outfit. The red coloring bled through the blue fabric and grew wider. *Great. My favorite dress, ruined.* Another thing I lost this month that I couldn't replace. Did the universe hate me that much?

"Of course, my apologies."

As I clenched my fists, I tried to swallow the dictionary of curse words forming in my mouth, but they came too fast. "Well, if you—"

I glanced up and locked eyes with the stranger. His sorrowful gaze pinned my insults to my tongue. Wide and bright, like old copper pennies worn over the years. A little damaged and dirty, but teeming with stories to tell.

"I really am sorry, miss. It's a little crowded in here and I…" He reached toward me but stopped before making contact. Instead, he slipped his hand into his pocket and pulled out a slim leather wallet with a faint monogram on the side. He slid a couple of hundred-dollar bills from inside and held them out in his long fingers. "Here, let me pay for the drink and the dress. I insist."

"Don't worry about it. It's just my luck, anyway." I shook my head, but he didn't waver. I could take it. After all, this was his fault. Besides, the money probably meant nothing to him. The way his navy suit jacket tapered on his broad shoulders screamed tailor made and, even though he'd tried to dress it down with jeans, they fit too perfect not to be high-end designer. He pulled the look off, but it tried way too hard for this town. I'd bet he wasn't from anywhere close to here and I'd likely never see him again. Except, it wouldn't be too bad if I did. I could get used to seeing that handsome face at the grocery store every once in a while.

"I feel terrible," he said, pushing the bills closer.

"Well, that's apology enough. If you'll excuse me, I need to take care of this mess."

He cast his stare to the floor, finally setting me free, as he slipped the bills back into his fancy wallet. I stuck close to the walls and slipped my way through the bar to the ladies' room at the back. After wadding up a handful of wet paper towels, I scrubbed at my skirt, but the stain didn't fade. Maybe I should go ask him for the money. I'd spent way too much on this dress the first time, and I was definitely in the mood to replace it with another for some retail therapy.

One of the bathroom stalls swung open and Nancy from the coffee shop near the park cast me a sweet smile. Her eyes caught on the stain and she cringed with pity, or maybe just embarrassment for me. I grinned back as I tried to keep tears from welling and watched until the door closed behind her. I collapsed against the dingy bathroom wall, the cold stone seeping through my thin disaster of a dress. A few wet lines tickled down my face. Maybe Claire was right. I should quit and start over somewhere else. Somewhere no one knew who I was. Maybe somewhere that didn't have Christmas.

My phone vibrated in my pocket. A few drops of red had splashed across the screen, but no major damage.

Claire: Where did you go? Are you okay?

Me: I'm fine. Just need a minute.

I wiped my face and held onto the porcelain sink for a couple seconds, letting my heart rate go back to normal. Glancing in the mirror, I tried to will away the lines starting to circle in my puffy eyes. Red swirling through green—even my own corneas had turned festive. Ugh. I forced a plastic smile. At least until I could get home and close the door on everyone else, then cry myself to sleep like I'd done all week. I'd hoped tonight would be the first good day in a while, but no.

As the door opened, the babble of the bar hit me in the gut. Enough for tonight. Time to go home. I slipped along the short hallway into the main room as a familiar bouncy head of chestnut waves sashayed past me. The synthetic scent of cheap perfume. The scent I remembered when I looked at engagement rings Fletcher would never buy me. Dierdre. Yes, definitely time to go.

I picked up my pace and glared back, checking that she didn't see me. She disappeared through the bathroom door and I exhaled again. Too close.

"Holly, I didn't know you would be here tonight."

The relief evaporated and my stomach twisted as a familiar deep voice cut through the din.

"Why would you, Fletcher? My schedule is no longer your concern."

I crossed my arms, bracing myself and putting as much distance between us as I could. He looked good. Too good. Ash blond hair stylishly slicked back, instead of flopping in his eyes. A new outfit that didn't look like he'd left it on the floor last night. Polished. Like he used to when we first got together. But it would fade, and maybe this time he'd be the one ending up with a broken heart.

"You don't need to be so rude. I understand you're mad, but—"

"But nothing. You're lucky I'm being this polite." I raised my voice. "You cheated on me. For months."

He slipped his hand over his coiffed hair and looked back over his shoulder. Only a few people seemed to hear, and he smiled back at them with a courteous wave. Coward.

"Calm down, alright. Can't we just be civil about this? It's a small town and we both have our reputations to uphold."

"What, like, first class asshole?"

I shifted right, but he stepped in front of me. I tried going left, but he blocked that way too.

"Holly." He hooked his fingers around my wrist. "Can I just talk to you?"

I yanked my arm away and held it to my chest as I scowled back at him. "No."

Over his shoulder, something red caught my eye. The handsome stranger stood swinging a holiday cocktail in the air trying to grab my attention. His stare narrowed on the back of Fletcher's head, then shot toward me. I looked away hoping to hide my shame.

A breeze whisked past, my hair blowing over my shoulder.

Dierdre slid beside Fletcher. She looked at me and her mouth fell open for a moment, before she quickly recovered. "Oh, hi. It's Hailee, right?"

"It's Holly," I grumbled. "And you know that. Everyone knows everyone around here."

"Oops, sorry." She giggled and settled closer to Fletcher, clasping her hand in his. The gaudy Christmas lights glinted off her ring finger. My stomach hollowed. A gut punch so forceful I struggled to stand. Fletcher had been ring shopping, just not for me. *Well played, Dierdre.*

The bar began to spin as this awful night kept getting worse. "I…"

"There you are, I started to think you weren't coming back." The navy suit jacket and jeans appeared by my side, handing me the cocktail. He turned toward Fletcher. "Ladies. Always keep you waiting, am I right? But this one is totally worth it."

The stranger nuzzled his nose in my hair as he stealthily slid his mouth near my ear. He whispered, "I can leave, but it looked like you might need a hand. Nod if you want me to stay."

Fletcher's clenched jaw cut sharp ridges in his cheeks as his glare swung from the stranger to me and back again.

Dierdre squirmed beside him and wrenched her hand out of his grip, flexing her suddenly scarlet fingers.

"Oh, you, always so sweet." I nodded and tapped my open palm on the stranger's taut chest. Clearly, he took care of himself. Nice. Very nice.

He tugged my arm and I stumbled closer into him. Fletcher's cheeks erupted, brighter than the artificially colored drink in my hand.

"I'm sorry, I don't believe we've met." The stranger stuck his hand out to Fletch. "I'm Ben."

He accepted the pleasantry, his arm pumping hard in some arrogant show of prowess, but Ben matched him shake for shake.

Fletcher's lips turned up into a sneer as something sinister flashed through his stare. "How long have you known Holly, exactly?"

"Well…" Ben gazed down at me. "Since…"

"Since college," I blurted. "Yeah, we knew each other in college and recently reconnected. Such great timing that we were both single again at the right time."

"Oh. That's convenient, since Holly's never mentioned you before," Fletcher said.

Ben's arm tensed around my back, but he regrouped and tilted forward toward Fletcher. "I doubt she would. I've always been crazy about her, but I didn't think she ever even noticed me back then. Whoever let her get away was an idiot, but their mistake was my good fortune."

Ben flashed Fletcher a refined smile. Perfect teeth peeked through his dark red lips. Why he defended me, who knew, but the pained look on Fletcher's face was worth more than the crisp bills in his wallet.

I took a sip of my drink to clear the lump growing in my throat and to, hopefully, get another hit of courage. "And just in time for the holidays too. It must be fate."

He turned his flawless smile toward me. "Absolutely. My Christmas Holly hanging out under the mistletoe."

I dropped my head back. The gaudy plastic green and white mistletoe hung above us in a nest of metallic silver garland.

Fletcher folded his arms as his smug, twisted smirk returned. "Sounds like we aren't talking about the same person. Holly isn't that kind of girl."

My blood boiled. His hurtful words, the alcohol, and the embarrassment blended in a dangerous combination. Without thinking, I raised up on my tiptoes and planted my lips on Ben's. His eyes widened and he froze under my touch.

Oh no. Oh no. What did I just do?

But he didn't pull away. His hand fell to the small of my back and tugged me closer as his lips moved against mine. Slow, but determined. Powerful. Fletcher wasn't wrong. I wasn't the kind of girl who made out in public, especially with mysterious strangers whose names I barely knew. But where had that gotten me? And now as Ben's arms encircled my waist, I couldn't come up with a reason I'd held back so long.

I slid my free hand to his cheek and he responded, taking more of my mouth as his slight patch of tasteful stubble scratched against my chin. The sweet sting of bourbon grazed the tip of my tongue as I drifted deeper into him. Away from this bar. Away from Fletcher.

Movement flashed beside us and I snapped back into the present. Dierdre spun around and disappeared into the crowd. Fletcher scowled, then tossed a hand in the air before chasing after her.

Ben's lips relaxed and he rested his forehead against mine. He chuckled, his warm breath stoking the fire smoldering in my chest. "Nice to meet you too, Holly."

CHAPTER 2

My hands slipped into Ben's silky chocolate locks and held tight to the back of his head as his kisses trailed down my neck. Tingles shot through my entire body and conjured thoughts I shouldn't have. I didn't even know him, but I didn't care. Lips, tongues, and teeth all whirled together in a tornado of sensation. So much better than Fletcher. So much better than any other guy I'd ever met. My hand met his face again, my palm burning hotter and hotter against his skin. The rest of my body blazed. I…

"Earth to Holly. Come in, Holly."

Claire's voice cut through the fog as her hand waved in front of my glazed stare.

"Wait, what?"

The harsh lights of Corner Brew flicked on and I slammed my paper coffee cup onto the wood-grained countertop. I blew against my palm, attempting to cool the growing patch of sizzling skin, scalded from my mocha latte.

Claire laughed and retrieved a cardboard jacket from the front counter, then slipped it over my cup. "That's why you need to start bringing your own mug. Way fewer injuries."

I rubbed my eyes and picked up the cup with my uninjured hand. "Yeah, right."

"Jeez. What's with you this morning? Do you seriously have a hang over? We only had a few drinks with that Ben guy, I didn't think you'd had that much."

"No." I scowled at her, but she simply rolled her eyes and poured a generous helping of milk into her green plaid tumbler. "I didn't sleep well."

"No kidding. You look like hell."

"Uh ... thanks?"

"You're welcome." She nodded and smoothed my hair over my ear, taming the stray strands that always shot straight up from my crown. "But seriously, this is supposed to be your big day. The day you stand up for what you deserve. I'd think you'd want to be on the top of your game."

I glanced at my reflection in the coffee shop window. She wasn't wrong. Bags drooped under my eyes and I hadn't even tried to cover them with makeup this morning. My eyeliner swooped in crooked lines and forget even trying lipstick today. I swept my caramel strands back and secured them with an elastic at the nape of my neck. Better, but not sophisticated like Claire. Her bright eyes, rosy cheeks, and sleek bun taunted me in the glass door as we pushed our way out into the street.

"Maybe I should wait to talk to Jenkins? I'm really not in the right state to do this now. I could always do it tomorrow."

Claire linked her arm with mine. "Oh no, I'm not letting you chicken out. Do you want to be a real reporter?"

"Of course, I do."

"Then get over yourself and ask for what you deserve.

Confidence is a very attractive quality, Holls. You'll be fine."

"Maybe I'm not that confident."

My feet nearly slipped out from under me as Claire crashed to a halt without letting go of my arm. "Are you kidding me? Where is the girl who was kissing hot strangers at the bar last night?"

My cheeks flamed. The fluffy snowflakes drifting through the sky landed and melted on my skin. "You mean the girl who kissed one hot stranger, chatted him up, then awkwardly left without her jacket or purse?"

"It wasn't that bad. Besides, I totally didn't mind walking the four blocks in the snow to your house to return your things when I have back-to back client meetings today." She grinned as her sarcasm hit its mark and stung between my eyes.

"I'm so sorry, Claire." I dropped my head on her shoulder. "I think I just got flustered. I don't know what it was about that guy, but I'm totally embarrassed."

She squeezed my arm and tugged me closer. "Like you already said, you have no idea who he is and you'll probably never see him again, so who cares? Besides, the look on Fletcher's face when he stormed out of there with Dierdre was one hundred and ten percent worth it."

"Really?" I perked up and pictured the delicious image in my head.

"Oh yeah. He's probably off licking his wounds somewhere right now."

"He totally deserves it," I said.

"Yep. He totally does. In fact, he deserves so much worse than that. If Austin ever—"

"Don't even say it. He would never. You guys are perfect for each other." I held my cup up in the air until Claire clinked her travel mug against it. "Besides, he knows he'd have to deal with me if he did and that wouldn't be pretty."

"Speaking of not pretty, we're finally going to do something about those awful honey oak kitchen cabinets over the holidays. Renovating the whole room actually. You should see my inspiration pictures." Claire held out her phone and clicked the power button on. "Shoot. It's later than I thought. I'll have to show you another time."

Claire tucked her phone back in her pocket and shuffled across the sidewalk toward the revolving door of the First Street Bank. "Now remember, eye contact, stick to the facts, and don't take no for an answer. Got it?"

"Yes, boss."

She winked and wagged her index finger at me. "And don't forget to text me when it's over. I want to hear all about your success."

"Bye, Claire."

She disappeared into the bank, off to save the world again, one checking account at a time. I let out a deep breath and watched the hazy steam circle around my head in the winter chill. I could do this. I'd asked Jenkins so many times before, but this one felt so final. The Havenbrook Herald meant everything to me. My life. If I couldn't make this work, I didn't have a clue what I'd do next. But it didn't matter, Jenkins was going to give me that position and I'd have a long, happy career here. I leaned against the building and took a sip of my latte as the rough stone bricks teased hair out of my haphazard ponytail. I closed my eyes and faced the sky, letting the snowflakes cool me down and, hopefully, calm my nerves. *That's it. I could do this.*

The image of Ben's delicious mouth on mine flashed through my memory. His hands on my skin. I snapped my eyes open again and pressed a finger to my lips. Like I could still feel him there. I groaned and took another sip of coffee. How was I going to focus enough to ask for a promotion when I couldn't get that kiss, or that guy, out of my head?

"Morning, Holly. How was your weekend?" Doris chirped when I walked in and it lifted the clouds over my tense mood a little. Twenty years as the receptionist at *The Herald* and never a complaint. Just a bright grin to greet people and a kind heart to back it up. She'd been the first person I met when I'd come here as a kid. And she'd sat with her encouraging smile as I pushed open that door, as a nervous rookie hoping for her hometown editor to give her a chance. Doris gave me the friendly push I needed to get through the interview that day. Maybe she'd be my good luck charm again?

"Uneventful." *If you didn't count last night.* "How are you doing?"

"Oh busy, busy as always. Getting gifts wrapped for the grandkids. I can't wait to see their darling little faces on Christmas morning." Her face beamed with pure delight, her short gray locks crowning her head like a halo. I almost felt bad about cringing when she mentioned Christmas, but it wasn't her fault I'd suddenly become a cynic.

"Sounds wonderful. Do you know if Jenkins, I mean Peter, is in the office yet?"

"Yes, he was in before I was this morning, but he left a note that he'd be in solid meetings until ten and not to disturb him." She adjusted her glasses on her nose and looked over a yellow post-it note with Jenkin's scrawl across the surface.

Strange. Peter Jenkins typically waltzed into the office right before the nine am pitch meeting without even a second to take off his coat. "Great thanks. Any chance you can squeeze me in at ten o'clock?"

She glanced at her computer screen and clicked around a few seconds. "You bet. All scheduled."

"Perfect. Thank you."

I pushed through the door into the office and settled into my typical dingy blue cubicle. Except today, a bushy strand of cheap plastic holly circled my space. Cute. Really. Whoever did this needed to be crossed off the nice list. I pulled it off the fabric walls and re-pinned it on the outside of my cube so I didn't have to look at it. Managing my own column meant that I typically didn't work in the office as long as I made it to the pitch meeting and met my deadlines, but it also meant the short lot on desk selection. Even Coby the intern's desk met the minimum requirements to be considered bigger than a closet.

After finishing the last of my latte, I fired up my laptop and sat back as the OS icons spun on the screen. I reached into the bottom drawer of my desk and pulled out a thick manila file folder. Some articles were from college, clipped from the campus paper. Others I'd written every time I thought I had a chance at a reporter spot. Every time I'd been let down. I flipped through a more recent one on the top about the union negotiations at the meat packing plant last fall. It was good. Tight prose. Good grammar. Eyewitness accounts. But it didn't matter. Jenkins wouldn't even look at them, he'd just sigh and run his wrinkled hand over his chin before he assured me that my day would come and I needed to be patient. But I couldn't wait any longer. Electricity sparked in my veins and prickled against my skin. Something had to change.

"Hey there, 'Ask Holly'."

I cringed at the nickname and spun around in my chair, as I closed the file folder, dropping in back into the bottom drawer.

"Morning, Jesse."

He leaned against the small entrance to my cube, the unsteady walls tilting and threatening to fall. He'd been here a few months less than me, moving from a stint in Chicago as a crime reporter, back to his hometown of Havenbrook and away from the buzz of the city. Also taking another reporter job I'd never get. But at least I couldn't argue with his credentials and he always went out of his way to be benevolent. Jealousy didn't stand a chance against his positive attitude.

"Have you heard that Jenkins is making a big announcement this morning?"

"No. I haven't heard anything. What's it about?"

Jesse shrugged, the kind lines around his eyes wrinkling. "Not a clue. My daughters did some baking this weekend, so I went by his house to drop off some cookies and his wife said he'd received a call from corporate on Friday night and spent the entire weekend in the office. I stopped by on Sunday to bring in a piece for the holiday issue and sure enough, the door of his office was closed but the lights were definitely on."

"Strange. Hopefully, it's nothing serious. Maybe he's retiring or something?" Which could be perfect. If I could convince him to put me in a reporting spot, the next editor would have to deal with that decision.

"Well, let's get going, I doubt we are going to want to miss this."

I snatched a notebook and pen from my bag, then raced down the hallway after Jesse. The board room had already started to fill, but Jenkins hadn't arrived yet. I took my usual spot at the far end of the table, next to the window, and positioned my notes in front of me. Then a lump of dread collapsed in my stomach.

"Shoot, Jesse. Save my seat, I forgot something at my desk."

As I rushed back through the office, I popped up on my tiptoes to see if Jenkins left yet, but his door remained closed. *Perfect.* I grabbed the folder from the drawer and quickly typed my password into my laptop. My latest article for my non-existent job appeared on the screen. I hit print. I couldn't risk going in with a dated piece. This one about the community center embezzling scandal would be sure to grab headlines. I sprinted to the printer on the far side of the room and stuffed the still-warm pages into my folder.

The board room door clicked closed across the office. Late. Not a good impression to make when you're about to ask for a promotion. I bolted past the cubicles and paused at the door to catch my breath. After swiping my hair back and straightening my skirt, I rapped my knuckles on the door and slowly crept in.

Jenkins stood at the end of the table and waved me in. "And this is our fantastic advice columnist, Holly Brighton of *Ask Holly*."

He rambled on about my accomplishments and my cheeks scorched. Normally, the attention would be enough to cause the blush, but I hadn't even heard Jenkins' words. Beside him, in an impeccable pinstripe suit and solid black tie, stood the stranger from the bar. His lucky penny eyes exploded as he caught my gaze.

"And Holly, please meet Benjamin Concorde from Concorde Publications Media. He's here to take *The Herald* digital."

CHAPTER 3

Wait, what? Digital? The *Havenbrook Herald* was an institution in this town. It predated the majority of print publications in the area. But the even bigger question? Out of the thousands of people who worked for head office, why did they have to send Ben?

Jesse pushed my chair back from the table and I dropped into my seat, as the folder made a loud smack on the table. I glanced down at my lap, wishing I could hide in my pocket until after the new year. And a Concorde? No wonder he had no issue shelling out hundreds like Halloween candy, his family owned half the papers on the East Coast and the ones they didn't own outright they had a considerable share in them.

"I know this will be a difficult transition for everyone, but advertising revenues are down across the country and we need to keep up with the times. We've converted papers in St. Louis, Charleston, D.C., and Detroit with amazing success and we'd like to continue that model with some of the smaller regional outlets."

I dared to look up. Ben stood with his hands in his

pockets, trying to look comfortable and failing miserably. His slicked back hair screamed of skyscrapers and working lunches, not small towns and their salt of the earth mentality.

"Excuse me." I raised my hand as I scanned the shocked and withering faces of my colleagues.

"Yes, Ms. Brighton, is it?"

His stare locked on my face and weighed heavy on my neck. A glimmer of a grin curled across his lips as he said my name. The lips that not even twelve hours ago were smashed against mine in the back of a pub.

"Are you sure this is the right move for Havenbrook? All those urban centers sound wonderful, but things move differently here. People are different around here. They still rely on a physical paper. Half the seniors in this town don't even own an electronic device."

He smirked as he watched me. The rest of the room seemed to fall away and I shook my head to break the eerie spell.

"Then they will need to get with the times, I guess. It's not feasible for this outlet to keep bleeding revenues with little hope of recovering them. I hear what you're saying, but sometimes change is a good thing."

"And sometimes change can kill a good thing," I added.

Ben jerked his head to the side, his brow furrowing as he glanced over at Jenkins.

I slapped my hand over my mouth. I'd crossed a line, and it didn't seem like anyone else planned on speaking up.

Jenkins shot me a stern glare. "Mr. Concorde will be meeting with each of you individually this week to go over the plan and to make a feasible route forward regarding the future of *The Herald*. I'm sure he would be willing to hear your concerns at that time."

"Of course, Peter," I said, then leaned back in my chair.

Ben nodded, his confident grin disappearing into the stuffy office air. "I know this might be a tough transition for some of you and there will be some changes coming." He glared at me and I focused on my pen, refusing to give him the satisfaction of knowing that he'd hit his mark. "But I assure you that I want to make it as easy as possible for everyone involved and ensure things go smoothly for our January 1st roll out."

Less than three weeks. How did he think he was going to make a change this dramatic in that little time? Especially with the holiday issue coming out so soon. Completely ludicrous.

Jesse shifted uneasy in his chair along with half of the other staff. I got it. I really did. Magazines went digital ages ago, but this wasn't Cosmopolitan or Vogue. This was *The Herald*.

"Watch for meeting invitations from me in the next couple of days. I look forward to hearing what everyone has to say."

Do you, Ben? Do you really, or is that what you've been trained to spew to the low-life peons who prop up your family's money? Whoa. I blinked and tried to clear my head. The cocktail of emotions surging through my head better get back in line or I was going to make a fool out of myself in front of this guy. Again.

Jenkins stepped in front of Ben, hiding him away like a puppet at the end of a show. "That's all for today. I know everyone is working on the holiday issue so we'll save pitches until later, but if you have anything in particular you need to address, come to me directly. Thank you all for your time."

Jesse shook his head and a low whistle escaped his lips. I pushed away from the table and collected my things, trying to get out of this stifling room as quick as possible.

"And Holly," Jenkins called, still standing at the front of the room. "I can meet now unless you'd like to wait right until ten for our meeting."

I glanced down at the file folder in my hand and my shoulders drooped. "Never mind, Peter. It sounds like you have more important things on your mind right now."

We retreated to our cubicles, wordless and sloth-like. Zombies. I grabbed my phone and texted Claire.

Not going to happen today. Long story. Talk later.

I didn't wait for a response, just chucked the phone back into my coat pocket and closed my laptop. If I wasn't going to be talking to Jenkins, there wasn't any reason for me to be here. I could go through my email and write my column at home. Besides, my stomach suddenly ached. I slid open the bottom desk drawer and flipped through the folder one last time. The ache deepened, spreading through my chest. Or maybe it was only my heart breaking again? It was so damaged now I doubted I would know.

"So, you're a journalist."

I jumped and the folder slipped from my hand. My articles flew through the air and scattered across the beige carpet and a pair of stylish black dress shoes.

"Are you determined to make me drop everything I touch?" I stooped down and scrambled to collect the pages, chucking them haphazardly into the drawer.

Ben crouched. "I'm sorry. I didn't mean to startle you." He picked up the last article, the one I'd just printed and hoped to present to Jenkins, even though that was never going to happen now. He skimmed the first few sentences. "I thought you were the advice columnist. Peter didn't mention that you wrote headline too."

"I don't." I snatched the pages from his grip and shoved

them in the drawer, then closed it with a metallic thunk. "I'm just 'Ask Holly'. That's it."

"Well, that story looked pretty good. Needs a decent polish, but a great start."

A great start? Fantastic. No wonder I hadn't been able to convince Jenkins to give me more responsibility.

"Not that it matters now. Once we go digital, we'll start cutting back on staff, start bringing in articles from Reuters and other presses until there's nothing left," I said.

Ben frowned and pushed back to standing with an effortless roll. "What makes you say that?"

"Because it happens all the time."

I followed his lead and stood, straight as possible to narrow the few inches he towered over me. Working in a pre-dominantly male office wasn't always easy, but I'd held my own. I'd been a wreck lately, but no way would one outsider knock me back down. Even if his smoldering stare made my knees shake and I couldn't forget the feel of those soft lips—which could utter my career death sentence at any moment. "I may not be as connected as you are, Mr. Concorde, but I can assure you, I have contacts at other publications. I know what the collateral damage of a restructure like this looks like. Pardon me, if I'm a little sensitive about it when my job could be on the chopping block."

He tensed at the accusation and stepped back. "That's fair. There will probably be some cuts, but I'm hoping to minimize that as much as I can. Maybe you could help me, since you seem so passionate about the project? I could use someone who knows *The Herald*, but has also seen some of the world past the county line. Sound like a workable plan?"

Ben extended his hand, and I stared at it. Sell my soul for a potential stay of execution? Maybe. But considering his only opinion of me was the train wreck of a girl who kissed people she didn't even know, I needed to make a better impression.

"Alright, Mr. Concorde. We have a deal." I shook his hand with my sturdiest grip. He raised an eyebrow as he studied me. Maybe I'd already made a statement. "Now if you could please excuse me, I have work to do."

CHAPTER 4

Dear Holly,
 I'm trying to plan an unforgettable Christmas for my girlfriend, but I...

I pinched the bridge of my nose and groaned, trying to inhale the scent of Mrs. Baker's blueberry pie to calm my nerves. Another Christmas romance letter. There seemed to be more and more of them every year. Didn't ... *what was his name again?* ... Smitten by the Season, know that he was cutting it a little too close to ask for my advice now and still plan on pulling anything off in time? Or that he could've simply read any of my articles from the past two months to glean ideas from? Articles I'd painstakingly written while trying to push down my nausea. But at least it would be a few weeks reprieve before the Valentine's requests started coming in. Assuming I still had a newspaper to write at by then.

As if sensing my uncomfortable tenseness, the tiny bell over the diner door chimed and Benjamin Concorde blew in on the winter wind, a trail of snowflakes following behind and dotting the checkered linoleum floor. He brushed the snow from his hair, then narrowed his piercing eyes to scan the restaurant.

The sight of him garnered a different reaction than a few days ago. Maybe hiding away from the office made it easier to forget his charming demeanor and let the memory of his touch work its way out of my bloodstream. An addiction that I just needed to quit cold turkey. A total mistake.

"Can I help you?" Mrs. Baker leaned against the counter, a half-filled coffee pot in her hand.

"I'm just looking for—" his stare continued my way until it landed on my face. "Never mind. I found her. Thanks."

He nodded with a warm, gentle smile, then swaggered down the row of red vinyl booths toward me, his lips spreading into an even wider grin. I smiled back, my mouth betraying the negative thoughts that clouded my brain since the moment I saw him standing at the end of that conference room table Monday morning. Mrs. Baker stretched on her tiptoes and leaned over the cash register, nearly dropping the coffee pot as she watched him walk away. I shook my head. She winked back.

I slammed the top of my laptop closed and slid it into my bag avoiding any more eye contact with either of them. I'd tossed and turned all night dreading this meeting. Picturing the worst-case scenarios and waking up sweating. I couldn't believe I'd agreed to help him tear apart *The Herald*. It had been my life for years, even beyond my own column. The more I thought about it, the more it stoked a dangerous fire inside me. Despite Ben's suave air and amazingly powerful lips—that I had not been thinking about at all—I kind of wanted to send this grinch packing before he stole the Christmas I didn't even want to celebrate.

He slid into the seat across from me followed by the intoxicating scent of his cologne. The notes were tasteful yet matched him perfectly, bold and urban like he'd just stepped out of a high-end downtown department store. Stores like that would be long decorated for the season by now. The intricate displays and immaculate designer trees would be lining every floor as old-time holiday classics drifted from the hidden speakers. Back in my college days, I spent hours wandering through the aisles, as the festive trimmings reminded me of home, but with a city flare. Like a perfect cross between who I was and who I one day could be.

"Thanks for meeting me outside the office. People seem to be pretty anxious with me around, so it's nice to get out and away from all that." He unbuttoned his jacket but kept it on, lacing his fingers on the table top in front of him and leaning forward. "Besides, this seems like a fun little place."

"And we make the best pie this side of the Mississippi." Ms. Baker appeared at the end of the table; her eyes glued to the new stranger. "Anything I can get you?"

"Yeah, I'll take a slice —" Ben glanced across the booth. I crossed my arms and glared back at him. "—or maybe I'll keep it simple and just take a coffee. Thanks."

"Sure thing, but you're missing out." She reached between us and flipped over a porcelain cup. She poured the hot coffee as she eyed my defiant stance and shook her head. She returned her focus to Ben. "If you need anything else, give me a holler. Sound good?"

"Absolutely. The coffee smells fantastic," he replied.

He beamed up at her, his warm eyes softening as he chuckled at her kindness. She smiled back and he flashed a glimpse of his perfect teeth, the sentiment seeming almost genuine. Eventually, she sauntered away leaving us to our business. Ben wrapped both palms around the steaming cup and arched his shoulders slightly forward as if absorbing the heat. My lips tried to smile, but I forced them to remain in a hard line, noting that he sat exactly the same way I did when the winter chill set in. The familiarity prickled in my brain. Maybe I was being too harsh.

"I'm sure you know why you have the office on edge. Everyone knows what your presence here means. Things are going to change, and I doubt anyone is going to like it." The words shot out my mouth like tiny darts aimed right at the bull's-eye that was his handsome face. So much for easing up on the harshness.

Ben sighed as his smile dissolved into a frown and he leaned back against the vinyl booth. "I know people aren't always thrilled to see me, but I'm not trying to be anyone's enemy. Honestly, this is just business. I figured if anyone would understand it would be you."

"Me? I have bills to pay too, you know."

"Of course, and I will do everything I can to keep people's jobs, but you're the youngest person on staff and you have experience in a bigger publication. I just thought you'd get that."

Any kindness I had left disappeared. "So you've been digging up on me?"

His left hand slipped from the coffee cup and he started to tap the table with his index finger. "It's on your resume, and I've looked into all the staff, not just you. It's my job. And speaking of jobs, I would like to know more about why you're working the advice column with your education and the internship you have under your belt?"

"Just because I love it. Best job ever." I grit my teeth and tried to hide any sarcasm by staring down into my lap.

"Okay... But if you love it so much, how come you have been trying to get a reporter position?"

I snapped my head back up. All humor faded from

Ben's manner, leaving only his questioning stare that burned the top of my cheeks.

"I saw the stack of articles you had the other day, plus Peter showed me a few of them. You're a great writer, Holly. He said you've been asking for a reporter job for a while."

"Well, thanks, but my time will come. One day. I just need to be patient."

He raised an eyebrow and kept staring until I looked away. "Really? With your talent, you could be at any national publication you wanted, not stuck at a tiny outfit like *The Herald*. You could be out there living a reporter's dream."

Through the window, the cheery sunshine glistened on the pristine blanket of snow accumulating on the side of the street. Another charming day in Havenbrook. Back at my old office in the city, if I looked out I could watch all of Kansas City go by. The hustle and bustle of the busy newsroom. The urgency of the next edition. The energy of it seeped from my memory and lit in my bones. I slid my hands beneath my thighs and bit down on the inside of my cheek.

"That's pretty precocious coming from you. I mean, are you living your dream, Ben? Ruining people's lives and destroying the careers that people have spent their lives working toward?"

"Of course not." He blinked for a second, slow and meticulous, then gazed out the sunlit window. "I don't enjoy breaking things down, but sometimes you need to cut off a few dead branches for the tree to grow. Personally, I'd prefer to be the one building things up instead of knocking them down, but Concorde is the family business, and sometimes you have to do what you have to do."

I released my tense shoulders and let out a sigh. "Yeah, family can make things tricky."

"Interesting comment. Does that have anything to do with David Brighton?" He shook his head and leaned back across the table, pinning me with his inquisitive gaze again. "When I was going through the financials, I noticed his name as the editor-in-chief before Peter. Any relation?"

I opened my mouth to speak, but nothing came out. Pulling my arms in closer to my body, I cleared my throat. "Yeah, something like that."

He hung in silence, the eager quiver of his top lip exposing his need to say something and the struggle he had to keep his mouth closed, waiting for me to elaborate. But I wouldn't. An old reporter trick. Let the silence draw out the truth. Very clever. But magicians aren't very mysterious when the audience knows their tricks.

After several uncomfortable minutes of the staring game, he sat back and drained the coffee cup with a loud gulp. "Okay, Holly, I've tried to be nice, but you clearly don't like me and that's fine. But I still need to do my job and I thought if you were willing to help, I could salvage a lot more of the paper than doing this on my own. I know you don't like this. I don't like this. But it's going to happen with or without you." He re-clasped the buttons on his coat and stood by the table as he slipped a ten-dollar bill out of his pocket and placed it under the empty cup. My entire body burned. I expected it to be anger, but it sure seemed more like embarrassment. What had I done?

He took a few steps toward the door, then halted and spun back around on his perfectly polished dress shoes.

"For what it's worth, I was excited to see you walk into that boardroom. I felt so lucky to have met a woman so intelligent and charming, not once but twice. It seemed like fate was trying to help me out, but I guess I was just being hopeful. Thank you for your time."

He raced to the entrance and nodded at Ms. Baker as he walked out. I winced at the tinkling of the bell as the door slammed shut behind him. *Why did I need to be so hostile?* I crossed my arms on the table and dropped my forehead on them, inhaling the lemon scent of the sanitized tabletop. What a complete disaster. Maybe I needed to lose this angry persona and find that amazing girl from the bar too.

CHAPTER 5

❄

Almost all of Havenbrook passed by as I hid against the brick wall near the bank. They waved and shone their carefree friendly grins as they shuffled down the snowy sidewalk, while I forced myself to smile back, my meeting with Ben still plaguing me. Ben with his dreamy hair and sexy quiver to his top lip when he spewed those words, assuming he knew all about me. But if he was so wrong, why did his assumptions still bother me almost five hours later?

A shock of red hair sticking out from a woolen beanie drifted by and snapped me out of my annoying thoughts.

"Claire, wait up." I peeled away from the wall and leapt two giant steps down the sidewalk after her, then clamped my hand on her shoulder.

She whirled around and gasped. "Jeez, Holly, are you trying to give me a heart attack?"

She clasped her mittened hand across her chest as small puffs of her breath hung in the frigid air.

"Sorry, I really need to talk to you about Ben."

"Ben? You mean the super-hot guy you kissed at the bar and turned out to be your boss's boss? That Ben?" Claire shot a naughty wink, then continued to scurry down the sidewalk.

I rushed along beside her avoiding eye contact and the small patches of ice along the concrete. "Well, clearly, that was a mistake. I met him for lunch today to talk about the paper, but I think I made things worse."

"I'm sure it's not as bad as you think. What did you say?"

I thrust my hands in my pockets and stared down at my feet. "Pretty much everything that came out of my mouth was a problem. I basically argued with everything he said and chased him out before he even finished his coffee."

"Yikes." Claire halted and grabbed my arm, yanking me back a step. She stared me down in the concerned way she always did when I put my foot firmly into my mouth. "That bad, huh? What did he say?"

"First, he mentioned the change to digital, which you know is just going to destroy *The Herald*."

She shook her head and started walking again. "Maybe not. But keep going."

"And then, he started talking about my writing and how I should move into the city and become a reporter."

"Well, that's good, right?" she said. "It's exactly what I've been telling you to do, anyway."

I locked eyes on the giant wreath hanging over the doors of St. Michael's Church, just behind Claire's head. I stared harder as a strange tickle started in my throat.

"But that's not what you told him, was it?"

I heard her sigh, but still couldn't look at her face. I shook my head. "No, I kept right on going. I'll be surprised if I even have a job by tomorrow morning."

"Seriously, Holly?" Claire stopped walking and tugged my chin down to her. "I know you've been going through a lot lately, with Fletcher and all, but if you don't stop being so dramatic you're going to end up hurting yourself more than that jerk ever could."

"I know, but you know how much *The Herald* means to me. I can't just let somebody come in here and ruin everything. It would be catastrophic."

"Yeah, but at some point you're going to have to let it go."

Her words stung like needles, delivering the harsh medicine I so desperately needed. "I need to apologize to him, don't I? Like possibly full out groveling?"

She nodded and squeezed my arm through her mitten. A comforting jolt of warmth sparked up my arm. "It might be just fine. I'm sure if you explain why you were upset, he'd understand. He actually seemed like a pretty reasonable guy that night at Danny's."

"Maybe. But how am I going to be able to convince him to stop messing with the paper and everyone else's lives here?"

Claire shrugged and dropped my arm as she continued up the sidewalk. "I don't know. Perhaps if he understood how much the paper means to Havenbrook and what people are really like here versus big cities, he'd reconsider."

The spark of an idea flashed in the back of my brain, growing larger and brighter by the second. "Yeah. You might be right, Claire. That's exactly what I need to do."

"Did you want to come for dinner? I'm sure Austin would love to see you, and I'm trying a new Mexican recipe that's going to be way too much food for the two of us. Besides, I want to show you the dress I got for the fundraising gala tomorrow. And don't forget, we are supposed to help set up just after lunch."

Details formed and clicked in place like puzzle pieces. A puzzle that seemed to look a lot like Christmas. If anyone could make Ben see this town for what it was, it would definitely be me.

"Holly?" Claire waved her hand in front of my face, barely missing my nose "What about dinner? Did you want to come?"

I shook my head as the final parts slid into place. "Sorry, I have plans all of a sudden. Or more like a plan."

Claire crossed her arms and narrowed her stare. "What are you up to?"

"Don't worry," I nodded my head and smiled broadly until her concerned face cracked into a laugh. "It will be fine, but do you think your husband would mind if I borrowed a few of his things?"

CHAPTER 6

The night sky settled around me, inky black and a little ominous, as doubts about my master plan crept into my brain. Everything seemed perfect when I left my house, but as I stood in the hotel parking lot with its instrumental holiday songs blaring through the front speakers, I considered turning around the way I came and curling up in my comfy bed until the new year. I'd already made things as bad as I could, why risk making it worse?

Except the knot in my stomach from my botched lunch meeting kept squeezing tighter and giving up might cause it to rip me apart. No turning back now. I took a deep breath and let it out slowly as I pulled open the door of the Starlight Inn.

"Good evening, welcome to the Star— Hey, Holly what are you doing here?"

I flinched at the recognition. Robbie Benson, clean-cut and all-business in his purple vest and gold name tag, launched a wide grin at me from across the lobby. The beauty of small towns was that you knew everybody. But the curse was also that you knew everybody. In Robbie's case, all the way back to kindergarten.

"Hey, I didn't realize you worked here." I did. "How is your mom doing?" Which I already knew.

"Better, she's back in remission, so that's something to be grateful for."

Tugging my tote bag closer to my body, I marched up to the counter and delivered my best courteous smile. "Well, that's amazing. And just in time for the holidays too."

Robbie's shoulders relaxed as a warm grin spread across his face. "Absolutely. We couldn't ask for better timing."

I stretched up on my toes and leaned over the counter. "So, is there any chance you'd be able to tell me what room Benjamin Concorde is staying in?"

His smile turned into a playful smirk. "Holly Brighton, are you stalking our guests? I might have to call the sheriff."

"Of course not." I forced a laugh, but it came out more nervous than I'd hoped. "It's strictly business. He works for the parent company that owns the paper. He already knows I'm coming, he just rushed out of the office so quickly I forgot to ask him his room number."

"Hold on, have we slipped back a few decades or can you not just text him?"

Think, Holly, think. "I…"

Robbie slapped his hand against the wooden counter and threw his head back with a guttural laugh. "I'm just messing with you. He's in 204."

I eased away from the counter, shrunk my neck into the collar of my coat, and ran for the stairs. "Thanks." I yelled over my shoulder as I bounded up the first flight.

Walking slow, I focused on catching my breath before I reached Ben's door. I'd already left enough bad impressions for one day. The television roared inside. It sounded like a newscast. Boring. Didn't he get enough of this at work every day? Maybe this wasn't really a good idea. Maybe I could just go and he'd never know I was here. Unless, of course, Robbie decided to mention it to him in the morning. I grit my teeth and shivered. That would be so much worse.

Another deep breath and I rapped my knuckles against the old oak door.

One second... Two seconds... Three seconds... Four. No answer. Fine by me.

I turned on my heel and rushed back down the hallway toward the stairs and my escape.

"Holly?"

I slammed to a stop, nearly falling over my own feet as Ben's deep voice called out my name. My shoulders eased, but I quickly tensed them back up. No. It didn't matter how sexily my name rolled off his tongue. I was here for one purpose only.

Plastering on my best small-town hospitality smile, I whirled around and strutted back toward Ben's door, exuding as much confidence as I could muster.

"Ben, so you are home. I mean, in your room. I guess this isn't really your home, now is it?" Seriously? For someone who worked with words all day, I didn't have a clue how to use them. My arm twitched, aching to hide my face in my hand, but I fought it down and kept it locked by my side.

He narrowed his questioning eyes then leaned against the open door, arms crossed. "Yeah, not really home. But for the amount I travel, it might as well be. What are you doing here?"

The soft scent of cucumber mint soap wafted through the hall. Ben's wet hair clung to his forehead and a small droplet of water trickled down his cheek. Instead of his tailored suit, he'd changed into a black T-shirt and a dark washed pair of jeans, his sleeves tugging just enough against his toned biceps. The whole look fit him well. Too well.

"I..." I peeled my eyes away from the contours of his shirt to ease my tongue and aid the words to flow. "I feel like we might have gotten off on the wrong foot today."

He frowned, but his eyes danced with curiosity. "I would say so."

"You asked for my help, and I didn't provide it. But, if you really want to know what *The Herald* means to Havenbrook, then you need to experience it. Get out of your closet-sized hotel room and be a part of the action."

"Sounds a bit like a sales pitch, Ms. Brighton."

Ms. Brighton? I really must've screwed things up today.

"No, just an opportunity. Besides, what else were you going to do tonight?"

His face furrowed for a second and then he shrugged, the frown melting away into the dim light of the hallway. "I guess I better take you up on your offer then. Just hold on a second and I'll grab my coat."

"Oh, and you'll probably need these." I slipped the tote bag off my shoulder and held it open.

He pulled the scarf, hat, and mitts I borrowed from Austin out of the bag. "Am I going to regret this?"

"Maybe. But we'll never know for sure if you don't come with me."

CHAPTER 7

❄

Strands of white lights twinkled above our heads and led us down the bustling street. Red bows dotted the pastel-colored awnings as we passed, while boughs of evergreens swooped between the candy cane striped tents lining the snowy sidewalks.

"C'mon, Mr. Concorde, we're almost there." I glanced over my shoulder and beckoned with my gloved fingers.

Ben rolled his eyes, but continued to follow me as I twisted our way through the crowd toward the town square and the heart of the Havenbrook Christmas Market. With his hair tucked underneath Austin's beanie, he almost blended in with the locals. Except he'd never be one of them. Ben stood too rigid for a small town. Too proper. Even in the door of his hotel room, hair a mess and wearing denim, he still screamed of the city. Of traffic and subway stations. High rises and billboards. So why did the thought of him seem exhilarating instead of exhausting?

Near the edge of the square, I slowed, taking in a deep breath of cool winter air. A crisp, clean taste skated over my tongue and memories of years of perfect nights like this one swirled in my head. The crunch of footfalls whispered behind me as Ben's warm breath rustled the hair near my neck. I shivered, but shook it off.

"I thought you hated all this Christmas stuff?" he said as he stepped beside me and put his hands on his hips.

I glanced around the square. So many happy faces that I'd known for my whole life, glowing bright with rosy frostbitten cheeks. "What makes you say that? Who hates Christmas?"

"You gave me that vibe when we met." Ben's face scrunched up in a failed attempt to hide his amused grin. "Plus, that night you announced to the bar that you hated it."

My stomach churned and I rubbed my hand over my face. I peeked out from between my fingers as the recollection came speeding back. "Seriously?"

"I wouldn't worry, it was too loud in there for anyone to hear you anyway."

"Anyone, but you, I guess."

Ben laughed. Light and airy. I must have been a bigger mess than I remembered.

I stared down at the well-trodden sidewalk, studying the imprints of the various boot grips that had come before us. "Well I didn't mean it … exactly. It hasn't been the best year for me and, well, you kind of came along when I was having a rough time."

He tucked his mittened fingers under my chin and tilted my head up to meet his gaze. The playfulness from the prior moment melted as his dark eyes softened and drew me in like a comforting cup of caramel hot chocolate. "I hope things get better. I don't want to be the cause of any more trouble for you."

"We'll see." My throat tightened, and I slipped out of his gentle grip to stare off toward the skating circle in front of the giant Christmas tree. "Now, I didn't bring you here to talk about me. I need to show you something."

I jerked my head to the left and started weaving through the crowd again. Along the side of city hall, full spreads of *The Herald* hung in giant wooden frames, their supporting chains wrapped in silver and gold ribbons.

"This is the holiday edition from 1984." I pointed at the black-and-white photo of handmade candy canes underneath the vintage *Herald* masthead, then slipped around the frame to the next one. "And here is 1956 and 1957."

The images of Christmas trees and sleigh rides burst off the pages. Headlines in their bold fonts followed by uplifting articles in their neat little rows. Just as they always were. As they always should be.

Ben stuffed his hands in his pockets and studied the pages, his eyes flitting back and forth as he read every word. "What is all this?"

"Moments captured in time and lovingly archived by the citizens of Havenbrook."

Ben coughed at the sentiment as his left eyebrow arched up. A puff of steam from his breath swirled around his head.

"Or if you like a more straightforward answer, this is an exhibit of all the yearend issues of *The Herald* as far back as they could find them. They are missing most of the ones from the early 1800s, but almost every other one is here. Framed and preserved, then put on display every Christmas for the whole town, or anyone who happens to come through, to see."

"That's incredible." He crossed his arms over his chest and leaned back on his heels to take in the entire exhibit. "They've kept them all in amazing condition."

"Yes. *The Herald* means a lot to Havenbrook. To me. It's one of the few things that unifies everyone here. Ever steady. I don't know where you're from, Ben—"

"Chicago."

"Sure." I shook my head. Just as I suspected. "But small

towns are different. They stand for tradition and revel in consistency."

I kept walking through the exhibit, running my fingertips over the frames as I passed and letting them swing slightly in my wake.

"Did you know if you walk into Mrs. Baker's diner on any Saturday morning, you will find every single person with their head down in *The Herald*? Every sports team has a sponsorship from the paper and any athlete that goes pro gives us exclusive access for their first interview. People maintain their subscriptions as part of their wills and pass it on to their children."

I rounded through the late 70s section and lingered in front of a familiar headline. My heart pumped harder in my chest as I struggled to breathe. I closed my eyes as the faded black and white smile beamed at me. Without looking, I remembered every detail of the photo. The curve of his brow. The tiny scar to the left of his nose. He looked so young then. No wrinkles or the worry lines that would soon etch themselves across his forehead. Pride and ambition, but with a warmth that melted even the coolest critic. *The Herald Announces New Editor-In-Chief, David Brighton.* I knew the words without looking. Each one seared across my heart. "For some people, *The Herald* means home."

A chill flitted across my cheek as Ben's shadow cast over me. "Seems pretty important to you too."

"It is." I swallowed hard and fluttered my eyes back open. "I owe you an apology. You asked for my help and instead of being honest I chose to be a little...well...hostile."

Ben snickered behind me. "Really? I hadn't noticed."

Peeling my gaze away from the frame, I whirled around, my face right against Ben's chest. I gasped, and stumbled a step backward, not expecting to be nearly so close. A warm rush bubbled in my veins, but I pushed the feeling down. "That wasn't fair to you. You're just trying to do your job."

"And you are doing yours. I wish you'd been more open with me, but I get it. You really care and it shows. Conviction and passion are not things to be ashamed of." He lowered his head as his dark stare locked on mine. Just as quickly the shadows flitted into the night and a softness eked in. "However, I was really looking forward to Mrs. Baker's pie so I think you might owe me a slice."

"Very funny. But I'm serious, how do you think the town is going to take *The Herald* going digital? They couldn't exactly have exhibits like this."

"No, I suppose they can't." He nodded and scanned over the years of history tied in metallic bows. A concerned frown grew stronger on his deep, red lips. "Except sometimes history is just that—history. The paper needs to generate more ad revenue. It can't be bleeding money like it has over the past few years. Digital could be a way to save the paper from an even worse fate. How do you think Havenbrook would feel if we had to close *The Herald* instead?"

The reality froze me in my boots. I'd visualized a world in which the paper went digital and that had been bleak, but I never imagined that closing the paper entirely would be an option. I wrapped my arms across my chest, then wandered away from the exhibit toward the bustle of the market again. People flitted in front of me. Blurs of festive colors moving far faster than I had time to process. Clenching my jacket sleeves in my hands, I shivered as the cold December breeze finally seeped into my bones and froze me to my core.

"Trust me, it's not something I would want to do." Ben's voice drifted toward me, but still seemed miles away. "But sometimes it's the way it is. I have to do my job too, even if it's not always fun."

I dug my fingertips into my arms and sighed. "So, why do you do it then?"

"Do what?"

"This job? If you don't like having to deal with these kinds of things, why don't you make a change? You're a Concorde. Your family owns the company. I'm sure if you wanted to do something different, you could."

Snow crunched behind me as he stepped up on my left. He didn't try to steal my attention, just stared straight out into the crowd as the night washed over him. The icy breeze nipped at his nose as a calmness cloaked his expression.

"You're not wrong. I do think about it sometimes. What it would be like to not live out of a suitcase for six months out of the year. To slow down and maybe stay somewhere longer than a week at a time. But my family depends on me. My mother runs the main office in Chicago, my sisters head the satellite offices on either coast, and my father spends his time between all three. They need someone in the field and as the youngest, I sort of fell into the role."

"And you get to be the sacrifice."

He chuckled, but the humor left his lips flat and jaded. "I guess I am."

I released the iron grip on my arms and nudged him with my shoulder. "See, was that so hard? Maybe there is a soul under that expensive suit after all."

"Maybe." He swayed toward me and bumped his shoulder into mine.

The chill in my limbs melted away as I tipped slightly to the right and my harsh frown slipped away. I chuckled softly and the sound teased a smile from Ben.

"Now you know about me, but I don't seem to know much about you. How is that fair?" he asked.

"What did you want to know?" A loaded question. A

deadly one if wielded properly. But maybe he could be trusted. Or maybe I'd unleashed a whole mess of trouble.

"Well…"

He rubbed his hand under his chin as his inquisitive eyes rolled toward the length of plastic candy canes strung in rows above our heads.

"Is it really that tough?"

He scanned over my face, his smile widening. "Don't want to waste this opportunity?"

"You shouldn't. You never know—"

The never-ending stream of people flowing behind Ben's head came into focus. Two familiar faces solidified in the crowd, grinning and giggling like teenagers. Fletcher and Dierdre. Why now? Bile rose in my throat. I grabbed Ben's arm and swung him around so we backed against the swarm of market goers, then tucked in closer to him.

He glanced back over his shoulder and almost immediately the light of recognition sparked across his face. "I'm assuming that means you two still aren't on good terms?"

I shook my head. "Not exactly. I'm pretty sure that's never going to happen."

His head swiveled following Fletcher, then swooped back down at my head cowered against his shoulder.

"All clear."

I exhaled sharply, and the feeling returned to my body. My numb fingers released their clutch on Ben's jacket near the zipper on his firm chest. "Sorry."

"It's fine. My ex is a nightmare too. How long were you two together?"

"Too long, I guess. Or at least I would have hoped he'd broke up with me before he started dating someone else."

"Ouch." Ben's face scrunched up. "Sounds like you're better off. Maybe it wasn't meant to be?"

I craned my neck and tried to get my blood flow back. The shock drained from my muscles and was replaced quickly with a new tension. One that made my knees quake. "Sounds a bit spiritual for a practical guy like you."

"Not really. If your processes are failing, it could be time to liquidate and move on. Spending too much time and money on bad investments just puts you in a worse position. Sometimes it's better just to start over."

"Sounds great, but it's not always that easy. How many times have you started over?"

His brows furrowed and his mouth opened, but only his breath came out.

"I thought so." I closed my eyes for a moment and took a deep, calming breath. "It's admirable advice. Thanks for trying."

Ben shoved his hands in his pockets and stared at the ground. "I guess I've never really lost anything that meant that much to me."

"Like *The Herald* means to Havenbrook."

I rocked back on my heels, as the words burned on my tongue. I shouldn't have said that, but it just flowed out before I could stop it. My impeccable timing almost uncontrollable. Too late now.

The melodic chime of carols wafted through the market, hiding the silence growing fast between us. I'd orchestrated this outing to help convince Ben that *The Herald* needed to stay as it was, but instead I'd only made a bigger mess. Shown him how big of a wreck I really was. How would he even consider listening to me now? I glanced around the square. The bright lights sparked a new idea.

"So, Mr. Concorde, how are you at ice skating?"

CHAPTER 8

"Oh no, you don't." I pushed down on my left foot and lunged forward with all my strength. Wind whipped my hair against my face as I glided faster and faster around the frozen pond, Ben's gray wool jacket less than an arm's length away.

He looked back over his shoulder. "Did you really think that challenging me to a race would end well for you? I'm a little competitive, if you haven't noticed."

I dug each foot deeper into the ice as I skated, forcing my legs forward. His long gait could only help him so much. His stride was too choppy. Sure, that might help with a quick start, but it wouldn't hold him for a long distance. The rented skates wobbled around my ankles but I pressed on, determined not to let him beat me.

The gap between us closed. A few more strides. Gritting my teeth, I gave it one last push to sail past him. I spun around on my toe and skated backwards for my victory lap. I pumped my arms in the air.

"Woohoo! Take that, Ben."

He tossed his head back and slowed down to drift lazily

around the skating circle in front of me. His deep laugh echoed throughout the square.

"Impressive. Seven years of hockey and I get taken down by a small-town girl. My father is going to be pissed when he finds out his money didn't prepare me for battle."

"Well, I'm definitely not one to be underestimated."

He dropped his chin and lunged toward me, gripping my jacket at my waist. "I'm starting to figure that out."

The air thickened. Heavy. Pressing on my chest and making it hard to breathe. Ben mimicked my reaction as his breath caught in his throat. Only the chill of the night remained between us—except I couldn't seem to feel it.

"Thanks for giving me a second chance," I whispered, low and delicate to not ruin the moment. "I shouldn't have been so rude at the cafe. It's not how I normally am, I just get a bit emotional about things sometimes. Things that are important to me."

He brushed my hair off my shoulder and inched closer. "It's not a bad thing. You can't teach people to be passionate about what they care about."

His words rolled off his tongue and warmed my cheeks. I didn't hate him. It would be easier if I did, but I couldn't. I held onto his solid biceps and stood up straighter. The distance between our bodies closed inch by precious inch. Ben's eyes widened, but instead of pulling back he held my waist tighter, drawing me in. An odd sensation pulsed through me as I melted into him and craved so much more.

"Look, Mom, he's going to kiss her under the mistletoe," a tiny voice shouted, cutting through the ambiance.

I turned to my left. A little girl, with two braids sticking out from underneath her fuzzy pink beanie, smiled at us with a dark gap where her top front tooth should be. Her mother gave me a shrug and pushed the little girl forward and out of the way.

"Ha. That's ridiculous." I let go of his strong arms and spun around to skate toward the side of the pond. "My feet are killing me in these borrowed skates. I think I'm done."

I shook my head and flopped onto the long bench beside the ice. Ben plunked down beside me and looked me over, quickly ripping the laces open on his skates.

"Why don't I grab some hot chocolate while you return these?" he said, passing me the snow-covered blades.

I nodded and leaned back as he walked away. He glanced over his shoulder and smiled until I waved at him. My lips started to pucker and the image of our kiss at Danny's flashed through my brain, mixing with the ones I'd found myself imagining in my dreams. What was going on? He worked for my employer. He was practically my boss. So, why did I suddenly want him back here on the bench with me?

After returning the skates, Ben appeared at my side with a steaming paper cup. "Here you go."

"Thanks." I took a quick sip and let the smooth liquid soothe my dry throat. "I should probably be getting you back to your hotel. I'm sure you have work in the morning and I hear the executives at head office are a bit conservative."

He narrowed his stare. "Is that how you see me?"

"Sometimes. But I think I might be able to be convinced otherwise."

"Then my master plan is working. I knew I could blend in."

I laughed. "You definitely don't blend in. Not even in that hat."

He frowned and adjusted the beanie on his head, his dark hair peeking out from underneath the sides.

We strode beneath the strings of white lights leading back to Main Street. The last few vendors busily packed up their wares, shoving items into boxes and rushing away. It must be later than I thought.

"So, how exactly were you able to find my hotel room?" Ben asked as he lined up and tossed his cup into a nearby garbage can. A perfect shot. He pumped his fist in the air at his victory.

"It's not like it was that hard. There are only three decent inns in Havenbrook." I shrugged and tossed my own empty cup into the same garbage can. *Swish.* I smirked. "Besides, the Starlight is the only place in town that offers us a corporate discount."

"Well, that is some pretty good investigative work there, Ms. Brighton." He stopped walking and leaned in closer, staring down into my eyes. The rich scent of hot chocolate still clung to his breath. Sweet and warm. "You really would make a great reporter."

"Maybe. But that's not my job, at least not at *The Herald*. So, why bother talking about it?"

I unlocked my gaze from Ben's and looked back toward the skating pond. A fresh batch of snow had started to drift silently between the buildings flanking the festive street.

"Peter told me you've been gunning for a reporter position for months. There are so many opportunities out there. Why not go for what you want? I really don't understand."

I swallowed against the lump growing in my throat. "Because it's complicated. Havenbrook and *The Herald* are my home. Sometimes I do miss working for a bigger outlet. The excitement of the city. But I can't just abandon this place."

"Havenbrook is amazing, but you won't be able to follow your reporting dreams here. Even if Peter gave you the job you asked for, it would be extremely limited on what you could achieve. Maybe your old internship would take you back at an entry level, just to get your foot in the door again."

I sighed and glanced up at the sky. The snowflakes fell on my eyelashes, creating a haze over my vision. "Because I wasn't there long enough to matter. I accepted that internship at the Kansas City Star, but only a few months after I started my dad got sick and I had to come back. My mom died when I was a baby and there wasn't anyone around to take care of him."

I blinked away the snow and shoved my hands in my pockets, pulling my arms tight to my sides. A cool, wintry wind whipped through the empty market stalls, swirling the snowflakes around my feet with every hurried step.

Ben walked along beside me in silence until he finally said softly, "I'm sorry, Holly. I didn't know."

"Why would you? It isn't a front-page news kind of story. I came back and started my life over again here."

"And your dad?"

I swallowed hard and blinked twice to avoid the inevitable tears from falling. "Three months. That's all he had left."

Ben wrapped his hand over my shoulder then quickly pulled his hand away. "I'm so sorry."

I swept my finger along my lashes and forced the painful memories back into their box in the deepest parts of my brain. "It happens."

"Well, if you ever change your mind, I could be a huge asset for your career."

"Oh yeah," I said, with a touch of intrigue.

"Yeah, I have a ton of contacts in the industry, not just at Concorde but other publications as well. And—" Ben rested the back of his hand against my cheek. The heat soothed the still fresh wounds and I fell into his touch. "I'm sure any paper would love to have someone like you working for them. We're lucky to have you working for us."

"Thanks. I—"

The world plunged into darkness as the lights of the markets flicked off. I tugged away from Ben's touch and looked around. The street was deserted and the skating circle lay calm and barren.

"I guess we've outstayed our welcome."

❄

The star-studded sky gave way to the neon sign of the Starlight Inn. Like the falling snow, we'd drifted here, slow and aimless, until our feet found the front door. The harsh artificial light of the lobby called, but the moonlit glow of outside wrapped us like a blanket and refused to let us go. Or maybe I'd just lost the feeling in my nose and toes.

"Here we are, Mr. Concorde. Safe and sound."

He glanced toward the front door and then back at me, still standing firm on the sidewalk. "Thanks. I think I really got to know Havenbrook a lot better."

"Yeah. I love it here. Plus, when it snows like this, it's kind of beautiful."

His eyes narrowed on mine. "It sure is."

Electricity pulsed through my body, awakening parts of my heart that had fallen asleep. Except, he couldn't really be the Prince Charming of my fairytale. We'd never be a happy ending.

"Um … that was—"

"Super cheesy. I'm so sorry." He emitted a low sexy growl and grabbed the back of his neck. His teeth caught on his bottom lip. The bright white mesmerizing against the dark red under the moonlight. A warmth rushed through me fighting against the cold night air and I jerked as I unintentionally bit down on my own lip, sending a jolt of pain through my chin.

"I should probably go." I pointed back toward town, but didn't move except to fumble my house keys in my hands. My empty house.

"Yeah, work in the morning. Of course. Thank you for saving me from a night of bad television and spreadsheets."

"You're welcome. I kind of owed you one, anyway."

He tilted his head and blinked.

"But before I go." I cleared my throat. "That first night. At Danny's. I never thanked you for helping me deal with Fletcher. I should have."

"No problem. I did spill a drink on you, so I had to make sure we were even. But after tonight, I think you're one up on me."

"Okay." I turned on my heel, but stopped. "But why did you do it? I know about the drink and all, but it was a bit of a risk. And you didn't really have to."

"I guess I like fixing things more than breaking them. Besides, if I remember correctly, it was you who kissed me."

Flames licked my skin as the memory of the night flashed back in my head. Flickers of embarrassment and excitement. Still confusing to me several days later. "True. Sorry about that."

"Don't apologize. It was the best welcome I've had my entire career."

"It was a pretty great kiss." One of the better ones I'd had. Maybe even the best. Or maybe I just remembered it that way. Then the memory dissipated as I faced him again.

"That was before I knew you were my boss. But, depending on how your restructuring goes, you might not be for long."

"Hey. I will do whatever I can to protect *The Herald*." He

took my hand and caressed it between his own, then placed his forehead against mine. "And you."

His lips rested so close to mine. I tasted them in my mind and ached for another bite.

"I believe you." I pushed up on my tiptoes and grazed my lips against his cold cheek, the barely there stubble scratching against my skin. "See you tomorrow."

CHAPTER 9

The sunlight shimmered off the pristine white banks that flanked the sidewalk on the way to the office. Each flake a twinkling diamond shining on my every step. A whole new, glorious world since yesterday. I sipped my mocha latte, letting the rich chocolate slide down my throat and warm me from the inside. A magnificent morning that would hopefully bring a fantastic day. Ben had promised to protect the paper the best he could, and the words played on a sultry repeat in my head from the moment they left his deep, delicious lips.

I took another sip and shook my head. I shouldn't be thinking about him that way. He controlled my career. My destiny. Any sort of feelings for him would be a huge mistake. I just wish someone could relate that to my dream brain before it worked overtime last night.

"Good morning, Doris," I said as I breezed through the front door of the office and stomped the snow off the toes of my boots.

"Good morning to you too, Holly. You seem in an exceptionally chipper mood this morning." Her befuddled look followed me across the lobby.

"A wonderful night followed by a good sleep. How could I not be in a great mood?" And for once it wasn't a lie or a polite put on. For the first time in the last several weeks, I finally felt hopeful. Like I could take on the world.

I slipped off my jacket as I scurried through the maze of cubicles toward my desk. Before I managed to duck into my cube, the boardroom door opened at the end of the hall. Peter and Ben filed out, heading my direction.

"Good morning, Holly." Jenkins scanned me over. "Don't you typically work from home on Thursdays?"

I stiffened for a moment, my back stick straight. "Sometimes, yeah. But I had some things to take care of here today."

"Just make sure you hit those deadlines." He waggled his finger at me as his stern face broke into a smile. "You've never missed one yet, and I would hate for you to break your streak."

Ben cleared his throat and moved to Jenkin's side. The soft casualness of last night 's demeanor had been smoothed back into its urban, hard style. Except this time his dazzling warm grin didn't quite match his cool exterior. "A pleasure to see you again, Ms. Brighton."

He nodded politely, then stared up at me through his dark lashes.

I swallowed down the ridiculous bubble of excitement threatening to burst from my mouth in a completely unprofessional giggle. I glanced up at the ceiling. "You too, Mr. Concorde. I hope you have been enjoying your stay."

He took a step forward, closing the distance between us. "Of course. I'm beginning to see how much Havenbrook has to offer."

"We have that conference call at nine in my office, Ben. Don't want to keep your father waiting." Jenkins sidled along beside us casting a questioning look for me to Ben and back again.

"Of course," Ben straightened his suit jacket and checked that the buttons were secure. "Wouldn't want that."

He followed Peter down the hall toward his office but glanced back to catch me watching him walk away. I smacked my hand against my forehead and dragged it down the side of my face. This was stupid. I was being stupid. Like a giddy teenager instead of the competent woman I knew I was. This, whatever this was, needed to stop. He controlled my career, and being unprofessional wasn't going to help anything.

I rushed the rest of the way to my cubicle and flung my coat over the back of my chair. A shaft of rainbow light painted across my desk. I glanced up at my desktop monitor.

A small crystal snowflake hung off the edge of my screen. I slipped its royal blue ribbon from its perch and dangled it in front of my face. The morning sun streaming through the windows on the far wall caught the edges and cast colored beams all around my cube.

I pulled at the tiny ring of paper looped around the ribbon.

For taking a second chance.

I replaced the snowflake on my monitor and peered over my half walls at Peter's office. Ben smiled as he nodded my direction and slowly closed the door. I flopped into my desk chair and pulled my laptop from my bag. If I didn't focus on work, who knew what trouble my brain would get into.

❄

The words flowed fast. Much quicker than they had in months. Inspiration fired out of my fingers like electricity. A superhero of syntax. I polished off five *Ask Holly* letters and still managed to write a brand-new article without even taking a break to breathe.

But the search for a synonym to 'repugnant' slowed down my process. As I surveyed the list of options, a strange buzzing noise rattled my concentration. The noise stopped. I glanced around, shook my head and went back to my thesaurus search. The noise buzzed again.

I listened for a second, then reached down into my purse and pulled out my cell phone.

"Hey Claire, what's up?" I asked as I spun my chair away from my desk and stretched out my stiff legs.

"I've been calling for like three hours. It's not like you not to pick up."

"Sorry, I was just in the writing zone today. I don't know what happened, but I'll take it."

"Does it have anything to do with why you absconded from my house with my husband's warmest mittens?"

"Maybe." I teased. "But I will get them back to you soon."

"No rush. But when are you going to get to the hall? I thought you said you had time to help set up?"

I glanced at the time on the bottom left of my monitor. Already 2:19. What happened to my morning? My stomach growled, asking the same question.

"I'm so sorry. I didn't notice the time. But if you give me about a half hour, I'll be there."

"Only if you can. But I'd really appreciate it. There's still so much to do and I need to get home to get ready."

"Be right there."

I hung up the phone and shoved it back into my purse. I shut my laptop and snatched up my coat as I lunged toward the cubicle entrance. A silhouette hovered over my escape.

"Leaving already?"

The coat slipped from my fingers and landed in a pile on the floor. Ben gracefully swept it up in his arm and handed it back.

"Thanks." My fingers lingered next to his, just like his gaze hesitated to leave my face.

"Yeah, I have somewhere I have to be. And I'm late."

He kept smiling, but a shadow fell over his expression. "Well, I won't stop you then. But what about later? I really wanted to talk to you some more." He leaned closer and dropped his lips close to my ear, his voice a seductive whisper. "I really had a great time last night."

"Me too." I slipped right to put some distance between us. "But I can't. There's a fundraiser for the children's hospital wing and I promised I'd be there. That's actually where I'm going now, to help set up the event."

"Okay. But maybe I could call later or something?" A strange new look overthrew his flirty demeanor.

"Is everything alright, Ben?" I rested my hand on his arm and he seemed to steady. "Wait. I can do one better. Here, if you don't have anything else going on, why don't you come to the fundraiser?"

I spun around and rummaged through my purse to find the tattered ticket envelope. I slid the red and white card stock tickets out into my fist. One of them was supposed to be Fletcher's, but there wasn't any chance that he'd go anywhere near me now. I held the extra ticket out toward Ben. "The paper sponsors the event, so I'm sure it would be fine if you came."

"But I—"

"It's a bit fancier, but one of your posh city suits would be just fine. You'll probably be better dressed than half the men there."

He puffed his chest and stood up straighter, brushing invisible lint from his lapels. "So, you do like this look."

"Don't get too far ahead of yourself, Mr. Concorde. I just said you would blend in fine."

"What's the point of blending in when you can stand out?"

I tapped him gently on the chest and brushed close past with my coat and bags. "Badly misquoting other writers won't impress me. But meet at The Havenbrook Museum at the end of Virginia Street. 7 o'clock. I might let you try again."

I hurried down the hall, fighting the goofy grin trying to plaster itself on my lips. From behind me, Ben yelled, "I'll be there."

CHAPTER 10

"What?" Claire's head jerked forward. "You invited him here? That Ben guy you kissed at the bar? The one who owns *the Herald?*"

"Shhh." I glanced over my shoulder. A few couples swayed on the dance floor, while everyone else huddled in private groups gossiping and cackling the night away. Glasses clinked. Wine flowed like water. And no one really cared about Claire's outburst. "He doesn't own *The Herald*. His family's corporation does. Totally different thing."

"Right. Absolutely. But at least it explains why you're dressed like that."

"Like what?" I scoured the lace bodice of my poppy-colored frock and tugged the tight fabric straight on my hips.

"Like that." She waved her hand in front of me as if performing some witchy magic. "Normally, when you attend a charity event, you remember to bring the back of your dress."

I stood up straighter, letting her snark roll off my half-naked shoulders. "Very funny. I think I look good."

"You do, Holly. Too good. But watch out, looking like

that, I might try to take you home with me at the end of the night."

"Wait, what did I just hear? Pajama party at our place?" Austin appeared behind Claire and slipped a flute of champagne into her hand. "It's fine with me. Am I invited?"

"Oh, stop." Claire playfully slapped her hand on his suited chest. He winked then clasped his hand over hers. She sure did a great job cleaning him up for the event. I rarely saw him without a hoodie or ball cap, so his slicked back blond locks and three-piece suit seemed exceptionally dashing.

"Besides, she's not wearing that outfit for either of us. She has a date."

"I don't have a date. It's a work thing." A sudden tremble shot through my arms and I eyed Claire's drink with immense jealousy.

"It isn't the guy who you stole my gloves for, is it?" Austin added. "Those were some of my favorites."

Claire glared up at him. "Why are you worrying about this? I've never even seen you wear them."

"I might wear them. One day." He shrugged. "But yes, Holly, you look pretty hot tonight." Austin took a sip of his own champagne as Claire nudged him with her elbow in his gut. He coughed and wiped the back of his hand across his mouth.

"Thanks. But it doesn't really matter, anyway. He's already over a half hour late so I doubt he's even coming."

Claire grabbed my hand and rubbed her thumb against my knuckles. "I'm sure he's probably just lost or stuck in traffic or something."

"Seriously? Havenbrook is the smallest town in the state and he doesn't have a car here."

She offered me a half-smile, which looked pathetic. I fought the urge to slouch and ruin what was clearly the perfect outfit.

"Or he just wants to make an entrance." Claire nodded her chin over my shoulder, then pointed with her immaculate French manicured finger toward the entrance.

I whirled around on my stilettos to see Ben standing in the lobby craning his neck to scan over the crowded room.

I shrugged and started for the door.

"Go get him," Claire said and tapped my butt as I walked away.

"Alright, Austin, she's cut off."

He ignored me as she settled back against his chest and he kissed the top of her head.

I rushed a few steps then slowed my pace. No reason to hurry. Might as well make an impression. Just like Ben already had. Every head turned to watch the mysterious man near the door. Poised, confident, and oozing enough charm to have every woman in a six-foot radius swooning in seconds. Half the room probably wondered where he came from, and why he'd stumbled into the event. The other half watched him with curiosity, wondering how someone could find a steel blue suit cut so perfect around his broad shoulders in a small town like this. And I just watched, still surprised that he actually showed up to meet me.

Ben swaggered a few steps into the room then stopped dead, his stare glued in my direction, his eyes wide.

"You made it." I asked, as I approached. His gaze dropped to the floor for a moment. "I'm so sorry. Meetings ran much longer this afternoon than I had hoped."

"It's fine. I had a bunch of administrative things to help Claire with for the event, anyway. We actually just finished up."

"Good. So, is it fine to say I lied and spent two hours trying to figure out what to wear?"

"Don't you have only about four or five outfits here anyway?"

He laughed, the light returning to his eyes. "Good point. But I thought you said it was only a little fancy?"

He took my hand and leaned forward as his cheek brushed against mine. I froze.

"Because, Holly Brighton," he whispered. "You look far too breathtaking for just a little bit fancy."

He backed away and released my hand.

"I try," I croaked, then cleared my throat, trying to shake the soft touch of his skin. "Now, why don't we head over and get you a drink?"

We maneuvered through the crowd as I tried to ignore the stares following our every move. He leaned into my ear.. "Everyone's looking at you."

"Yeah, I doubt that." His hand rested near the small of my back as we navigated our way, not daring to touch but the heat of his palm scalding the naked skin near my waistline. My little secret as I passed the familiar faces of everyone I'd known since I was a child.

"Well, hello there, Ben." Claire inserted herself between us and the bar, extending her hand in his direction. "It's so nice of you to be able to make it to our little event."

"Not a problem." He took her hand and shook it. "Claire, right? We met at the bar?"

"That's right. However, I didn't realize that I would be seeing you again so soon."

I dropped my head into my hand and wished for the world to open up and swallow me.

"This is my husband, Austin."

Austin shuffled up behind her like a good escort. "Nice to meet you."

She nudged him in the side. "Why don't you run and grab drinks for our friends?"

"It's fine, Claire," I said. "I was just taking Ben over to the bar myself. Thanks though."

"Don't worry about it, it's fine." Austin nodded, his

impeccably styled hair starting to come undone as a small piece flipped down onto his forehead, before he disappeared into the throng.

The second he was gone, Claire edged up beside Ben and hooked her arm with his. "So, Ben, Holly really hasn't told me too much about you. How long do you expect to be in town?"

He glanced up at me and froze. "I don't know yet. Things are still kind of up in the air."

"Well, Havenbrook really does a great job with Christmas. If you aren't in any hurry, maybe you could hang around through the holidays. Unless you have somewhere to be? Family, girlfriend, whatever?"

Seriously, Claire. I should've known she'd fall into big sister interrogation mode. But, I guess sometimes blunt had its advantages.

Ben stood straighter and politely made some distance between the two of them without being too obvious to Claire. This guy sure knew how to handle himself. Probably years of training from his family's glamorous events.

"Like I said, not really sure where I'm going to be at." He locked eyes with me. "But I don't have a wife or girlfriend to rush back to, if that's what you're wondering."

Claire winked at me and I grimaced.

"Two glasses of champagne, coming up." Austin, thankfully, arrived and thrust over-filled glasses into our hands, then slipped his arm over Claire's shoulder. "What did I miss?"

Ben shuffled closer to me and shoved his free hand in his pocket, his elbow brushing against my arm. I shivered in the swelter of the crowd.

"Not much. I was just going to ask about this gala. What exactly is the charity again?" Ben asked.

"Well—" Claire shuffled out of Austin's grip. "All the

money we raise goes toward the children's wing at the hospital."

Ben nodded and rolled his head back, taking in the chandeliers and ornamental sconces on the wall. "Sounds admirable."

"Absolutely. Years ago they were going to close it down, but instead they created this charity to pay for the operating expenses. Every year the whole town comes together to keep it running," I added.

"Don't be so modest, Holly."

My breath caught in my throat and my eyes widened, glaring down at Claire. No. I screamed with my mind hoping she would get the hint. She didn't.

"It's really Holly's dad who got all of this going. That first year he went door to door in a snowstorm to collect pledges to keep the lights on for all those sick children. He's really the one who kick started this whole movement. Now it's a great way to get together before the holidays and for a great cause."

"Really?" Ben nudged me with his shoulder and I crossed my arms over my chest. "Sounds like big hearts run in the family."

"Absolutely. Everyone loved Holly's dad. He was an extraordinarily great man."

I waved my right hand across my neck, signaling for Claire to stop, but she didn't notice. Instead, she raised her glass and held it up to Ben. "To David Brighton, the kindest man Havenbrook has ever known."

"Excuse me?" Ben leaned closer to Claire.

She lifted her glass in the air again. "To Holly's dad, David Brighton."

"To David." Ben clinked his champagne flute with hers and glared over at me. I refused to meet his questioning stare and joined the toast, guzzling back half my drink afterwards. The bubbles hit my brain immediately, but only made things fuzzier.

"Well, this sounds like a wonderful cause, I'm sure Concorde Publications would love to make a donation. Do you know where I might be able to do that?"

"I'll show you." Austin cut through our little group and turned Ben toward the donor station. He slapped him on his back, then glanced back at Claire. She shrugged.

"He seems great," Claire said as soon as both men disappeared.

I turned on my heel and stared at her.

She jerked her head back. "What?"

"Nothing." I sighed and let my shoulders sink, the straps of my dress dangerously close to sliding off. "I just hadn't told him about my dad yet. Or at least not the part about him being editor of *The Herald* for over a decade. It was before Concorde bought the paper, so I'm sure he's figured out we're related, but not how close."

She slid in beside me and wrapped her arm around my waist as she rested her head on my shoulder. "I'm not sure how he would've figured that out from what I said, but I wasn't trying to make you look bad. I was trying to boost you up."

Scooping my arm around her waist, I gave her an awkward half-hug. "I know, thanks for trying, but I'm sure I just look like a weirdo now. I should have just told him when he asked about him a few days ago. I just didn't want him to disregard my opinion because I was the editor's daughter. I wanted to save the paper because it deserves to be saved."

"He'll get over it. He seems pretty normal. Charming. Sophisticated. Sexy as all hell. You might have just stumbled upon a winner."

"You forgot to mention that he's also practically my boss."

She pinched my chin and steered my face down to meet her eyes. "Then I think someone needs to tell him that. Because the way that man is looking at you, is definitely not suitable for work."

"Yeah, right."

She crooked her eyebrow then drained the rest of her champagne. "I'm not blind, Holly." She took my hand and raised it above my head forcing me into a twirl. "And neither is he."

It shouldn't matter. It couldn't matter. But her words swam through my limbs and made them twitch. There were so many reasons why he and I were a bad idea, but why did I not seem to care?

Across the room, Ben stood talking to Jenkins. When did he get here? Must've been in those late meetings too. I took a deep breath and shook out all the weird vibes building up in my blood. All those things I shouldn't feel, but couldn't help myself.

"Well, maybe you should have thought of that sooner," Jenkins muttered as I approached.

"Hello there, Peter. I didn't see you come in. Is Isabelle here as well?" I joined the conversation with a smile making sure not to stand too close to Ben, but aching not to be too far from him either.

Jenkins plastered on a smile, but the expression stopped at his lips and didn't quite match the harsh deep-set lines puckered around his eyes. "Why, Holly, don't you look lovely. Yes, Isabelle is around her somewhere. Probably talking to our neighbors again."

Ben watched Jenkins with an icy glare, except he seemed to be more collected than Peter.

"I hope I wasn't interrupting anything?" I backed up a step. "Maybe I should go find her."

"No need. I think we've said all we need to say." Ben

cleared his throat and shook off his harsh expression, replacing it with a polite grin.

Jenkins' stare flit between him, then me, and back again. I leaned away from Ben, trying to put as much space between us as possible. Whatever it was, I'd never seen Jenkins this angry, at least not outside of the office. Both men held each other in silent gridlock until eventually Jenkins scoffed and conceded.

"Enjoy the rest of your evening, Holly." Jenkins marched away and disappeared into the crowd.

Ben's shoulders dropped as the tension dissipated.

"What was that all about?" I asked.

"It's nothing." He sounded calm, but couldn't meet my eyes.

Putting my hands on my hips, I tapped my foot. "Peter Jenkins doesn't just give people the death stare. Especially not in public. What's going on?"

He leaned closer, the smell of his expensive cologne clouding my head. "Is there somewhere we can go? To talk."

I pointed at the balcony surrounding the event hall and rushed toward the hidden stairs leading to the upper level. He followed close behind, keeping each step in time with mine. My heels sunk into the plush carpet and I gripped tight onto the banister to keep myself from falling. The thoughts bouncing through my head weren't helping my concentration, nor was the thought of being up here alone with him.

As we crested the top stair, the din of the gala muted into a blur of incomprehensible sounds. The lights faded, leaving both of us draped in shadow, save a few slivers from the chandelier that cut across the angles of Ben's perfect face.

"Why didn't you tell me that David Brighton was your father?"

I crossed my arms and walked silently over to the balcony, watching the people below us swirl about. Colors and sounds, mixing and melding together, but nothing giving me any more clarity.

"Because I didn't want you to know. *The Herald* has always been a huge part of my life. I grew up in that office. I sat on his knee as he edited. I played pretend under the desks when the regular staff went home for the night or on weekends when the edition wasn't as perfect as he'd wanted it to be. It really is my home."

Heat prickled my back as the soft cashmere of Ben's jacket brushed over my skin. His hand appeared next to my waist on the railing as his breath tickled the small hairs on the back of my neck. I shivered and sunk deeper into him. Expensive notes of bergamot folded over the distinct clean smell of the cucumber mint soap from the Starlight. I closed my eyes and inhaled.

"Why did you think I wouldn't understand that? I grew up in a boardroom. Hockey games and soccer practices were cut short by conference calls and last minute trips. Both my parents worked hard for what they wanted and they built something amazing. It sounds like your dad was just like them."

"Maybe. But I didn't want it to seem like a weakness. You flew into town for business and I'd have hated if you thought I was only doing this for my father. I'm not."

"I know that." His hand moved from the railing and clutched my hip, then he spun me around until we stood face to face. "You have a heart bigger than this whole town, Holly. Maybe this whole state. I wouldn't expect anything less from you."

He lowered his head and the tip of his nose ran down the bridge of mine. Skin on skin. Slow and electric. My hands splayed across his chest as he tugged me tighter, his fingertips lighting sparks like cherry bomb fireworks up my spine.

"I never expected to meet someone like you," he breathed against my cheeks.

"Maybe I should've started kissing random strangers years ago."

He pulled his head back and gazed down at me. His copper eyes appeared endless, as if they actually pierced into his soul and let everything pour out. "I'm glad you didn't."

I pushed up onto my toes and let my lips brush against his. Asking. Waiting.

He released his grip on my waist and jerked away. I sunk down onto my heels, wishing I could fall even further through the floor.

My mouth dried as the sting of rejection shot through my limbs, my knees threatening to give way. "I'm sorry. I just thought…"

"Please don't apologize." He let out a long sigh. "I just need to tell you something first."

Pulling back, I leaned against the railing as his face scrunched while he battled whatever he needed to say.

"Remember how you said you would consider taking a reporting job if it came up."

"Yeah, but there isn't one here."

"No, but Peter let me have one of your articles and I sent it to my friend Marcel at the Boston Trumpeter."

I shot up straight, nearly tripping in my heels. "You what?"

"I know I should've asked first, but the good news is that he loved it and wants to offer you a job."

"You had no right to do that." Ice formed in my veins as my stomach hollowed. I clenched my hands into fists. "Is that why Peter was so mad at you? Did you tell him that you were poaching his staff? Please don't tell me he knew about this before I did?"

"Of course not. I wouldn't betray you like that."

"But you would share my work with another editor without my permission and ask them to hire me."

"I didn't ask him. I just sent it along and told him to keep you in mind, but he had a job opening and he loved your work. You should be happy."

I stuck my finger in his face. "Do not tell me how to feel."

"Then don't take the job." He held his hands up in surrender. Except even though he backed down, I still didn't feel any better.

I gripped my arms, suddenly exposed. Nearly naked and humiliated.

"Why couldn't you have just asked me first? Do I really mean that little that I can't have an opinion on my own life?" Who did he think he was? Did being a Concorde suddenly make him the king of all things? Not to me. And I actually trusted him. I was so stupid.

"No, Holly." He stepped forward with his arms open, trying to touch me, but I pulled away. "There just wasn't enough time. I needed to do this now."

"Right. It's almost the holidays and most people are taking vacation, there really isn't any rush."

Ben rubbed his forehead and placed his other hand on his back. His suit jacket rode up as he paced in front of me. "Yes, there is. Remember I told you that *The Herald* needed more ad revenue. Well, we looked at the books again. They need one hundred thousand dollars just to make it until next quarter and nearly five times that to survive for the upcoming year."

"Which means?"

"We're closing *The Herald*. The holiday edition will be its last run. I'd planned on announcing it tomorrow at the morning staff meeting. That's why Peter was so angry, and that's why I rushed out to try to find you that job. After tomorrow you won't have one."

I couldn't breathe. Each word pressed on my ribcage and closed in around my lungs. Heavy. Cement bricks weighing me down. A few tears broke past my lashes and I wiped them off. Mascara streaks painted across my hand, but I didn't care. Nothing mattered right now.

"Why didn't you tell me?"

"I planned on it. I really did, but then I walked in the door and I saw you. So excited to see me and so absolutely gorgeous. All the things I wanted to say didn't matter because I just wanted a few more minutes, or hours, or whatever we had left, seeing you happy. To just be with you."

His compliments died at my feet as I seethed. "Then what? We drink, we dance, you walk me home and then 'oops, I forgot to mention I'm closing down your entire life in the morning'. Erasing my father's legacy."

He stopped pacing. "To be fair, you didn't tell me about that. At least I planned on telling you about all this. And I really did try to help you out by sending off your article. I wanted to keep you from the fallout."

All this time, I'd fought to keep the paper running. To keep everyone's jobs. My job. But none of it mattered. And how long had he known? Was he plotting all this while we skated in the market? Or maybe while we stood under the stars and he told me how beautiful I was? Did it mean anything or was it just a way to placate me while he razed my whole career to the ground? Except it meant something to me. And he just broke that something, then crushed it under the heel of his expensive designer shoes.

"I don't need you to swoop in and save me. I can handle things myself," I said.

"I know you can. But I was looking out for you. Why can't you just let someone care about you?"

"Why? Everyone who cares about me just sets me up and then leaves. Hell, this time I knew you were leaving and still managed to walk into this with both feet."

My hands gripped the banister, hanging on to keep me stable as the room spun around me. Everything crashed and shattered in one moment. The paper. My job. Even my heart. Although Ben, clearly, didn't deserve it in the first place. I hadn't even realized how hard I'd fallen for him until the thought of him leaving cut deep instead of being a relief.

"I hoped we could work that out, but you knew that one day I'd have to go," he pleaded.

I pointed toward the stairs, tears streaming hard down my cheeks and I didn't care to stop them. "Then why don't you get a head start."

He dropped his head to his chest, but didn't argue. Each plodding step took his lying mouth further away from me. So, why didn't it feel like a win?

❊

The cold, blustery wind followed me from the cab to the door, nearly pushing me inside. Strains of Christmas music whined from the jukebox, but I didn't have the energy to stumble over to that side of the room to make it stop. Instead, I clicked my stilettoed feet up to the bar and swung myself around on a stool.

I flopped my arms on the bar top without removing my jacket and stared at the lines of brightly colored liquor bottles along the far counter. Lights glowed from beneath them, adding to the show, and making the thought of a drink all that more enticing.

"You look like you've had a rough night." Danny rested

his hands along the bar rail and leaned over me. The soft hint of concern helped ease the strain in my muscles from clenching tight since I raced from the ballroom balcony.

A rough night? To be honest, I wasn't sure. I got my dream job, but I lost the paper. My father's paper. This town's paper. No matter what I might have gained, I'd still lost and let everyone down. If *The Herald* had been suffering so badly, why didn't Jenkins tell anyone? Did he even know? That man worked as hard as any editor in any city, but maybe the finances weren't really his forte. Or was shuttering the paper really the Concorde plan all along? I trembled. Ben could have been lying to me this entire time. Lying to us all.

He didn't seem like he could do something like that, but how much did I really know him? He'd only been here for a couple of days. One knee-weakening kiss and a few conversations didn't make him innocent. Plus, imagining him as the villain made it so much easier to erase the image of him descending those stairs, broken and defeated. If only there were a way to keep us from being on opposite sides of this?

"Hello, earth to Holly." Danny waved his hand in front of my face. "Can I get you anything?"

I snapped out of my thoughts and looked around. I wasn't used to the place being so quiet. Granted the fundraiser was on tonight, but Danny's Pub was always packed. Successful. An idea started rolling around in my brain. I pushed it down at first, but it roared back, begging to be fleshed out.

"Maybe," I said, drumming my fingers along the wooden bar top. "Have you ever considered advertising?"

CHAPTER 11

Alright, Holly. Deep breaths. I closed my eyes and breathed in slowly, trying to calm my racing heart. The plan backfired, as my jaw thrust open in a deep, almost painful, yawn. I'd barely slept a wink last night, and for the few hours I may have, I tossed and turned more than an ocean in a hurricane. Plus, getting started at 5 AM didn't help matters.

I ran the rest of the way and yanked open the front door of the newspaper office. Doris looked up with her courteous smile quickly morphing into a concerned frown.

"Holly, the meeting has already started. You're late."

"I know," I said as I raced across the lobby. "But there was something I needed to finish. Trust me, it was worth it."

Or at least I hoped it would be.

I chucked my coat and my laptop bag in my cubicle as I rushed toward the board room. Before I reached the windows, I slowed to a relaxed walk, straightening my barely worn suit jacket and pushing my shoulders back. I expected at least a few sets of eyes to notice me, but everyone seemed locked on Ben as he leaned against the head of the table, leading the charge. Wide-eyed expressions and frowning wrinkled mouths hung on his every word. If there was any doubt that he hadn't made the announcement yet, Jenkins' glassy broken stare proved otherwise.

I clutched tighter onto the file folder in my left hand. Only one chance to get this right. Rapping my knuckles on the door, I pushed it open without waiting for an invitation.

Ben halted mid-sentence and glanced up at me. "Thank you for joining us, Ms. Brighton. Now if you could please take a seat so we could continue."

His words came out firm and calm, businesslike to a fault, but his face gave his emotions away. The awkward curl of his bottom lip. The pained glint in his eyes. He'd probably hoped I wouldn't show this morning. Probably would've made this announcement so much easier. But I wouldn't let closing *The Herald* be easy on anyone.

"Thank you, Mr. Concorde, but I think I'd prefer to stand."

He shifted his weight from foot to foot but didn't argue. Instead, he crossed his arms and paced the front of the room, refusing to look in my direction.

"As I was saying, I know that this isn't exactly the news anyone wants to hear, especially before the holidays, but we—" Ben nodded toward Jenkins for support, "—don't have any other options. Effective December 24—"

"I do," I said, raising my hand then feeling silly and dropping it to my side.

"Excuse me?" Ben shook his head and blinked. "You what?"

"I have another option. A few of them, in fact."

I spread the manila file folder open on the board room table and plucked a contract from the top.

"You said we needed to generate more ad revenue, is that correct?"

Ben stood up straighter and crossed his arms. "Of course, but I don't see how—"

"Then here is an order for $60,000 of ad space between now and March."

"That's great, Ms. Brighton, but it's not nearly enough to cover the paper's needs."

"Oh, I know." I grabbed a stack of contracts held together by an overextended binder clip. "That's just the first one. I have over $250,000 of advertising in my hands."

"But—"

"And I know that's just a start. This here—" I pulled the rest of the pages from the file folder, "—is a list of local business owners willing to provide angel investments to keep *The Herald* running."

Jenkins bounded across the room in two quick strides then plucked the list from my hands. He quickly scanned the pages as his eyes widened.

"It all looks pretty legitimate here, Ben." A wary smile whispered across his mouth, but he pushed it back down.

"Oh, it is. Communities like Havenbrook take care of each other. They trust each other's judgement." I dropped the stack of contracts back on the table with a thud and stared back at Ben. "When everyone heard we needed help, they jumped to offer. They believe in what we're doing here. What this paper means to the people who live in this town."

"So, does this mean we get another chance?" Jenkins gazed between me and Ben. Each of us in the triad of information refusing to make any quick moves. Ben strode toward the exterior window and pressed his fingers along the sill. His knuckles blanched white from the pressure. White as the fluffy flakes of snow falling just outside. He let out a deep controlled sigh, then turned and placed his hand across his forehead.

"Can you all please excuse Ms. Brighton and myself for a few moments? I need to review this new information before making any further comment."

Voices rumbled around us. Concern bordering on hope. Hope I'd given them.

Ben raised his hand toward the door and nodded. As I collected my paperwork, a hot surge rushed through me. Like getting sent to the principal's office for the best senior prank in history. Except I'd never been one to get myself in trouble before. Head held high, I marched toward the door as the dread of confrontation started to claw its way in. Jesse flashed me a thumbs up and a wink as I passed, helping my steps stay light and pushing me forward.

"We can take Peter's office." Ben's voice commanded behind me. I didn't turn around to see his angry expression. I could hear it. Picture the distortion of the face as he realized I'd destroyed his plans. He probably regretted meeting me now.

❋

I hurried into the small office as the door shut hard behind me. Not quite a slam, but enough to make Jenkins' wall of framed diplomas rattle against the eggshell painted wall.

"What exactly was that in there?" Ben pointed toward the closed door as red seeped up his neck into his defined cheeks.

I crossed my arms and backed up until I leaned against the far bookshelf in the corner. "I just found a way to save *The Herald*, that's all. Doing the work you refused to do."

"And you didn't think to tell me before you stormed into my meeting and made me look like an idiot in front of everyone?"

"Just like you consulted me before sending my private work to a stranger to apply for a job I never asked for?"

He dropped his chin into his chest and grabbed the back of his head. "I said I was sorry about that. I was just trying to help you."

"And I was just trying to help *The Herald*."

"Except this isn't the way it works, Holly. This is a business, not a charity pet project. The advertising revenue is great, but what happens when the investors' pockets are empty or they get tired of supporting a losing cause?"

"Well, at least we will have a chance to turn it around first. You wrote the paper off before they had the opportunity." And us.

"If you'd just told me your plan, I could have helped you. It might not have worked, but you didn't need to shut me out."

Ben quieted and circled around the office running his index finger around the edge of Jenkins desk until he flopped down in his chair. "When I met you, I was mesmerized by your passion, your heart. The way you care so deeply about things, but I'm starting to think that maybe you're just stubborn. Holding on too tight to things and never letting them breathe. It's exhausting to watch you throw away so much potential that I doubt you even know you have."

I pushed off from the bookcase and walked toward the opposite side of the desk. "What's that supposed to mean?"

"If I need to explain, then you clearly don't get it. The paper, your ex, this whole town, it's just you could do so much...and we could..." His stare dropped to his hands knitted in his lap. "Never mind. Obviously, everything I've done since I got here was a mistake. You can dismiss everyone from the boardroom while I sort through this mess you left for me."

I stood in silence for a moment, but he never looked up.

Eventually, I placed the file folder on the desk in front of him, my hand pausing on the papers for much longer than necessary. I'd walked in here this morning with one mission in mind, but now it didn't feel quite as victorious. The tightness growing in my chest hurt more than it should.

"Ben, I…" Except there was nothing more to say. At least not right now.

My hand lingered on the doorknob but eventually made the move to turn it. "This probably means nothing, but if we were on the same side maybe things would've been different."

"Except that you couldn't see that we always were." He finally looked up. I expected anger, but only pain shone through his eyes. "I get that Havenbrook and *The Herald* are your anchor, but if you don't let go, you're just going to drown."

"Maybe, but at least I have something I'd be willing to risk my life for."

The hollow thunk of the door closing between us echoed through the office. Ben on one side and me on the other. It was probably for the best.

CHAPTER 12

❄

Stubborn? Who was Ben to call me stubborn? Mr. I'm-all-corporate-stooge-all-the-time telling me I need to relax. I wrote the word down in thick block letters on my notepad and traced them over and over again until the pen tip cut through the page. Clearly, I'd moved on to another stage of processing our argument in Jenkins' office. Already lunch time and he still hadn't emerged. The door remained closed tight. Even Jenkins sat in an empty bullpen desk to avoid disturbing him.

An unusual silence fell over the office. Whispers and hushed tête-à-tête's wafted around, but no one seemed to dare to speak aloud.

I'd tried to write several times, but the words just wouldn't come. Most of them were tied up in my head, piecing together all the things I should have said when I had the chance. When I could have told Ben what I was really thinking. Except I still hadn't sorted that out yet. I scrolled mindlessly through my email. So many "Ask Holly" questions punctuated with the desperate junk mail pleas of stores trying to get those last-minute sales less than a week before Christmas. My computer dinged as another email arrived.

MDupre@BostonTrumpeter.com
Job Offer

I hovered my mouse over the hyperlink as my fingers twitched. It wouldn't hurt to just look at the message. Obviously, I wasn't going to take it, but it didn't mean I couldn't find out what the market looked like for my level of experience. To be honest, it would almost be irresponsible of me not to read it. I clicked the mouse button.

Ms. Brighton,

I received your information from Benjamin Concorde, and...

I hit delete without reading any further. No point. Just seeing his name sliced deep into my heart. Scars that I should get started on healing.

After slamming my laptop shut, I wrestled my phone from my purse.

Coffee? I texted.

Three little dots appeared immediately.

Sure. Meet you at Corner Brew in 10.

❄

A hit of roasting espresso blasted my face as I pushed open the door. Instead of jumpstarting my pulse, today it had the opposite effect. Claire waved from her favorite table by the window as she sat, her chin propped up on her hand, watching the town go by.

I popped up on the bar height chair and flipped open the plastic lid on the coffee cup already sitting in my place.

"I guessed it was a double shot mocha kind of day." Claire shrugged and scanned my face looking for clues. "So, what is going on with you? I saw you rush out of the gala last night and then you don't answer any of my calls or texts. What happened?"

I took a long sip and let the chocolatey goodness roll down my tight throat. My shoulders sank, a slight pain prickling through the muscles I'd held taut for the whole morning.

"No, it wasn't you. It was that Ben guy I invited. Big mistake," I said.

"Really? I kind of liked him. He seemed kinda nice."

"Yeah, a nice guy that was about to close down *The Herald* for good."

Claire slammed her palm on the table and it echoed through the small café. The barista behind the counter glared at us.

"You're kidding? And you're just saving that piece of gossip until now. Why didn't you tell me yesterday?" Claire asked.

"Because I had to do something. I couldn't just sit back and let this happen, so I spent all night calling and visiting half of Havenbrook to get the money we needed to stay open."

"Wow. You're kind of amazing, you know that?" She winked at me and took another sip of her Chai latte. "But why didn't you ask me for help?"

"Because apparently I'm selfish and stubborn." I took a giant gulp of my coffee and let the burn sting all the way down.

"Says who?" Her face soured as she sat up straight in her chair. If anyone would throw down for me, it was Claire. It's a good thing I didn't call her back yesterday, she might have hunted Ben down.

"Ben." I dropped my head and picked at the adhesive order label on my cup. The cutesy little hearts and snowflakes drawn on the side didn't even lighten the heaviness bearing down on my ribs. "I might've, kind of, thrown my entire save *The Herald* plan at him during a well-attended staff meeting."

Claire sucked air through her teeth as her face mimicked how awful I felt. "Yikes. Not a great move, but everyone should still be pleased with what you've done. Besides, that wasn't any reason to call you selfish. Saving *The Herald* is a pretty selfless act, or at least I think so."

"Okay, maybe he didn't exactly call me selfish, but definitely stubborn. Those words 100% came out of his mouth."

"Why do I feel like there's more to this then you're telling me?"

"Not really." I set my elbows on the table top and held my head in my hands trying to make the thoughts stop. "Only that Ben submitted my writing to an editor in Boston and they offered me a reporting job."

Claire's expression perked up. "Holly, that's fantastic."

"But I'm not taking it."

She leaned back on her chair. Her nose scrunched up, like it did when she needed to pick her words carefully. "And why, exactly? You've been talking about a reporter job forever."

"Yeah, but not like this. I'm not just going to up and leave everything I know for that."

"No wonder he called you stubborn."

I crossed my arms and scoffed at her insult. "Wow, that's fair."

"Seriously, you've been going on and on about how you wanted this job and you haven't gotten it. Heck, the night you met Ben you'd gone off on one of your rants about how you were going to look elsewhere if Peter didn't give you what you wanted, now all of a sudden you're doubling down on staying here in Havenbrook? I'd be pretty confused too, if it weren't for the fact that I knew you were all talk about leaving."

I pushed up from my chair and snatched the cup off the table. "So, you've just been humoring me this whole time? Nice."

"Sit back down, drama queen. I have supported you through everything, and I knew you'd finally leave when you were ready. Everything you've been through has held you back here, but other than me, what is really holding you back now?" She shook her head as if I might answer, but I stayed silent. "One of the things I love most about you is how you dream so much bigger than the rest of us, but it breaks my heart to see that most of the time they're just dreams. You got out of here once and I was so, so proud of you and I get why you needed to be here for your dad. But then you met Fletcher, and he just held you back and I hoped that, finally, now that you'd ended things you'd be able to move on, but you're still just as stuck."

I stood still, one foot facing the door but refusing to move. Her words washed through me filtering through many levels of my heart. Anger filtered into irritation into sadness, into something that might have resembled acceptance, but I wasn't sure yet.

Claire placed her hand on mine and gripped my fingers. "You are my best friend in the whole world, and that is never going to change, but you have to stop letting good things pass you by because the last time you left things didn't work out how you planned. I'm telling you this, because I care about you, and because I know you'd tell me if I needed to hear the same. But don't lose out on your future because you can't let go the past."

Was she right? Was I sabotaging my entire life to hang on to my dad and this town? My mind raced, picking apart every decision I'd made over the past few years. Every little choice I made kept me here, but is this really where I wanted to be or because I felt I needed to? Maybe. Maybe not. Everything blurred. Claire's words mixed with Ben's that mixed with all my messy emotions in one big cocktail that I needed to swallow. And even though things hadn't become completely clear, my heart knew I'd made a huge mistake.

"Holls, say something to me." She tugged at my hand as she cast me a teary gaze.

"I…" I grabbed my coffee and chugged back the rest of the cup. Words jumbled in my head. So many things to say. So many apologies to make. I grabbed her hand and tugged her close, burying my face in her shoulder. "I love you the most, you know that, right? I'm really sorry."

She squeezed me back. "It's okay. I know I'll pay you back with a crisis sooner or later. I always do."

After letting go, I rubbed my hands over my face and tried to collect myself the best I could. "There's something I've got to do. I'll call you later, okay?"

"Go make things right, Holly," Claire said, as she waved me toward the door.

Bursting out onto the busy sidewalk, my feet ran faster than my brain could catch up. He had no right to call me out, but clearly Ben saw what everyone else did, and that I somehow couldn't. It didn't make things better, but I needed to talk to him. Needed to hear more. Needed to apologize.

"Afternoon Doris," I called as I raced through the lobby.
"Holly, wait."

I skidded to a halt.

"Didn't you get the message? Peter has just recalled everyone to the boardroom. Hurry up, dear."

I bounded through the empty office and whipped out my phone. Yep, eight missed messages from Jesse, two from Jenkins, and fifteen from Doris. Shoving the phone back in my pocket, I crept into the boardroom.

"Just in time." Jenkins said from the head of the table. "I'm happy to announce that due to Holly's hard work and ingenuity, *The Herald* will remain open."

Cheers erupted around the table and Jesse patted me on the shoulder.

"Good work, 'Ask Holly'," he said.

Jenkins raised his open hand in the air and the voices stopped. "This doesn't mean we don't have a lot of work to do. This experience should teach us all how important it is to make sure we are taking care of our business, as well as doing the best job that we can. We owe this community more than ever now. So, let's go forth and make this the best holiday edition of *The Herald* that they've ever seen. A giant thank you card to Havenbrook."

Everyone rose and headed for the door. I looked around again, however the likelihood that I missed him in the small room seemed impossible. "Peter," I whispered across the table. "Where's Ben? ... I mean Mr. Concorde."

Jenkins smirked. "He already left. Said there wasn't anything more he could do here."

My feet tapped below the table. I'd missed him. I wasn't even gone that long.

"Okay." I jumped up and weaseled my way into the main office then zig-zagged through the cubicles to get back out the door.

"Where are you going now?" Doris called after me.

"To fix things," I yelled back, even though I had no clue how.

I dashed through the snowy streets, the sun reflecting off the white banks and nearly blinding me without my sunglasses. But I knew this town better than anyone, even if I couldn't see, I could still find my way.

In the distance, the neon Starlight sign glowed dim in the daylight. My stomach twisted and turned, my typical regret trying to eat its way into my bloodstream, but I wouldn't let it. I didn't have time.

I slowed near the lobby and struggled to catch my breath, as I pushed the door open in front of me. I speed walked my way to the left passing the main check-in counter, my head down on a mission.

"He's not there, Holly."

I wretched my head back. Robbie stood behind the counter with his hands on his hips.

"What?" I said.

His wide sympathetic stare weighed down on my shoulders. "You just missed him by about twenty minutes. Some fancy car service came by and collected him."

"How did you know that's—"

"Don't try to pull one over on me. I see all sorts of people every single day and there is no way that the devastated look on his face when he left could match the one on yours right now without there being a story behind it."

I tripped forward and slammed my hand against the wall as the world began to spin.

"Are you okay?" Robbie rushed from his post to pour me a glass of lemon water from the public dispenser.

The swirl of emotions finally caught up with my feet and ricocheted through me. I was too late. All the things Claire said about giving up on what I wanted and the only thing I knew for a solid fact seemed to be that Ben was one of those precious things. I'd messed up. I'd made an idiot of myself. And who knew if I would ever get a chance to make it right.

CHAPTER 13

"It's going to be strange without your smiling face around here, sweetie." Jesse blinked as he rolled his wet eyes up toward the ceiling.

I wrapped my arms around him and inhaled, trying to lock more memories into my brain for a rainy day. I'd have to grow into a city like Boston and lonely days would definitely be on the horizon. "I'll miss you too. Give me a call if you are ever up that way."

"Of course. And remember to have a Merry Christmas."

He flashed me a kind smile and rushed out the front door toward the street. My shoulders sank. I thought I'd have more time after I accepted Marcel's job offer, but he wanted me by the new year and I'd already written enough columns to last that long for *The Herald*. With the holidays thrown in the mix, it just made sense to go while I could. Besides, if I waited too long, I'd have too many chances to talk myself out of leaving. Although, Claire would probably shake me senseless if I did.

I shifted back and forth on my feet, scanning the office for something or someone I might have missed, but with it already Christmas Eve, no one really worked much today anyway, so I had the entire day to get myself organized. Only one thing left on my list. The one goodbye I'd been dreading.

Rapping my knuckle against the flimsy door, I peeked inside Jenkins' office. Bottles of scotch with brightly colored bows sat in a perfect line on the side of his desk, but he ignored them, poring over a printed copy of last quarter's financials.

"Do you have a minute?" I asked, opening the door wider and edging into the office.

"Absolutely, Holly. C'mon in." He pulled his reading glasses from his nose and rubbed his eyes. "Just finishing up."

"I won't be long. I just wanted to say goodbye before I left."

I tucked my hands behind my back, suddenly unsure what to do with them as Jenkins stretched out in his chair. A sigh erupted from his lips as his body deflated like a giant man-shaped balloon.

"I guess that's it then?" Jenkins scratched the back of his head and looked toward the floor, as a sheen slid over his gaze. "I know I can't convince you to stay, so I won't try, but thank you so much for all you've done for this paper and for me. These last few weeks have been the most stressful of my life and somehow you managed to make things better. At least for now."

"Of course, Peter. You're the first one who gave me a chance and I love it here, but..."

"You don't need to explain. I get it. You've given me an amazing gift, now it's my turn to make sure I keep things in line and maintain *The Herald* legacy. I owe you that." His throat bobbed as he swallowed, then he extended his hand. "I might have given you your first chance, but your talent is much bigger than Havenbrook. I'm sure we won't hear the last of you, and whatever comes out, we'll all be proud. I know your father, wherever he is, sure will be. He always knew you were destined for greatness."

"Thanks. That means a lot." I took his hand and shook it while his soft wrinkled fingers trembled in my grip. His soft green eyes misted over completely and my throat ached harder with each welling tear. He opened his arms wide and pulled me into a hug. My ribs tightened around my heart as it threatened to burst. "I'll miss you, Peter. Merry Christmas."

"Merry Christmas to you, too. Now go, before I regret not begging you to pass up that fancy city job."

I nodded, my words sticking in my throat like shards of glass. Besides, nothing I could say would be enough. Wiping my hand over my eyes and casting a few stray tears to the carpet, I rushed out of the office.

"Oh, Holly, one last thing."

I froze, but refused to turn around.

"Could you answer one last 'Ask Holly' letter before you go? I think it would be an amazing addition to our holiday edition."

"I've already turned in my laptop and—" I glanced at my phone and tapped the screen, "—it's almost six on Christmas Eve, haven't we closed the issue already?"

"Do an old man a favor and give it a read. I left a copy on your desk. If it's not something you're interested in doing, I'm sure I can find someone else to answer the poor soul."

I peeked back over my shoulder. A strange smile twisted on Jenkins' face as he pulled my strings. Couldn't let me walk away, could he? But one last letter couldn't hurt. Besides, I didn't have anywhere to be. What would I do tonight, anyway? Go home and pack my bags just to sit and wait for the next week to pass before my flight?

Eerie silence settled over the office. The last of the late staff had left, probably off to family dinners or other gatherings. The emptiness hollowed my stomach. This was it. I was finally going. I scurried to my empty desk, the weight of my decision boring down on my shoulders. A folded piece of crisp white paper sat in the middle of my barren desk. I eyed the letter and shook my head. No. Why drag this out and make it harder to leave? I needed to be done.

While shrugging into my jacket, I scooped up my purse and unclipped my office pass card then rested it on the desk next to the crystal snowflake I didn't need to bring with me. I sighed. A new beginning. Shouldn't this be easier? Or maybe it wasn't that I didn't want to move on, but that I'd hoped a certain someone would have waited around to see me off. But that would be too much to ask for someone like him.

I marched through the office for the last time, slowly taking every detail in. The cluttered maze of the bullpens. The earthy smell of printer ink. My home for so many years, except now it wasn't, and for the first time since I'd finally made the decision to go it didn't seem so scary anymore.

Red and green lights from the street reflected across the shiny reception floor. Another Christmas in Havenbrook. Possibly my last, who really knew? A strange calm settled over my body. But whatever happened, I was going to be okay. My hand hovered over the doorknob heading out into the snowy twilight. Maybe I should answer just one last Christmas wish.

Ripping off my coat, I stormed back through the office, grabbing a pad of paper and a pen in my fury. Just fifteen minutes. That's it. I'd put together an answer and the team could edit it to polish later. I settled into my chair and clutched the letter in my hands. Even if I couldn't have everything I wanted this holiday, it didn't mean that I couldn't help someone else have theirs.

Dear Holly,

I met the most amazing woman. Intelligent, charming, and the biggest challenge I've ever encountered. But I've completely blown my chances with her. She's the advice columnist at The Havenbrook Herald, and I'm starting to think I should have listened to her more. The entire town trusts her opinion, why didn't I? I let my work and my ego affect my judgment and I regret it.

If I stand under the mistletoe in the middle of the skating circle at seven o'clock on Christmas Eve, do you think she'll show up so I can tell her how I feel? If she doesn't, maybe I already have my answer.

Sincerely,

Needing Just One More Chance

CHAPTER 14

❄

The festive lights of Havenbrook glinted and glittered along the snowy sidewalk, casting a celestial glow against the empty streets and darkened shop windows. The whole town had already closed down for the holidays. Except for me, as my boots slipped and slid on the ice in my frenzied rush toward the Christmas market. At least if I fell, no one would be around to see me land on my butt.

As I rounded the final corner, I wrestled my phone from my pocket and slowed to a walk. 6:58. Right on time. If I hadn't sat in my desk reading Ben's letter and letting my thoughts play out all the different things I could say, all the ways this could go, I wouldn't have had to run. I also wouldn't be gasping like a weirdo trying to calm my heavy awkward breaths before I made my way to the end of the market. And even worse, I still didn't have a clue what to say.

Bright white snowflakes glowed against the backdrop of city hall and the soft chords of a soulful jazz *Jingle Bells* echoed off the brick buildings from the skating pond, beckoning me closer. Drawing me in. Ahead, the shiny surface of the ice glimmered in the moonlight, casting shadows around a figure standing stoic in the center. My face warmed. Like the hot July sun kissing my cheeks amidst the December frost. He was really here. I wrapped my arms around my chest, clutching my coat closer to my body, and picked up my pace.

I reached the edge of the skating circle and eased my toe out onto the slick surface, as a strange weightless sensation flowed through my limbs.

"Hey," I called out as I slipped my way across the pond.

Ben's head rose from his chest and a flicker of hope lit in his eyes. "You came."

"Yeah. I received an 'Ask Holly' letter asking for help, and at *The Herald* we take our advice column very seriously."

He nodded. "Well, in that case, I have a huge problem."

"Oh, yeah?" I narrowed my stare and thrust my hands to my hips, as I finally closed the gap between us. "Tell me all about it."

His lip twitched as if he might smile, but it faded as quick as it appeared. He hung his head again. "There's this woman. She's smart, strong, and stubborn as hell, and I just can't seem to get her out of my head."

"So," I nodded and tapped my finger across my lips, "what exactly is the problem?"

"I hurt her. I shouldn't have, but I did, and now I'm supposed to be on a plane halfway across the country, but I couldn't bring myself to board. I regret how I treated her, when she was only trying to help. If I'd just listened to what she'd been trying to tell me the whole time, maybe I wouldn't have made such a huge mistake." He lifted his head and pinned me with his stare. Wide-eyed and open. Fragile. Like whatever I said could save him or shatter him into a million unfixable pieces. "What do you think I should do to get her to forgive me?"

I studied his face. The hard cut of his jaw that I ached to rest my hand against and let it melt into my palm. His deep, dark lips I dreamed of kissing again since the night we met.

"First of all, I'd apologize and make sure I told her everything you've just told me. I'm sure she's been waiting to hear it," I said.

"Holly, I am so—"

I raised my hand and rested it on his chest. "I wasn't finished. I'd also make sure that she apologized for her own behavior. I shouldn't have made such a scene in front of everyone. When I knew about the sponsors I should have tried to talk to you in private or at least given you a heads up. I was angry and frustrated and I made a bad decision."

"Maybe, but it's your decision that rescued *The Herald*. You asked me to help save the paper and that's not what I did. It wasn't on purpose, I just followed the regular Concorde business model and didn't open my mind to the other possibilities. Sometimes community support is bigger than facts and figures. I only tried using my head, you used your heart as well."

"Well, now you have a second chance with them too." I tugged at the collar of his jacket. "I've only bought the paper a few years to turn things around and they're going to need someone to help them through it. Unfortunately, I won't be here to do it."

He nodded. "I heard. Marcel told me you took the job in Boston. What changed your mind?"

"You did…with a little help from Claire, of course. You were right about me. Havenbrook is my home, but my future isn't here. Just my past. I thought I needed *The Herald* because it kept me closer to my father, but I think I'm a lot more like him than I originally thought." I glanced out toward the newspaper exhibit near city hall. I didn't need to see his picture; it was already locked in my memory. Forever. "He'll always be with me, even if I'm not here. It's time to start my own life and make my own dreams come true."

"I'm really happy for you. I think you are going to love it there and Marcel is amazing. But, I won't be the one handling Havenbrook anymore."

"What?" My hand jerked, but he rested his gloved fingers over mine, keeping me from yanking it away.

"The thought of getting on another plane and leaving everything behind again made me sick to my stomach. I called my parents and told them I needed to start living my life, one that is more than offices and hotel rooms."

I gasped and squeezed his hand. "You quit your own company?"

"No, of course not." He laughed. "But we're going to make some changes. Starting with distributing some of my responsibilities to others in the organization. Then I'll have my pick of any home office under the Concorde umbrella."

"That's amazing, Ben." I smiled, but my throat clenched. Both of us seemed to be getting exactly what we wanted, so why did it feel like a loss? "Where are you going to choose?"

"Anywhere I want. There's a new office opening in San Francisco that could use my help. Or—" His voice lowered. The tone shaky, for once, uncertain. "There's a struggling publication just outside of Boston. I think I could do a lot of positive things there if I had a good enough reason to go."

"Wouldn't that make you direct competition for my new employer?"

"Probably. But it would also mean that we'd both be in the same city." He dragged out the final words. A question without actually asking. So much more than a business decision.

The streams of Christmas carols echoed on the breeze, but neither of us made any other sounds. Could he really be serious? Could he honestly want to be with me?

"But I also hear there's a spot for me in Florida. A lot less snowy than the east coast, unless…"

His burnished copper eyes begged me to say yes. To tell him what he wanted to hear. That one little word sat so ready on my tongue, but I bit it back.

"This is an important change for you. I shouldn't be part of your decision, Ben."

"But what if I want you to be?"

And I wanted to be. But after being burned by Fletcher, could I take another blow if he decided he missed his jet set former life? But Ben wasn't Fletcher. He wasn't anything like any other man I'd ever known.

"Fine, then tell me one thing." He released my hand and backed up a step. I shivered as the cool breeze between us brushed against my skin. "What would you tell one of your readers if they sent you this question?"

I paused. It was so easy. I'd had so many similar questions over the years. "I'd tell them to follow their heart."

"And I know what my heart is telling me, what's yours?" Ben pulled off his glove and pressed his hand against my cheek. I leaned into his touch as all my worries drained and pooled at me feet.

"It's telling me that you'll really love it in Boston."

He smiled; his lips so close. His soft breath fell on my frozen nose, warming me from the outside in.

"I think so too. I'll have them finalize the transfer next week."

"Wait. You already knew I'd say yes?"

"No. I just hoped. But there is one more thing to deal with."

I frowned and glanced around the empty square.

Ben pointed his finger to the sky. I tilted my head up toward the white berries and dark green leaves of mistletoe tied to the string of lights above our heads.

I chuckled and shook my head against his palm. "Are you going to make me kiss you again?"

"I think this time it's my turn. Besides, I've been wanting to kiss you for so long now."

He pressed his full mouth to mine, and I pushed up on my tiptoes to meet him halfway. My hands laced around the back of his neck, as his strong lips massaged away the last of my doubts. I let go, falling deeper into his soft rhythm, the real thing so much better than in the dreams I'd forced myself to forget. Now all my dreams seemed to be coming true and I couldn't wait for the future. But I doubted it would have any moments more perfect than this.

I broke my face away and whispered, "Merry Christmas, Ben."

He smiled and kissed me gently on my forehead. "Merry Christmas, Holly."

ABOUT THE AUTHOR

SCARLETT KOL

Scarlett Kol is the USA Today Bestselling Author of dystopian, paranormal and fantasy novels for young adults. Born and raised in Northern Manitoba, she grew up reading books and writing stories about creatures that make you want to sleep with the lights on. She believed that the treasures in her mother's jewelry box were magic amulets that would give her immeasurable power and old books could transport her to secret worlds. As an adult, not much has changed.

Connect with Scarlett on social media or on her website www.scarlettkol.com.

facebook.com/scarlettkolauthor
twitter.com/scarlettkol
instagram.com/scarlettkol
bookbub.com/profile/scarlett-kol

ALSO BY SCARLETT KOL

Never miss a new release from Scarlett Kol by signing up for her newsletter.

DYSTOPIAN

Mercury Rises

PARANORMAL

Wicked Descent

Keeper of Shadows

FARAWAY HIGH FAIRYTALES

Falling

Dreamer

A Christmas Mulligan
by
Stella Brecht

PROLOGUE

Shot after shot rang out over their heads.
Ginny sat, unflinching, watching the casket in front of her.

The guns seemed like a lot.

It was all part of the military funeral, Ginny had been to them before, watched it all happen, but as she stared at the box that her daddy laid in, it seemed over the top.

He hadn't died in combat. Her daddy wasn't shot by the enemy. He died during a training exercise. A stupid mistake made by a kid he'd been training to ship off to unknown parts of the world. He'd died saving them all.

Everyone but himself.

Her father was selfless. He was a hero.

And she hated him for it.

For sacrificing himself and leaving them behind.

He promised to come home. Every time he walked out the door, he promised.

Then, instead of her daddy, two men in uniform came to their door.

The guns firing the salute might as well have been aimed right at her heart, because she would never recover.

Not from him being gone, or from the sight of her mama breaking in half when those men came to tell them.

The bugle played the worst song she'd ever heard. Their fifth grade teacher had taught them about it a month earlier. Ginny didn't expect to hear it played for her daddy, ever. Let alone so soon.

Silent tears slid down her face as the men folded the flag. Each snap of the fabric reminding her of the gun shots.

Ginny's best friends, Alice and Lacey, squeezed her hands as the men gave her mama the folded-up flag from his coffin. Any words they'd spoken were lost. All she heard was Mama sobbing.

As the coffin slipped lower into the ground, her mama's sobs became hysterical. Ginny couldn't breathe, her heart skipped a beat as her mama fell to her knees. Her grandpa and uncle rushed to her sides, trying to help as Ginny dropped her friends' hands and numbly bent and picked up the folded flag.

Her mama and daddy had been so in love they had been the talk of the town, made other people jealous. Lacey's Grandma Annie always said it was a once in a lifetime love story.

The price her mama had to pay for that love, it was too much. Ginny had watched her mama's heart break in half. Now as her grandpa tried to soothe her mama, Ginny understood that far more than her heart was broken.

As her mama dropped a rose onto the retreating casket, Ginny squeezed her daddy's flag and made a promise.

She'd be damned if she ever let it happen to her.

GINNY

❄

Fifteen years later...

Ginny couldn't remember ever being around so many people.

"You'd think they'd have some sort of capacity for this type of thing."

"It's an outdoor event, so they don't have to. I'm sure they worked with security and the Tour to figure out a number that would be safe, but until they hit that, everyone is welcome," Alice answered while studying the sheet that listed players' names and pairings.

Ginny smiled at her friend as she led the way. Although she didn't share Alice's enthusiasm about sporting events, the promise of beer and attractive men was enough to convince her to tag along. And because it's what you do for one of your best friends.

Especially after they threaten to release precious secrets if you don't.

Ginny sipped her beer as they sauntered along the food tents. The TV screens that showed the players' names with their scores alongside them were huge. Ginny stood frozen in the center of the walkway as the men kept flashing across the screens.

"Alice," she hissed. "These are some seriously good-looking men."

Alice laughed as she braided her long chestnut hair, pulling it to the side.

"Did you think they wouldn't be because they were golfers? Golf is quite the sport these days. Good-looking and athletic guys, major sponsors, and beautiful venues."

"Well, I'm just happy to be looking at men that aren't from Artis."

Ginny adored her small town and the life that went along with it. Well, everything except the fact that she knew every man who lived there, which made it very hard to date. Or fall in love... get married... have children.

Not that Ginny was interested in any of that.

"So, how does this work? Are there bleachers? Assigned seats? Is it like a track and field event with different things going on all day?" Ginny asked Alice as she looked around for any official with a whistle.

"Ok, so the golfers have been playing since about 7 a.m. The group that's in the lead doesn't tee off—sorry—that means start, until about 2 p.m. So I think we go post up at one of the holes and if one of the groups catches our interest, we can follow them around. If not, we'll just wait for the leaders, who will be the last ones out, and follow them."

"So the leaders are last?"

"Yea. Confusing, I know, but there's a good reason for it. Which I'm happy to share if you're even slightly interested."

Ginny smiled as she sipped her beer.

"Right, didn't think so. Ok, Gin, follow me."

Alice grabbed her hand, and they were off. Ginny stumbled after her, trying to sip her beer and keep up the pace. She spilled twice before finally focusing on Alice instead of the beer. With legs twice as long as hers, Alice often forgot to accommodate for Ginny's vertical challenges.

"Slow down! Five foot person back here!"

Alice laughed but didn't slow down. "Don't you mean 'a respectable five-foot-two inches'."

"We all can't be Amazonian-size goddesses, Miss five-foot-ten-inches."

"Sorry, sorry. I just have the perfect spot for us and want to beat the crowd."

Ginny had just focused back on her beer as Alice came to an abrupt stop.

"Geez - give a girl some warning," Ginny muttered, as she wiped the beer from her chin.

"Perfect," Alice was examining the course map. "This hole is a par five, which means they should be able to get their ball in the hole in five shots. Well, if they're really good then it would be less than five. With the length of the hole, this is where the second shots should land. With where that bunker is most of them will play short..."

Ginny's eyes darted back and forth as Alice continued explaining the hole. She took Alice's aluminum bottle, and shook it slightly.

"What are you doing?" Alice asked with a healthy dose of side-eye.

"Trying to find an explanation for the words you're saying," Ginny teased as a small white ball landed ten feet in front of her.

"Told you," Alice smiled as she took a swig of her beer.

Ginny and Alice stood rooted in the same spot as five players hit shots near them. Ginny listened intently as each golfer man spoke to the golf bag handler man talking about the wind, grass, distance to cover and how the ball would run out on the green. She felt her eyes cross as she asked Alice to explain how the ball would run on a green for the third time.

"I'm going to need another drink to keep interpreting this," Ginny groaned, rubbing her temple.

"If we leave, we'll lose the spot and it's a prime location," Alice looked at the crowd that had gathered around them.

"Not a problem. We can take turns going to the bathroom while the other saves our spot. I'll go now, get us another round of beers and find an air-conditioned bathroom," Ginny explained, taking Alice's empty aluminum bottle.

The slight widening of Alice's eyes at the mention of air conditioning told Ginny all she needed to know about the prospects of something better than a port-o-potty.

"You owe me so big," she breathed through her teeth as she pushed her way through the crowd.

Ginny followed the ropes that looped around the course, unsure if they were meant to provide a path or a barrier.

Why would they have a thousand miles of ropes and not a single freaking arrow pointing to a bathroom?

Ginny stood staring at the fork in the path she was on. She was almost positive she'd gone to the right already. With a confident nod, she began heading down the left side of the path. She checked the course map Alice had given her, unable to make heads or tails of it without knowing which hole she was on. As she looked for a sign of any kind, the people standing around her all ducked and scattered. Ginny did what seemed appropriate, she looked up and around to see what the hell was going on. She figured it out just as the little white ball came falling from the sky and hit her on the forehead.

As darkness tinged her vision, she fell backwards with one last coherent thought, *Do not pee your pants, Ginny!*

"Stand back, give her some room."

Ginny flinched as the voices boomed in her ears.

"Did you see how hard she hit the ground?"

"I know, she hasn't really moved either. She's been out for a while. Should we check for a pulse?"

"She's breathing, check out her chest."

"Oh, damn, check it out indeed."

If her eyes had been open, she'd definitely have rolled them. Maybe even flipped the men off.

Asshats. Unconscious woman in need and I get stuck with the dumber than mud tools.

"Sir, have you called for the medics?"

Thank God for women or no one would ever get to the important parts.

"Yes, medics are coming folks, please stand back and give her some room. Don't touch that ball either!"

Glad they've got their priorities straight, Ginny thought as she assessed herself mentally. *Nothing feels broken, at least. Am I paralyzed?*

"Move out of the way! Let me through!" A fresh voice broke through the crowd, louder than the others.

It sounded mad. Interesting. She could hear and fully process everything happening around her, but she couldn't open her eyes.

Oh, God, why can't I open my eyes?

"Has she been out this entire time?" The angry voice was officially in charge.

A warm hand touched her neck, as a cologne that was woodsy, and distinctly man, filled her senses.

Sure. You can't open your eyes for like a minute and suddenly you're a freaking savant of touch and scent.

"She's breathing and her pulse is steady. Where's the medic?" Angry man sounded relieved.

"Man, how'd you know to do any of that?"

"I'm from California, Jimmy. We all take the same lifeguard course when we turn fifteen."

Well, Jimmy is officially not the white knight.

"You'd be the hero of the day if it hadn't been your ball that hit her."

"Yes, thanks, Jimmy. Can you just go find the fucking medic? And get a glove and anything else in my bag that I can sign."

Swag to sign? I'm laying helpless on the ground and he's passing out autographs? All right, time to open your eyes and tear this asshole a new one. Can't he aim the little ball when he uses the club thing? It doesn't seem that hard.

"You'd be surprised," the husky voice chuckled.

Ginny's eyes shot open. She instantly regretted the motion. Her brain had obviously been trying to protect itself by sealing her eyes shut. The sun and brilliant blue sky had her squinting and shading her face.

"Yea, that last bit was out loud, but just a whisper so I'm the only one who heard. Oh, here, let me." The golfer repositioned himself, shading her head.

Her entire body relaxed as she eased her eyes fully open, relieved her poor manners weren't broadcast for all the world to witness.

"How's your head," the golfer asked gently.

"I haven't had any complaints."

Ginny slammed her eyes shut again and groaned at herself. The large and extremely good-looking golfer holding her hand burst out laughing. She allowed herself a small smile as she cracked open her eyes and studied her rescuer. His deep brown eyes crinkled at the corners as he laughed. It was a deep and heady noise that sent a warm pulse of energy straight to her chest. He dropped her hand as he pulled off his hat, revealing a major tan line across his forehead. His light brown hair fell across his forehead as he pushed his hand back through it, replacing his cap. Ginny was mesmerized by the motion, forgetting her anger as his laughter died down.

"Oh my God, that was amazing." He chuckled again.

"Yea, well, thank the next drag queen you meet for that one." Ginny touched the throbbing spot on her head.

"Easy, it caught you right in the forehead. You're going to have a big ole goose egg."

"Yea, well, that's what happens when you're wandering a golf course looking into the sky. Serves me right."

"No, it's my fault. I hooked that last shot and it got away from me."

"Sir, I have no idea what any of that means, but I doubt you meant to knock me out with your golf ball." Ginny eased herself into a sitting position, thanking all the entities she'd ever heard of that she'd chosen to wear shorts instead of a dress or skirt. She spotted the two asshats still staring at her chest and aimed a very pointed glare as she pulled at her top. They had the decency to look ashamed, or maybe that was just because they got caught.

"Freaking men," she muttered as she moved her head side to side, suddenly aware of the crowd that had gathered. A rather large one.

"Uh, what's going on?"

"Oh, them? Yea, a professional golfer hit you with a golf ball and you were unconscious for a bit. Tends to draw a crowd."

Ginny gave him a healthy dose of side-eye as she readjusted herself.

"All right, well, I'm alive. Go ahead and hit the ball again." Ginny waved him off as the medics weaved their way towards her.

"I'm Greg," the attractive golfer with sparkling brown eyes held out his hand.

"Ginny spelled like the liquor, not the Forrest Gump character," she answered automatically, shaking his hand.

"Well, Ginny," he squinted at her odd answer. "You've certainly made this an interesting round of golf. Thanks for not dying or anything."

"Happy to help," she winked as she released his hand.

The medics got to work shining lights in her eyes and asking her weird questions.

"I have no idea who is in the lead, but I would never know that," Ginny sighed with irritation.

"GINNY?!"

Ginny closed her eyes against the loud noise.

"Who yells at a golf tournament?" Medic number one asked medic number two.

"That would be my best friend who apparently discovered I was knocked unconscious. Brace yourselves."

"Ginny! OHMYGAWD! I was looking everywhere for you and then they showed you unconscious on the big screen and I couldn't figure out what hole you were on and oh my God are you ok? Your head doesn't look right! What's wrong with her head?!"

Ginny let Alice go until she ran out of breath.

"OK! I'm fine. My head looks like this because a golf ball hit me there. Everything is all right. These wonderful medics were just about to tell me I'm fine, to not imbibe in any more alcohol and to go to the hospital if I'm not feeling well, right?"

"Uh yes, actually," medic number one answered, finishing filling out his paperwork.

"Great, thanks!" Ginny pulled herself up and stumbled back.

"Oops. Caught you." Greg, the hunky golf ball assassin, caught her around the waist.

Ginny straightened up quickly, moving out of his reach. She didn't want to think about, let alone acknowledge, the goosebumps she experienced when he touched her.

"Thanks. Good luck out there. Hope your ball goes where it's supposed to next time."

He shook his head as he smirked at her.

"I take it you don't watch a lot of golf."

Ginny shrugged, offering him a "what can you do" half-smile.

"Right, well, customarily when someone is hit by an errant shot the golfer gives them a glove or ball, or whatever is handy in their bag. Autographed, of course. So here you are."

He handed Ginny a ball, a glove, and a large coin looking item.

Ginny bit her lip to keep from laughing or asking what the hell she was supposed to do with any of it.

"Thank you. Best of luck."

Greg offered her another smirk as he signaled to his golf bag handler man and they returned to play.

Ginny held back with Alice as the group of people dispersed.

"I'm never going to the bathroom alone again." Ginny sighed.

Alice hugged her tightly.

"Well, if it means you get physically injured, I don't want you doing it either. Do you want to head home?" Alice asked as she released Ginny, just enough to inspect her forehead.

"Actually," Ginny pulled away from her probing eyes and put her new random golf items into her purse before readjusting the strap across her body. "I want to follow these players. After we find that elusive bathroom."

"This group? Seriously?"

"Yea, why?"

"Well, they're not doing very well. They're going to miss the cut."

"Alice, the look I'm giving you is because I don't know what that means. And it is not because I have been hit in the head."

Alice laughed and hugged Ginny again.

"Ok, we'll follow these guys. Just duck if everyone screams 'FORE' ok? You have no survival instincts."

"No one was screaming, thank you."

"Really?"

"I mean, they were all scattering and ducking but there were no screams."

Ginny didn't wait for Alice to comment and trudged off in the direction she'd seen Greg go.

"Any reason you want to follow them? Greg Hix - that's the guy who hit you, in case you were wondering - hasn't made a cut in three months." Alice interjected as she jogged to catch up, gently steering Ginny towards the row of port-o-potties she'd missed before.

"Well, no reason, really, I mean. I don't know, it's just nice to recognize someone out there. Makes it feel like you've got something to cheer for."

They spent the next two hours trekking across a never-ending field of varying shades of green, oohing and aahing as the players took their shots. Ginny studied Greg more than the other two players he was with. He'd been gentle with her, funny and kind, but as he missed shot after shot he was aggressive and rude. The brown eyes that she'd seen sparkle held no joy.

After they made it to the last hole, *praise all the entities*, Ginny and Alice posted up at one of the picnic tables in the main fan area to watch the next several groups come through.

"All right, I'm going to the bathroom, no bad jokes please," Ginny teased as she wandered away from Alice, who seemed torn between staying and going. A scowl from Ginny seemed to help her make up her mind, and she turned back to the large screen.

Ginny found the bathroom this time, it had a mirror and working water even if air conditioning was missing. As she assessed herself in the mirror, it relieved her to find her light blonde curls still intact after spending time on the ground. Her oversized sunglasses had created funny tan lines, but the pupils of her pale blue eyes were a standard size and not dilated from the golf ball-to-head trauma. She breathed deeply, regretting the action as the chemical smell hit her. She applied a light pink lip balm and quickly headed back into the crowds.

And somehow, even retracing your steps, you're lost.

"It's like they don't want you to find your way. What a great way to hold people captive at a boring event. First, get 'em lost, then drown 'em in booze." Ginny muttered to herself as she wandered behind another large tent. She came up short when she found Greg sitting on the ground, leaning against a golf cart and drinking a beer. There were no other players around, so she suspected this was not the typical post-golf playing activity.

The brown eyes that had sparkled at her a few hours ago were dull.

"You always drink alone?" She interrupted his drinking, unable to just turn and walk away.

"Ginny like the liquor - how was your day? Better than mine, I'm sure."

She walked over and sat down beside him.

"Well, I followed a couple of groups then got sucked into watching this one in particular."

"Oh yea? Let me guess, the leaders?"

"Do I seem like I'd be that predictable?" She nudged him, watching as his smile didn't quite reach his eyes. Eyes that were red, and a face that was splotchy, from frustration or tears she couldn't be sure.

He downed what was left of his beer. "You seem anything but predictable."

"Smart man," she smiled at him. "I was actually following this one person in particular. It was pretty peculiar to watch. Almost like self-sabotage. You could just tell he was miserable every second he stood out there. He seemed testy and aggressive. Every shot seemed like a chore. Every miss was expected. I've never seen someone so unhappy. Not what you'd expect from a professional athlete."

Unshed tears glistened in his eyes as the silence stretched out between them.

"I don't know you at all, Greg," she spoke softly, picking up his hand, holding it in both of hers. "But you deserve to be happy. Look around at where you are, it's amazing. You must be a great golfer, but even if you aren't that's okay. If this isn't what brings you joy, then don't do it."

Ginny wiped a tear off his cheek, replacing it with a gentle kiss, and stood to leave.

"Since you gave me all sorts of trinkets earlier to remember getting hit in the head with a golf ball, take this to remind yourself to be happy. To not take a second of life for granted," she added quietly as she pressed her favorite black bear shaped key ring into his hand.

"Here I was drinking a beer when all I really needed was a shot of Gin," he smiled at her through his tears, holding onto the bear keychain.

"Never underestimate what top shelf can do for you," she winked at him, turning to go find Alice. She'd never admit it to her, but she was actually sad that the day was over.

GINNY

Seven months later...

Living on this mountain is going to keep me celibate, Ginny thought with a mental sigh as she sipped her wine, contemplating looking up local nunneries when she got home.

The latest attempt at finding someone to spend the cold nights with was going as well as the last 437. But who was counting?

The man sitting across from her had presented well. When he'd introduced himself at the company holiday party, it surprised her to find out he actually worked at the resort, too. A new single man had moved to the mountain. There should have been a ticker tape parade. They'd had a brief conversation, and she'd found him charming.

There had been booze in the eggnog. It was the only excuse Ginny could come up with to explain how she was on a date with him.

The first sexual innuendo had seemed innocent enough. Many people loved sausage, and The Black Bear Tavern had a great German sausage entrée. The second innuendo was her own fault. She'd asked what his favorite animal was. Although she wasn't expecting his answer to be a beaver, she could forgive the immature attempt at a joke. They'd reached their third mere minutes later. And, while Ginny loved pearls, she knew he wasn't being thoughtful in saying how good she'd look in a pearl necklace.

Zach was also picking his teeth with his fingernail.

A girl could only take so much.

Ginny wasn't looking for a husband, she wasn't even trying to find a boyfriend, but she was hoping for a semi-decent and respectful man to fill her time with.

Ginny mentally slapped herself as she thought about what Zach would say about a man filling her.

The lewd and lingering look he'd given their server as she bent to pick up the knife he'd "dropped" had been the nail in the coffin.

I cannot believe I'm stuck working with this douche canoe.

In theory they didn't work together since he was a cook for one of the restaurants at The Artis, but that didn't mean she wouldn't see him around the property. Or around the small town. The Artis was the high-end golf and spa resort in town that employed a large group of the locals. She wasn't sure how the people she'd known her entire life could hire someone like Zach to work with them.

Ginny glazed over while he rambled on about his existence before coming to the mountains of North Carolina. The Black Bear Tavern was the locals' spot in town, one of the few restaurants where you wouldn't find a ton of tourists. She saw several familiar faces as her attention wandered. She prayed they wouldn't recall she'd been out with Zach. The Christmas trees spread around the room decorated with garlands in the shape of bears brought a smile to her face. She loved how her town celebrated Christmas. Whether it was the Christmas festival or the tree lighting ceremony, it was always big and thematic. Realizing Zach had stopped rambling, Ginny saw the check had arrived. She tried not to seem overly excited.

As they made their way toward the front door, Ginny paused, touching his arm.

"Listen, Zach, dinner was lovely and I appreciate you asking me out, but I don't think there's any spark here. I'd like it if we can be friends?"

Ginny had given this speech at least two dozen times after a first date. She'd seen some interesting reactions.

"So, what, you think because I'm new in town you can get a free meal out of me? That you can use me and show me off around town so no one thinks I'm available? Then when you're bored or have gotten your night out, you're just going to throw me to the side? Without even a little under the shirt action?"

Ginny had never seen a reaction like this. A grown man throwing a hissy fit because she wouldn't let him touch her boobs. She couldn't process the situation.

A beer flew by her face, bringing her back to the present.

That's what best friends are for.

Alice stood behind the bar with the empty mug in one hand and her cell in the other.

"Listen, jackass, I'm a second away from sending this recording of your little outburst to the owner of the resort. He's known us since we were five years old, so I doubt he'd appreciate you speaking to one of his beloved employees like that. Now get out of here and don't come back until you've apologized."

A dripping and eggplant colored Zach ran from the bar.

"And you," Alice shouted above the laughter that echoed through the space. "What in the hell was that? You'd never let someone get away with speaking to you like that."

Ginny turned a confused face towards Alice as she made her way to the bar.

"Honestly? I have no idea. I think I was stunned? I've never had someone react that way to me before. Maybe I'm in shock?"

"Usually someone sasses you, you hit them right back, what made this different?" Alice asked, setting the glass down and wiping her hands.

"Maybe I reached my limit of bullshit with men? There are only so many pointless dates and ridiculous men a woman can put up with. I mean, that guy was angry at me because he couldn't touch my boobs?" Ginny was shouting and she didn't care. Until she looked past Alice and recognized the face looking back at her from two bar stools down.

For fuck's sake. Greg Hix.

Ginny's jaw might have been scraping the bar at that point, she wasn't sure. She quickly spun forward and plopped down onto the bar stool closest to her.

"Alice," she croaked. "G and T, please."

"Top shelf," the familiar voice added.

Alice turned towards Ginny with a look of confusion. Ironic, since she was the one who had dragged her to the golf event to begin with.

Of course, Ginny was the one who'd been in his arms and staring at his face for a prolonged period. She was also the one who'd kissed him on the cheek. So she'd be the one to recognize the elite athlete wearing non-golf clothes.

Thank you, Universe, for such a wonderful freaking evening, Ginny silently chided as she grabbed the gin and tonic from Alice's hand, downing a large sip.

"I've recently become a bit of a connoisseur of gin and the top shelf stuff here is some of the best." Greg said smugly.

"Yes, well, I've enjoyed gin for quite some time and I know they have an excellent selection here."

Couldn't she just sip her drink and die of embarrassment in peace?

"That your boyfriend earlier?"

Nope. Clearly not an option.

"Oh, the jerkwad who was pissed off about not being able to feel me up tonight in exchange for a meal? No. No, that was not my boyfriend. Just another failed outing." Ginny sighed, rubbing her temple.

Greg tried to stifle a laugh. Ginny couldn't decide if loud guffaws would have been better or worse.

"Well, I'm with Alice. Except I'd have thrown something with a spice in it so he'd be dealing with a wounded ego and painful eyes." Greg cleared his throat as he picked up his own glass.

"Damn, why didn't I think of that?" Alice wondered aloud as she drifted by filling pint glasses.

"This is a pretty random place to stumble across you," Ginny accused, sipping her drink.

"You'd think so, right? Well, in case you were wondering, I did not come here looking for you."

"Good to know. It had crossed my mind, since, ya know, what the hell?"

"Yea, this is weird. I really didn't know you'd be here. Just saw you sitting at a table while I was eating dinner." Greg explained as if that answered all her questions.

"Oh great. Did you witness all the glory that was Zach?"

"Oh, yes. Zach was hard to miss."

"Yea, I figured. Alice," Ginny shook her now empty glass at her friend. "So, what brings you to Artis?"

"We're going to gloss over Zach that easily?"

"I'm not sure one can gloss over a mega-douche such as Zach. Can't we just not talk about what happened there?"

"I could go find him, beat him up for you?"

"Really?" Ginny's eyebrows shot up. "Now that could be useful, but douche canoe could be a secret black belt or something and then you'd be wounded."

"I'm not sure I'm too worried about his skills. He was about half your size. And you're half my size."

"Uh huh. And what is that you're drinking?"

"Skipping over the size of your date?"

"I'm not sure how big he was, Greg. It was only our first date." Ginny flashed her doe eyes and sipped her fresh cocktail, blinking innocently.

If Zach could see her now.

Greg smiled at her, sipping his own cocktail. The holiday playlist Alice curated filled in the gaps of conversation creating a comfortable silence.

"Nice to know you remember me. Wasn't sure a sap crying on the ground would warrant a second look from someone like you."

Ginny flinched. Greg had seemed wounded that day, and the fact that he was making light of it made her uncomfortable.

"Don't worry, you won't find me that way again. I've been seeing a lovely doctor. He's not willing to put a ring on it or anything," he added with a saucy wink, bringing a giggle out of Ginny. "We've realized I hated being a professional golfer. That day was a bit of a turning point for me."

"Interesting. Still doesn't explain you being in North Carolina again. Or what you're doing on this tiny mountain top."

"Well, that tournament day was the best day I'd had in, I'm not sure how long, so when the opportunity came to be in the same area, I jumped." Greg motioned to Alice for his check.

"If memory serves, you didn't exactly do well in that tournament. Why would you want to be in the same area?"

Greg laughed. "Yea, I missed the cut. Like I said, it was a

turning point. A positive turn in my life. Why wouldn't I want to return to the same area for the mulligan?"

Alice laid his check in front of him, casting a curious glance in Ginny's direction. Ginny could only shrug.

She watched Greg lay down a large bill, probably three times what his check was.

"Until we meet again?" He winked at her as he put on his jacket.

"In Artis, you won't have much of a choice," Ginny smiled at him, remembering the last time they spoke.

Greg returned the smile, his brown eyes once again sparkling.

"Well, I might like the choice," he pushed in his bar stool, making his way towards the door behind her. "To see you again. Maybe we could plan on it this time? Not rely on golf balls or douche canoes?"

"No douche canoes?" Ginny laughed. "I'm not sure, whatever would we spend our time discussing then?"

"I'm confident we'll figure something out. So yes?"

"Can you assure me there will be no hissy fits if you're unable to touch my boobs?"

"No promises," he replied dryly.

"Hmm…" Ginny teased, sipping her drink.

"How about dinner? Tomorrow night?"

"I'll meet you here at seven?"

Greg gave her another big smile before heading into the night.

Ginny couldn't stop her own smile as she stared at her drink, stirring the metal straw in mindless circles as she mulled over what had just happened.

"Since he didn't answer your question, I can," Alice interjected.

"What question?"

"Well, you asked what he was drinking? I figured out who he was. Can't believe I didn't recognize Greg Hix the second he walked into my bar." Alice shook her head, disgusted with herself.

"I do expect more from you, Alice. You not recognizing a star athlete? Tsk. Tsk."

"Excuse me, but not all of us reminisce about meeting him like some people…"

Ginny shot her a glare.

"All right." Alice raised her arms in surrender. "Well, in case it means anything, he was drinking a Gin Rickey. Top Shelf. All night. Mentioned something about how he picked up a fondness for it a couple of months back and ever since he's been trying any and every gin drink he can find. We even chatted about his favorite gins and what we had in stock. I figured he was a random sales guy trying to unload some cheap booze. Go figure, he's just obsessed with my best friend."

Alice ducked back into the kitchen before Ginny said or threw anything at her. Which just left Ginny sipping her drink, contemplating the man she'd thought of more than once in the past several months, and that she'd get to see him again so soon.

And just what is he doing on this mountain?

GREG

Greg had been beyond pleasantly surprised when he'd stumbled across Ginny at The Black Bear Tavern. He'd accepted the fact that he'd never see her again. That the day they met was a random gift, a day he'd forever celebrate as 'Gin Day'. When he'd accepted the position in Artis, he admitted - even if just to himself - that the proximity to the tournament had played a minor role. He'd let himself hope that he'd run into Ginny again.

He was not expecting to find her in the small town on top of a mountain.

Freaking fate.

He'd found her once by hitting her with a golf ball. The second time by wandering into a random restaurant. He was damn well going to be sure there was a third time.

The coffee dripped into his mug while he worked through a light stretch. Even if he wasn't playing golf professionally anymore, he wanted to stay in shape and needed to be at the top of his game to be successful as the new golf pro at The Artis.

Sleep hadn't come easily for him. Excitement at starting the next chapter in his life mixed with his eagerness to see

Ginny again kept him too pumped up - like the night before the first day of school.

He sat on his back porch and sipped his coffee. The house overlooked the seventh hole of The Artis' golf course. Perfect proximity to work. Greg took a deep breath, enjoying the chill in the air, something he didn't experience in Southern California.

The buzzing of his cell broke him from his peaceful reverie.

"Hey Jason, it's early for a call from the west coast," he answered.

"Well," Jason yawned. "When one of your biggest clients moves to the east, you adapt."

"You mean former client," Greg downed the last of his coffee, and went inside to dress for work.

"Yea, whatever you want to call yourself."

Greg could hear the eye-roll through the phone. "You have a reason for calling besides busting my chops? It's my first day at the new gig, I want to make a good impression so need to get moving."

"I'm still getting offers, even better than the one you accepted."

"I told you to tell them no. I'm happy with my decision."

"Maybe I should send them to you for you to review? Never hurts to keep your mind open. Especially with stepping into something new."

Greg sighed. Jason was a decent guy, but the reminder of his former life was unwelcome on the day he was starting over.

"Send them if you want, but I told you, I'm happy here. Gotta go, I'll talk to you."

Greg started the shower, eager to rinse away the call.

❅

Six hours later, Greg yawned for the tenth time in as many minutes. He mentally shook himself.

C'mon man. This guy is doing you a favor by telling you all this. Least you can do is pretend to find it interesting.

Chad, the HR guy who had gone over all his paperwork with him, was in the middle of a never-ending tour of the people that worked at The Artis.

"It's a small town, man. The people who work here make up most of the locals, so it'll be good to get to know them right away," Chad explained as they made their way to the laundry rooms.

Greg nodded with a smile as they entered the space and Chad introduced him to three more people.

Greg never had a sense of community as a professional golfer. He craved roots. As a golf pro, he'd be stationary, living in a single place. He was looking forward to knowing his neighbors - to Artis becoming home.

The staff of the restaurants had been his favorite group to meet. They were welcoming and seemed genuinely excited about what he'd be able to do with the golf course. He'd even seen Zach from the night before. He didn't say much to Greg, he was too busy checking out one of the female servers to be bothered with the new guy. It was just as well, as Greg could never look at the man with a straight face. There were several restaurants at the resort, and he made a note of the one Zach worked in. Definitely wouldn't be taking Ginny to that restaurant.

Greg's mind wandered back to Ginny sipping her drink and making innuendos about size when the gust of icy wind snapped him back to the present. They'd gone through a door that led to an interior courtyard. The small space was a cheerful garden. Peaceful as a bubbling hot tub covered any unwanted noise. Live garlands and berries were decorating the space, with mistletoe hung in the doorways. The same high-end Christmas decor had been throughout the resort, but outside in a natural environment, it took on an even more fantastic effect. It transported Greg to a European village at Christmas.

It enchanted him.

"It's really something, huh?" Chad asked as he folded one of the blankets on a lounge chair.

"Spectacular," Greg answered. "Breathtaking really."

"One of my favorite places to show people. Really shows how serious we are about creating the five star experience for our guests."

"This is part of the spa?" Greg wandered to a table with a bouquet of winter flowers on them. He smiled as he pinched a flower petal.

Of course it's real, everything is the real deal here.

"Yes, this is a space the spa guests can visit before their session starts or even when they're done. An additional relaxation area." Chad said as he held the door open for Greg.

The smell hit Greg first.

"Wow, what is that?"

"It's great, right? You immediately feel peaceful. It's one of our private label essential oils. All locally sourced ingredients and handcrafted," Chad said proudly.

"That's impressive. I'll have to stop in and pick some items up. Can't hurt to talk up the products at the course. In fact, if we don't have any in the pro shop we should. Lotions, oils, sunscreen, and hand cream, any of that stuff will be an easy sell to golfers."

"Your first day and you're already coming up with great ideas! Our last pro was more concerned about making his own connections with the wealthy clients that passed through than with the success of the course. The design of the course and the other staff thankfully made up for it. I'm not sure what's out at the course's shop, but we'll get you set up with the spa sales manager to figure it all out."

Chad punched his arm playfully as they continued their tour of the spa.

They ran into a few of the spa technicians as they made their way to the Director and Manager offices. After some polite and, thankfully brief, conversation they made it to the last stop of the day, the spa boutique.

"Ah, and here is our sales manager, Lacey Edwards. Lacey, this is our new golf pro, Greg Hix."

A high-pitched gasp sounded from behind the desk. Greg cocked his head as Lacey shook his hand, ignoring the strange noise.

"Oh, how nice to meet you! I've heard so much about you—" Lacey flinched. "You know, from around, about how you're working here now. As the new golf pro."

Greg's eyebrows quirked in confusion as he shook her hand. She was cute in an eccentric way, with a mess of red waves around her head.

"Nice to meet you too. I was hoping to speak with you about possibly selling some products in the pro shop. Sun block, lotions, hand creams, those sorts of things would sell well. Even some of this essential oil that smells so amazing. I'm not sure what's stocked out there already, but would love to go over everything with you."

"Well, I'll let you guys talk shop." Chad thumped him on the back. "Greg, if you need anything you know where to find me. Best of luck!"

Greg smiled, shaking his head as he turned back to Lacey. She didn't avert her eyes as she studied him.

"Nice guy," Greg offered, motioning to the door.

"Oh, Chad? Yea, he's a lot."

"A lot is definitely how I'd describe him." Greg laughed. "You've got quite the team up here. Place looks great. I was hoping to purchase some items. That way I can talk them up out at the course."

Greg wandered to the far wall, looking at all the shelves.

"Oh, yes, let me grab one of our spa concierges to help you. It's their job to help understand a client's needs and recommend the appropriate products. Most of them are also technicians here, so either massage therapists, estheticians, stylists, something like that. So they're very good at their jobs."

"Oh, that's such a good idea, personal touches like that are probably why you guys are so highly rated. Plus, then I can sell the golfers on stopping in for a more customized set of products."

"You're very smart, Greg," Lacey mused.

"Thanks?"

"I'll just go get someone to help you."

Greg was smelling a different oil as he heard the hushed yet loud muffled conversation coming from the door Lacey had slipped into. Looking over his shoulder, he almost dropped the small bottle as he saw Ginny step out.

"You break it, you bought it," she teased, walking over to him.

"You're a spa concierge?"

"I am. I'll be the one to assess your needs and make recommendations."

"You were very good at it last time," he smiled, unable to help himself.

Ginny offered him a soft smile and shrug as she reached into her pocket.

"OK, Greg Hix, let's get down to business. I'm going to ask you a series of questions and we'll get you set up with some products."

Ginny peppered Greg with questions about his skin and how he cared for it.

"Is that a real thing," he asked.

"A T-zone? Yes, it is." Ginny laughed.

Greg couldn't stop his smile. The sound of her laughter did something to his stomach.

"It's right here," Ginny leaned towards him, moving her finger across his forehead.

Goosebumps erupted down his arms.

"Got it," he breathed, staring down into her eyes.

A soft blush lit her cheeks as she pulled a product from the shelf.

Goosebumps and a quickened pulse were his constant companions as the conversation continued.

Ginny teased as she taught. Enlightened, Greg's basket overflowed with products. The clock above the check-out space showed twenty minutes had elapsed. Greg wanted to spend the rest of the evening listening to her. He grinned, remembering their date.

"So, I guess this explains what you're doing on my mountain," Ginny picked the conversation back up as they walked to the counter.

Greg shook his head, averting his eyes from her ass as she interrupted his appreciative thoughts.

"Your mountain, huh?"

"Born and raised on it, so mine."

"Yea, new job, new life, new hometown."

"Got tired of the old job and life?"

"Had an interesting experience at a tournament some months back. Had me reflecting on my choices and path. Made some changes and discovered some things about myself. Now, here I am."

He smiled as he paid, Ginny's kindness had played in his mind for months, and now here she was again. Her lips on his cheek had also been on a bit of a loop since then. He'd stopped with the wild lifestyle and flings that day and now found himself staring at the lips he hadn't been able to forget.

"Well, the new setup looks good on you," Ginny handed him his receipt with a wink.

"No longer miserable looking?"

"You had a sparkle in your eyes when we first met that wasn't there throughout the rest of your day. Looks like you got it back."

"Or, maybe, it's just there when I'm looking at you?"

Ginny bit her lip, but the smile still came.

"So, Greg," Lacey interrupted their staring, causing them both to jump.

"Yes, hi Lacey, just finishing up my purchases."

"Uh huh," Lacey smiled, her eyes going back and forth between the two of them. "We're about to lock up for the day. You have dinner plans?"

Ginny's head snapped to the side, suddenly glaring at Lacey.

Well, that's an interesting look.

"Well yes, I do have plans for the evening," he answered looking at Ginny.

"Really?" Lacey's eyes flashed as she turned to Ginny.

"I was going to tell you," Ginny was busy stacking the oils on the counter.

"Sorry, didn't mean to get you in trouble," Greg grimaced.

"Oh, she's not in trouble," Lacey waved him off. "Well withholding information about a hot date with the new guy in town is a punishable offense per the best friend code."

Ginny groaned, dropping her head into her hands.

"Greg, would you like to come over to our place for dinner this evening?" Lacey smiled, her eyes dancing between Greg and Ginny.

"Is this how you make amends?" Greg stage whispered to Ginny while looking at Lacey.

Lacey nodded with a grin as Ginny groaned again.

"Ah, then yes, I'd love to. Whatever makes Ginny happy."

"Oh, good answer. I think I approve already. Ginny and I live with my Grandma, and we're making margaritas and fajitas tonight."

"Sounds delicious."

"Margaritas?" Ginny's head shot up, and she looked a shade paler.

"Uh huh," Lacey continued smiling as she jotted down their address and handed it to Greg.

Ginny's wide eyes found Greg's.

"Should I be concerned about the margaritas?"

Ginny nodded as Lacey shook her head no.

"All right. Well," Greg shook his own head in confusion. "I'm looking forward to seeing you tonight, Ginny, and Lacey, can't wait for those margaritas. I think?"

"We'll see you in about an hour?" Lacey suggested as she followed him to the door.

"Yea, that works, gives me time to get cleaned up. See you then, Ginny?"

Ginny twisted around to meet his eyes as he backed out of the boutique.

"Uh, yea," she sighed in defeat, offering him a smile. "See you."

Greg turned and left, heading for his car, chuckling as he imagined the hell Ginny was about to give Lacey for turning their date into a family affair.

GINNY

❄

Ginny pulled the third dress back over her head, hurling it across the room. Suddenly nothing in her closet was appropriate or cute enough.

Maybe it's not the clothes, maybe it's because he's the most attractive man you've ever met? And he's on the mountain, permanently.

She shook her head, trying to clear her thoughts.

Lacey sashayed into Ginny's room, taking in the pile of discarded outfit options and smiling smugly.

"Don't say a word," Ginny ground out through clenched teeth as she pulled a sweater over her head.

"Oh, I wasn't going to say anything," Lacey plopped down onto Ginny's bed.

"I still don't understand why you had to invite him over for dinner when we had plans already."

"You weren't enjoying the show I was watching. If you were, you'd have wanted it to continue, too."

Ginny gave one of her oldest and best friends in the world the death stare.

"He was flirting with you, Ginny. And you were flirting

right back. Plus, you didn't even tell me you made a date, so I needed to see what was going on."

"He's an attractive man, we should all be flirting with him. Why don't you flirt with him?"

Ginny regretted the words the second they slipped from her lips. The last thing she wanted to watch was Lacey flirting with Greg.

"Uh huh. Well, judging by that grimace, I don't think you're too keen on me flirting with him. Although if you wanted me to, I could…" Lacey trailed off with an innocent look.

"Shut up, Lace."

"I think you should wear the navy blue sweater. The slouchy one that falls off of one shoulder. And the tight, high waisted jeans. Super sexy, yet gives off the 'I'm not trying' vibe. The navy with your hair and eyes is always a killer."

Ginny gave her a shy smile.

"Thanks. Not sure why I care so much."

"Maybe you like him?"

"I don't know him, Lacey."

"Ginny." Lacey gave her a look that shouted 'puh-lease'.

"I don't, Lacey."

"Well, Alice and I have heard enough about that day all those months ago."

"I can be curious about someone I met in such a crazy way."

"Curious, that's what we're calling it?"

"He was a professional golfer, Lacey. I had never even been to a tournament. I was just interested in how it all worked."

"Damn, I always forget how good you are at deflecting. Well, that guy you were curious about has made a lot of changes. He's a golf pro now, and at our course no less.

Gin, if that's not fate slapping you in the face, I don't know what is."

"It's a coincidence, Lacey. No such thing as fate."

"Sure," Lacey pulled herself off the bed and out the door. "Keep telling yourself that, Ginny. No such thing as fate. You just so happened to get hit on the head with his ball that day, and he just so happened to show up in Artis all these months later."

"Even if there is, I'm not interested in anything long-term. You know that and you know why," Ginny sighed, closing the door.

Ginny wriggled into her jeans, thinking about the strange situation she found herself in.

She had followed Greg's career after meeting him. She'd seen the sudden change in his demeanor out on the different courses. What she hadn't seen change was his eyes. They were still sad. Miserable.

When she'd read he was retiring she realized how much she'd miss seeing him each week, even if it was through the TV screen. She hadn't even clued Lacey and Alice into how much of the sport she'd been watching since that day. The other players never gave off the aura Greg did. It had only intrigued her more.

She swiped blush across her cheeks as the doorbell rang.

Well, let's see if that secret misery still lurks behind those eyes.

Ginny found Greg with his face pressed firmly into Lacey's Grandma's bosom.

"What a handsome young man, Lacey. I'm so glad you brought him along to dinner."

"Oh no, Grandma, I might have extended the invitation, but he's friends with Ginny." Lacey helped Greg free himself from her Grandma, shaking his hand and taking his jacket.

Ginny hadn't moved a foot in any direction as the commotion played out before her. She took the time to examine Greg. His sun kissed skin, even in the dead of winter, the brown hair styled back from his face, the thick beard that was new since their first meeting, his full pink lips and those shining brown eyes. She assumed her imagination had exaggerated his eyes, but here they were in real life, just as beautiful as they'd been that day. This time, devoid of any sadness. Filled with mischief as he kissed Lacey's Grandma on the cheek. Filled with something much more primal as they found her, causing her cheeks to heat.

"Hi Ginny," he smiled at her, breaking eye contact as he took in the large room.

"Greg," Ginny smiled with a nod.

"Well, Lacey was just about to mix a big ole batch of margaritas, weren't you dear?"

"Sure, Grandma," Lacey laughed as she headed for the kitchen. "Be on your guard, Greg. She just wants you to herself."

"Oh, Lacey Rae, aren't you just the worst. Trying to give away all my womanly secrets. I obviously don't stand a chance here when he's looking at our Ginny that way," Grandma added innocently as she tugged Greg to the dining room. "You can call me Annie, young man."

Ginny took a deep breath, more than capable of handling Grandma and Lacey for the evening. She was very wary of handling Greg when he kept looking at her like he was hungry for much more than what was on the table.

Not like you're so innocent, Ginny. You're staring at his ass in those jeans like they're the last piece of cake.

"So, Greg, tell us all about your gorgeous self," Grandma added as Lacey passed around the margaritas.

"Welcome to the mountain, Greg," Lacey laughed as she toasted the group. "We're a strange group, but a good one."

Ginny sipped her margarita, reveling in the fact that the smile he'd offered had reached his eyes.

"Greg, you were about to tell me all about yourself," Grandma Annie encouraged.

"Ah, yes ma'am. Not much to tell. I used to play golf professionally, out on the Tour. Got tired of the lifestyle and made some changes."

"I see, and where are you from?"

"California. Went to school out west, too. But home hasn't really been a thing for a while."

"Your parents don't have a place out there anymore?" Grandma Annie prodded.

"Well, they each have their own place now. Split up when I was in high school."

"That must have been hard for you," Grandma Annie nodded to Lacey to refill their cups.

Ginny tried to feel bad but was enjoying the intel too much.

"Yes, well, they weren't a very good couple. Not what you'd call a shining example of a loving marriage. Lots of cheating, fighting, yelling." Greg took a rather large gulp of his drink before Lacey refilled the glass.

"Well, that's too bad. So not a lot of love in your life then?" Annie offered a look that would put Dr. Phil to shame.

"No, actually. But I don't want to hog the conversation. How did you all come to live together?" Greg sipped his drink as he turned the interrogation around.

Grandma Annie licked the salt off of her rim as she took a large sip.

"Well, let's see. Lacey and Ginny have lived together for a few years now. Alice used to stay in the third bedroom but she moved into the loft above The Black Bear Tavern about a year ago, which worked out well for me as I had an offer on my home so Lacey and Ginny took me in. These girls keep me young," Annie offered a smile to Lacey and Ginny.

"Oh Annie," Ginny rolled her eyes before taking a gulp of her own margarita. "You keep us on our toes and you know it." She turned to Greg, "A month ago, I came home early from a long weekend at the beach with Lacey and Alice because I wasn't feeling well and Annie here was having a rager."

"A what?" Greg stopped mid-sip.

"A rager. I pulled in at 12:30 a.m., and the music was thumping. There were at least fifteen cars on the street. I got inside and the alcohol is flowing. I've never seen the 'grown-ups' of this town party like that before." Ginny shook her head, her eyes unfocused as she recalled their preacher doing a beer bong.

"Wow." Greg said, finishing his second margarita. "My grandma was never that fun."

"See? Fun!" Grandma Annie said to Ginny as she motioned for Lacey to give her the pitcher.

Ginny rolled her eyes, unable to stop the giggle that followed.

"Well, that's nothing compared to some of the things we got ourselves up to when you kids were young."

"Grandma, that's ok," Lacey held up her hand.

"You three girls and the hijinks you constantly got into outdid anything we ever did."

Ginny imagined her eyes were as large as Lacey's at that comment.

"I mean, this one," Grandma motioned to Lacey. "Gets a degree in botany and then is surprised when I find her weed plants in my garden."

Lacey turned purple as she gulped her drink.

Ginny sipped her drink to suppress her own laughter. Greg didn't bother, he laughed loudly with Annie.

"And then my Gin here gets arrested for skinny dipping because she didn't realize they were doing baptisms at the river that day."

"Oh, please, I was there with the preacher's son." Ginny winked at Greg over her glass as they all laughed.

Lacey and Ginny served the fajitas along with another pitcher of margaritas as Annie and Greg continued exchanging stories.

Ginny stopped drinking after margarita number two, keenly aware that Annie would push drinks on Greg all night.

"Ladies, it's been wonderful. The food was delicious and the company even better, but I should get back before it's too late."

Greg offered hugs all around, saving Ginny's for last.

"Oh, uh, I'll walk you out?" Ginny offered awkwardly. "You sure you're ok to drive," she asked as they made their way down the stone pathway.

"Oh, yea, I only had two drinks. Every time she'd look away to set the pitcher down, I'd pour it into that centerpiece bowl thing. You'll want to empty that when you go back in. She's quite the woman," Greg laughed.

Ginny doubled over laughing.

"Damn, that is clever. I'll have to clue Lacey in for future situations. And yes, she is quite the woman. Been like a second mother to me since we were little. Although, Lacey's mom was like a mom to me too. So maybe I had three?" Ginny wondered with a small laugh.

"You were lucky. I always wanted to have a family like this when I was little."

"That bad for you when you were young?"

Greg sighed as he leaned against his car door, pushing his hands into his pockets.

"Not unhappy. I never wanted for anything. Well, nothing besides a family. My parents won't be winning any awards for their past. Affairs and leaving me to be raised by the nanny. A divorce that rivaled the civil war. I don't really keep in touch with either of them anymore. Although I wish it was different."

"I'm sorry," Ginny offered as she crossed her arms to keep warm.

"Don't be. I appreciate seeing love like this out in the world. It gives me hope for my own."

They stood staring at each other for a few moments. Ginny appreciated the silence and enjoyed just being in his company as the snowflakes slowly fell around them, swirling in the light from the porch.

"I should get going," he offered quietly.

Ginny nodded, unwilling to break the silent spell around them.

"I'd really like to kiss you before I go."

Ginny hadn't stopped nodding and only bobbed her head faster as he approached.

Greg's hands found her hips as he reached for her. His eyes danced as he looked down at her.

Ginny drew in a quick, cold breath as his lips lowered to hers.

The kiss was tender. Ginny sighed into his lips as she pulled him tighter and wrapped her arms around his neck. One of Greg's hands wandered lower, finding her ass and squeezing. Ginny gasped and Greg pounced, his tongue sliding in her mouth. The sweet kiss was quickly becoming too hot for her driveway. Yet, Ginny couldn't bring herself to stop.

Greg pulled back first, leaving Ginny feeling cold and empty.

Their heavy breaths created clouds of fog in the frosty air as they untangled their limbs from each other.

"I should really get going," Greg said as if to convince himself.

Ginny nodded again.

"Right." She shook her head. "Um, well, maybe I'll see you at work tomorrow?"

Greg just nodded as he got into his car. Ginny stood unmoving, waiting for his car to start. Watching as his forehead hit his steering wheel in frustration.

She laughed loudly as she realized what was happening.

"Need a ride?" She teased, tapping on his window.

"Car died," he lamented, leaving his head on the wheel.

"I'll get my keys," she smiled as she turned for the house, thrilled to spend more time with him.

❄

"I do not understand what happened to my car," Greg commented for the tenth time since they'd gotten on the road.

"It's really not a big deal, sometimes the cold weather can drain a battery."

"Well, you've seen me in enough embarrassing situations, it's definitely unfair."

"What? You think this is embarrassing? You just listened to my pseudo Grandma go on and on about stupid situations the three of us got ourselves into and you think your car battery dying is embarrassing?" Ginny shook her head.

"Well, it's not manly."

"Oh my God, you are not that type of guy are you? Can't be rescued by a girl?"

"It just seems like you're doing all the rescuing. Might be nice if it was flipped once, is all."

"What do you mean all the rescuing? This is the first

time I've driven you home. Confusing me with someone else?"

"Not likely, Ginny," the teasing tone had left Greg's voice.

Ginny looked at him questioningly and quickly averted her eyes back to the road. Those charming brown eyes stared at her, raw and vulnerable. Wide open.

"Well then," she cleared her throat. "You'll have to expand on what you mean."

"I'm not sure I should clue you in. I mean, I thought it was embarrassing already, and you didn't even know you'd rescued me then," the teasing tone returned.

Ginny smiled into the dark, liking the lightness in his tone.

"Oh c'mon, can't leave a hero hanging!"

She turned the car into his driveway and placed it in park, turning to Greg as she waited for him to reveal her heroic measures.

"Hmm." He took a deep breath, unbuckling his seat belt and copying her posture. He moved his hand to her head rest, turning to face her.

Ginny squinted, challenging him.

"Even though it's dark out and there's barely any light coming from the console, I know your eyes will be a little lighter. Because when you get worked up, that's what they do. I've seen it happen three times since I've known you."

Ginny's breath caught as he played with a strand of her hair, leaning forward towards her slightly.

"Yours sparkle," she said, sounding breathy.

"My eyes sparkle?" He didn't believe her.

She nodded, transfixed under his gaze.

"Not sure anyone's ever told me that."

"Well, most people are idiots."

Greg laughed. Ginny grinned, pleased with herself for bringing a smile to his face. Ever since she'd met him, she'd been trying to wipe away any trace of sadness. Whether it was a tear on his cheek or a shadow in his eyes.

"You rescued me the first day we met."

"I'm pretty sure you were the one to give me first aid. Considering I was unconscious and all," she rested her hand on the arm playing with her hair, relieved to be touching him again.

A smirk played at his lips. "Well, you might have been the one who needed resuscitating, but I was the one drowning. It wasn't clear to anyone, not even me, but you realized it." He placed his other hand on hers, squeezing. "I was sad. Depressed, if I'm honest. My golf game suffered, I spent more time living the life of a wannabe famous play boy than focusing on my job. A kind stranger recognized the pain, the hopelessness. Wiped my tears away and told me what I needed to hear to turn my life around."

Greg cupped her face.

"I can never thank you enough for what your kindness meant to me, Ginny. I won't stop trying though." He placed a gentle kiss on her cheek before getting out of the car.

"I left a note with Lacey to give to you. Has my number on it. I'd really like to hear from you. Good night, Ginny. And thank you, again."

"Good night, Greg," Ginny said as he closed the door.

Ginny watched him as he walked up the steps to his front porch and sat a minute longer collecting herself once he was inside.

When she got home, she found the note on her pillow.

Today was wonderful. Thank you for the smiles and laughs. I'd love to take you on a proper date. Tomorrow? Xx Greg

Ginny didn't hesitate to send him a text.

Hi. This is your friendly neighborhood hero. Just letting you know I'm home, safe and sound.

Thank you for saving me again tonight. I had a wonderful time.

Me too. And just so we're clear - you're not the only one who needs rescuing every so often.

Sweet dreams, Ginny.

Xo

Ginny sighed as she put her phone on her charger and scrubbed her face. A hero was the last thing she wanted to be in life, but with Greg she found herself desperate to keep rescuing him, to keep that smile in place on his handsome face.

She'd hoped she'd just misremembered that day all those months ago, those feelings and thoughts about him, but being in his arms tonight she realized she'd downplayed it all.

She liked him. A lot.

She smiled as she traced her lips, remembering his against hers. She pulled her pajamas from the dresser, and the smile slipped.

Her mama and daddy, frozen in time, staring at each other while Annie took their photo. One of her treasured possessions, and a mental bucket of ice water over her head as she relived her mama answering the door all those years ago.

Tears filled her eyes as she recognized the look her mama gave her daddy.

Staring at him, smiling, oblivious to the world around them.

"Oh, no."

GREG

❄

*G*reg had one of the best night's sleep in his life.

His first staff meeting went smoothly. The first lesson of the day, a chance for him to review some of his assistant pros, had been flawless. The staff had impressed him.

Flashes of kissing Ginny popped into his mind sporadically.

It was an excellent morning.

He felt so good that he broke out his clubs to hit some balls. There was only one explanation for his mood.

Funny how someone so small can make such a big impact, he thought as he teed up the next ball, thankful for the covered hitting bays. It wasn't snowing at the moment, but the overhang prevented the driving range from ever needing to close.

He was enjoying working through his rotation of clubs, the cold air stinging his face. No pressure on how he performed or which swing he used. He was getting back to golf basics and loving his time at the course, not only playing but working.

"I wasn't sure you were capable of that."

Greg spun around, already smiling as he recognized the cheerful voice.

"Hitting the ball straight?" He asked as he walked towards her, pulled like a magnet.

"Looking happy while holding a club," she said as he reached her.

Greg hugged her, unable to help himself. He hadn't realized how anxious he'd been to see her.

"I think I probably look happy all the time since I got to this mountain," he replied, releasing her, and carefully avoiding her spot on observation.

"Uh huh," she said. "We'll circle back to that later then."

Ginny walked over towards the various hitting bays.

"You interested in hitting some balls?" Greg asked. He hoped he hadn't sounded too eager.

"I've never used a golf club before." Ginny grimaced. "Wasn't exactly high on my list of activities to pursue while growing up."

"Nothing wrong with that. Always a first for everything." Greg winked at her. "Lucky for you, I'm an excellent teacher."

"That is your job, now isn't it?"

"As a matter of fact, it is."

Greg pulled some women's clubs from their rental area and carried them over to the bay next to his.

"I'm really not sure if I should," Ginny took off her gloves and wiped her palms on her pants. "I just came to drop off your car. Alice had a look at it this morning and now it's running with no problems."

"Thank you. The least I can do is give you a quick lesson," Greg held out an iron towards her, knowing she'd be unable to walk away from the challenge.

"Ok, just duck," Ginny said, grabbing the club from him. "So what do I do here?"

"All right, watch me, I'll use the same club."

Greg slowed his speed so Ginny could see every move he made.

"You make it seem like it's just swinging a club at a ball," Ginny accused.

"Well—" Greg laughed. "—it is?"

"No, it's not. It's perfectly moving your arms, hips, hands, and feet through a swing while holding onto the club and keeping your eye on the ball."

Greg watched Ginny approach the ball. Her stance and grip were good for someone who had never held a golf club. She looked like she was working through something in her head as she looked out at the range, picking a pin flag to aim for.

Greg was going to suggest one within an attainable distance when Ginny began her swing. It wasn't the smoothest thing he'd ever seen, but the mechanics were all there. She even hit the ball. While it didn't go as straight as she'd wanted, or as far, it was damn impressive for her first time.

"So? How was that?"

It took Greg a minute to process that she'd spoken to him. He was still in awe.

"You've never held a golf club?"

"You don't believe me?"

Greg loved the shy smile that accompanied her words.

"Most people don't make contact with the ball, let alone have a proper swing. You sure you've never done this before?"

"Positive. Although…" She trailed off as she placed another ball in position, ready to go again.

"Yes?" Greg encouraged her, setting himself up for another shot.

"I might have started watching golf pretty avidly a few months back."

Greg looked up from his shot, eyes and mouth wide. He

watched as she adjusted her stance and this time, the ball went sailing through the air straight at the spot she was aiming for.

She turned to him, a look of delight on her face. Whether for how well she was hitting the ball or because she'd left him speechless, he was unsure.

"Why did you start watching golf?" Greg asked as he picked at the old grip on his club, eager to hear her answer. Hopeful, that maybe their meeting impacted her as much as him all those months ago.

"Well, Alice dragged me to a tournament. I don't mind telling you, I was dreading it," Ginny turned back to her bay and set up another ball. "It was a boring day, but there were lots of cute men to ogle, which was a pleasant change of pace from up here on Mount Celibate, so I didn't complain. Then, of all the things to happen," she paused, ripping the club through the air.

The ball didn't go where she wanted again and she bit her lip in frustration, a look of confusion etched on her face. Greg moved from his own bay, ready to help her, but she just lined up another ball and tried again. He stood outside of her bay, watching her body work through the swing, and contemplating her celibate comment.

"Some guy hit me with an errant shot," she continued after her swing. "I mean, I don't have weird things happen to me like that. So, I was pretty surprised by it all. Not to mention, he was probably the most attractive man I've ever met, so opening my eyes to find him leaning over me administering first aid was interesting."

After her next shot went wild again, Greg snapped himself back to attention, leaving the attractive comment for later, and stepped into the bay, setting another ball down for her.

"So, golf was entertaining for the rest of the day,

following this guy around," Ginny continued, stopping on a quiet gasp as Greg stepped behind her.

He placed his hands over hers on the club, impressed that she held the club properly.

"When you're swinging down, you've got to move your hands like this," he murmured, his chin resting on her shoulder as he showed her how to rotate her hands through the swing. "That way your clubface is open the right amount and the ball will go where you want it to."

Greg took pleasure in the light pink that stained Ginny's cheeks and how her chest rose faster as he spoke. Her hair brushed across his cheek, the smell of berries tickling his nose.

As he stood back up, he moved his hands to her hips, missing the warmth of her body.

"And be sure to finish rotating these through your swing."

"Uh huh," Ginny's voice was breathy. She nodded as Greg released her.

While she focused on her ball, Greg took the opportunity to adjust himself.

For fuck's sake, ten seconds of touching her and you can't control yourself.

This time when Ginny hit the ball, it went exactly where she wanted it to.

"It worked!" She jumped up and down celebrating.

Greg smiled, nodding.

"Ok, again," she lined up another ball.

This was exactly why Greg could be happy teaching the sport for the rest of his career. The joy people had when they got it right. The excitement they had to keep going and to get better.

Her next ball landed in the same area.

"But that's not why I started watching golf," Ginny continued her story, lining up another shot.

"No? You weren't intrigued by how good and bad different players could be?" Greg had moved back to his own bay, wanting to keep his hands busy since they were itching to touch Ginny again.

"Well, that was fascinating, but no. I started watching golf because I got to see the ridiculously attractive man again, up close and personal."

They'd both stopped swinging, just standing in their bays looking out over the range.

"Why would you want to watch a sport that made a grown man cry?" Greg tried to tease, the lightness never quite reaching.

Ginny turned to face him, gripping the club.

"I ..." Ginny swallowed hard, the look on her face a mixture of guilt and embarrassment. Greg wasn't sure he wanted to hear her answer, but couldn't take his eyes off of her.

Ginny looked down to the ground, and Greg braced himself.

"I wanted to watch because I wanted to see him again. Even if it was just on a screen. I couldn't stop thinking about him. Wondering if he was happy. Wondering who would encourage him and easing his worries after a round. So," Ginny cleared her throat, closing her eyes.

Greg couldn't move, could barely breathe. He hadn't let himself hope Ginny remembered him, let alone that he'd had any impression on her.

"So," she opened her eyes and straightened up, steeling herself as she looked him in the eyes. "I became an avid golf watcher. I tuned in every week, for every round. Sometimes I couldn't watch them live, but I'd record them and watch before the next round. Usually, if he missed the cut, I'd stop watching, but he was suddenly making more cuts. He just wasn't happy when he made or missed the cuts. And then he was retiring, and it scared me. That he was finally unhappy enough to do something dangerous."

She swallowed, a sheen of tears in her eyes.

Greg thought of the moment he'd changed his life. Retiring is not something pro-athletes do when they're young and healthy, but Greg had never been good at being a pro-athlete. It was the best decision for him - it made him happy. He'd been in a poor mindset all those years. He lost himself in partying, making one poor decision after another. He took strange women back to his hotel room; he let people drive him home after they'd been partying. He made decisions that could have killed him. Even if he wasn't hurting himself on purpose, he had been.

"Mostly," Ginny interrupted his thoughts. "It scared me that I wouldn't get to see him anymore. Even if it was just through the TV screen. Which, I admit, sounds crazy and is embarrassing because I met him once. So, there you have it. That is why my swing is semi decent. I watched a lot of golf."

They stared in silence for a minute longer.

"Right," Ginny nodded, her cheeks stained pink. She dropped the golf club and turned to leave.

"Ginny."

She stopped, not looking back. "It's ok, Greg. Don't worry about it. It's nuts, I know. I swear I'm not a stalker and I can leave you alone."

"Ginny," he called again, smiling.

This time she turned towards him, watching as Greg slowly approached her.

He didn't speak as he reached her, gently pushing her hair back from her face. His eyes never left hers as his hand rested on her cheek, his thumb tracing a freckle lightly.

His thoughts were a jumble, running in circles in his mind. Unsure of how to explain to this woman how much her words touched him, how her concern was the most beautiful gift he'd ever received.

Unable to put anything into words, he did the only thing that made sense.

He kissed her.

The night before had been gentle and timid, becoming passionate quickly, his desire for Ginny pushing through. This time, Greg kissed Ginny with the awe and hope he felt every time he got to see her. He kissed her deeply, reverently.

As he pulled away from her, her eyes fluttered open, unfocused.

"Have dinner with me tonight?" While it was a question, he hoped she understood there was little control over what was happening between them.

A horn honked twice, and Ginny jumped.

"Oh shoot," she slapped her forehead, stepping out of his arms. "Alice followed me up here to drop off your car and has been waiting for me the whole time."

"Ginny, dinner, tonight."

"Can't wait," she smiled as she backed away.

"Thank Alice for everything. I'll pick you up at seven. We'll leave Annie and Lacey behind this time."

Greg chuckled as he went back to the empty bays and began collecting the clubs they'd used. He wasn't sure what he'd expected when he arrived on this mountain and began his life over, but it wasn't for fate to intercede again.

Well, the least you can do when fate keeps dropping the answer to all your hopes and dreams in your lap is not to fuck it up.

If this was his mulligan, he was planning on holing out.

Damn, that's the dirtiest sounding sentimental thought ever.

Greg laughed at himself.

"Careful, you do that too much and people might think

you're crazy." Lacey teased him as she approached, a giant bin in hand.

Greg rushed out to help her with whatever it was.

"Oh, thank you." Lacey gladly handed it over. "Ginny couldn't be bothered to help me as she flew out of here. Something about Alice kicking her ass? Anyway, these are your new products."

"Wow, that was fast."

"Well, it helps that I'm the sales manager, one of your new best friends since you're in love with my best friend and the person who makes the products." Lacey led the way into the pro shop, holding the door open for Greg.

"Wait, you make these products?" Greg put the bin down on the counter and pulled out small containers of sunscreen, hand cream, lotions, and lip balm. He opened a few and smelled them as Lacey set up a display case by the counter when her words finally registered.

"Yes, I make everything right here on the mountain—"

"Whoa, you think I'm in love with Ginny?"

Lacey stopped building the case and slowly turned towards him, a huge and devious smile on her face.

"Wondering how long it would take you to catch that. Are you denying it?"

"We just met—"

"Oh, bullshit, you met months ago. And even if you had just met, who cares? The way you two look at each other? It's like there's no one else in the room. Alice told me about your fascination with gin, too. It seems like you've been thinking about Gin ever since then. Not to mention Ginny has mentioned that golf tournament at least 300 times. So there's definitely something major between you two. We've heard how you guys met, but I have the feeling Ginny left out quite a bit..." Lacey let the words hang in the air, looking at him expectantly.

"Not sure what she told you..." Greg trailed off, looking

at a very interesting container of lip balm. "This smells amazing."

"Thank you. That's one of my favorites—wait, no, damnit. Ginny now, products later. We know about the ball hitting her in the head, the valiant first aid, even though you're the one that hit her." Lacey gave him a pointed look with that comment. "I also know that she and Alice followed your group that day, but Greg, there has got to be more to it. I've known Ginny since we were three years old. That girl would not be watching golf like she is if that was it."

"She told you she started watching golf?"

"Hard to miss when she's suddenly busy every Thursday and Friday afternoon or evening and occasionally Saturday and Sunday too. Not to mention she started using a lot of golf terminology in her day-to-day interactions. When Ginny Wellner starts using terms such as 'duck hook', you realize something is up."

Greg couldn't help but smile as he organized the products.

"Uh huh," Lacey looked at him with a knowing grin. "So, spill."

Greg weighed his options carefully. Would it be wrong to share with Lacey before Ginny? Or would he ever even get the chance to share with Ginny if he didn't talk it through with someone else first? And who the hell else would he confide in?

"You can trust me. I can see the wheels spinning from here," Lacey added as she went back to the display case.

Greg took a deep breath, readying himself. He spent the next ten minutes telling Lacey about the day he met Ginny, how she found him behind the tent and the impact she'd made.

"Did you really come to this place by chance, Greg?" Lacey asked.

Greg laughed at the look on her face.

"I did not know Ginny lived here. I was not actively looking for her. The position was available and it was close to where everything had changed for me. Not to mention thousands of miles away from my past. Seemed too good to be true. And then I walked into the local bar and she sits down a few tables over."

Lacey sighed dreamily.

"What?"

"Oh, Greg. Well, first, I'm relieved you're not a stalker. Second, I am loving how this is all unfolding."

"If you make these, why isn't this label yours? It says it's the spa's?"

"Nope, no getting away from the topic at hand. So what's your next step in wooing Ginny?"

"Well, we will come back to this label topic because that's weird, and I think you're trying to avoid it. But I am planning on seeing Ginny tonight."

Lacey's eyes lit up.

"So, as her best friend, or one of them, maybe you can clue me in to what she might like to do?"

"Christmas! It's her favorite holiday, so the date should be all about it."

Greg smiled as Lacey filled him in on Ginny's favorite things. He liked Lacey and Alice. It was another reason he liked Ginny. She surrounded herself with good people, something he hoped to get better at.

❄

Eight hours later, Greg had to remind himself to breathe as he drove to Ginny's house. Watching a TV monitor to see if they listed your name among the players who made the cut at a tournament was an anxiety-riddled activity. This was fifty times worse. He'd never felt so on edge. Considering his entire life had been about making a small white ball fall into a tiny hole, he'd dealt with anxiety before. His first official date with Ginny seemed more important than anything he'd done.

As he pulled into the driveway, he took another deep breath, grabbed the bottle from the seat next to him and sent a silent prayer into the universe.

Grandma Annie and Lacey had the door opened before he could press the doorbell.

"Ginny! Greg is here!" Annie shouted as she pulled Greg into her bosom for another suffocating hug.

"Annie, Lacey, lovely to see you two again," Greg gasped as Annie released him.

"We're just stepping out for the evening ourselves," Lacey said as she pushed Annie out the door past Greg. "Have a great time."

Lacey's one major role was to help Ginny get ready for the evening and therefore be sure she was dressed appropriately for what he had planned.

"Did you survive the bosom bombardment?"

Greg was certain he'd swallowed his tongue.

Ginny was breathtaking in skintight black jeans, a plum peacoat, gray slouchy hat and knee-high boots.

"You are the most beautiful woman I've ever seen," Greg confessed as she reached the spot he was glued to. "Oh, this is for you."

Greg handed the bottle of gin to her. The floral label seemed more fitting a gift than a bouquet.

"This is one of my favorites. Did Alice tell you?"

The bright smile she offered was blinding. She was wearing a pink gloss on her lips, and her eyes had a smokey shadow.

"No, although I should have asked, it's one I had the other day and really enjoyed." Greg couldn't stop staring at her lips. "Listen, I'm sorry to do this to you."

Ginny's smile slipped as confusion filled her face. Greg grabbed her by the pockets of her jacket and pulled her into him, tipping her chin back, relieved to find her smiling once again as he claimed her lips.

Her free hand found his back pocket and pulled him to her tighter as the kiss grew hotter.

"Never apologize for doing that," Ginny breathed as they pulled apart.

"Oh, no, I was apologizing in advance for smearing your lipstick," Greg winked at her.

Ginny laughed. She placed the bottle of gin on the entry table, fixed her smudged lips, and locked up.

Greg grabbed her hand, only letting go to get into the car.

"Ok," Greg picked her hand back up once the car was in drive. "Twenty questions. You go first."

Ginny beamed at him. "Favorite movie?"

"Fargo," he answered quickly.

"Wow, you didn't even have to think about it?"

"It's a classic."

"I've never seen it," she turned in her seat, facing him.

"Ginny. C'mon. Unacceptable. We must reconcile that immediately." He smiled, waggling his eyebrows at her. "Maybe tomorrow night. But it's my turn now - are you a dog or cat person?"

Ginny laughed. "With that eyebrow move, I figured you'd be asking me something scandalous about the bedroom. I like both, but I want a dog."

Greg sat unmoving, not speaking.

Ginny squeezed his hand.

"Oh, sorry, yes dogs are great, I love them."

"Where'd you go there?"

"Just, imagining bedroom questions to ask."

Ginny leaned across the dash, kissed his cheek, and

whispered, "Maybe we should save bedroom questions for later."

"I might crash the car if you do that again," he groaned, squeezing her hand.

Ginny laughed, and Greg beamed. As the game continued Greg learned that Ginny secretly loved emo music, to his delight. He revealed that he got pedicures regularly, to Ginny's relief.

"Men's feet are the scariest thing, I swear," Ginny shook her head and Greg continued the drive down the mountain.

"Ok, now you have to close your eyes."

"Is this when you murder me and bury me in the woods and you don't want me to know where we are so my ghost can't tell any future mediums?"

Greg stared at Ginny, mouth gaping at her as she laughed.

"So true crime shows are one of your favorites?"

"Guilty," she smiled and closed her eyes.

Greg pulled off the main road, turning toward the home of a local private chef.

As they approached the residence, Greg smiled. The chef had done exactly as he'd asked. He parked so that Ginny could see it all before getting out of the car.

"Ok," Greg turned the car off. "You can open your eyes."

Greg kept his eyes on Ginny as she opened hers, reveling in the sheer delight that filled her face as she saw what he'd done.

"You did all this for me?" Her voice was tinged with disbelief.

"Ginny," he pulled her hand to his heart. "This is a tiny offering of what I'd do for you. Come on, let's enjoy it."

Greg walked around the car, opening her door and picking her hand back up as the chef came out to greet them.

"Ginny, Greg, welcome! We've got your table all set up. Have a seat and we'll bring out the first course and drinks."

The table for two sat in front of a stone fireplace in a courtyard. Stockings hung from the mantle as a fire roared. Christmas lights covered the trees and furniture, with one fir decorated as a Christmas tree. Mistletoe hung on almost every surface, per Greg's request. As Ginny pulled him closer to the table, he stopped every time there was mistletoe. The kisses had started light and playful, but as they neared the table, the heat level reached toe curling. Ginny wrapped her arms around his neck and practically climbed him as they reached the table. Her tongue swept into his mouth when he gasped at her move. She stroked his tongue with her own and he almost came apart. He had to pry himself away from her or he would embarrass them both when the chef and server came back out.

Ginny's hair was mussed and her lips swollen as she looked happily across the table at him.

"Do we get to do that in reverse when we leave?" She asked, taking a gulp from her water glass.

"We'd never make it to the next stops." He downed half of his own water as the chef and server brought out appetizers and a flight of small glasses for each of them.

The chef explained the appetizers but left before mentioning the drinks.

Ginny's head was on a swivel, trying to take in all there was to see. Her eyes were wide, her smile huge. "Ok, so this is the most beautiful date I've ever had."

Greg picked up the first small glass and motioned for her to follow suit.

"What are we drinking?"

Greg winked at her as he sipped his.

Ginny gave him a saucy look as she licked her lips and tasted hers.

He watched, waiting, his eyes unable to look away from her mouth.

Ginny set the glass down and offered him an appreciative smile as she shook her head. Greg took another sip of the gin cocktail.

"You're spoiling me with your cuteness."

"Just wait," he said, picking up the second glass. "Five different seasonal gin cocktails. All made with top shelf. A Christmas themed menu that pairs with all of them."

The chef paired the crab cake appetizers with a Christmas gimlet. The pairing highlighted rosemary in each.

Ginny told Greg about Lacey's passion for botany and about their friendship.

The goat cheese salad paired with a Hanky Panky - a new drink for both Ginny and Greg. A sweet version of a gin martini with Italian bitters, created at The Savoy Hotel in London.

Greg told Ginny about his first trip to London, the first time he played golf internationally.

Mushroom risotto paired with a classic Tom Collins.

Ginny shared stories of Alice learning to tend bar. Greg spoke of the mixologists he'd watch flair in Vegas.

Greg thought Ginny's cheeks must hurt from all the smiling and laughing. When the chef brought out the main course and sides - a traditional turkey dinner - and explained the Thanksgiving Cocktail paired with it, Ginny's smile grew five times bigger.

They took turns sharing their favorite Thanksgiving memories.

Fried strawberries stuffed with cheesecake and mini pies were for dessert. The classic gin and tonic paired well with the fruit. The chef insisted on espresso to warm them after their meal and to energize them after so many calories.

As they finished sipping their cappuccinos, Ginny got a mischievous twinkle in her eye.

"Time to leave?"

"Yes, on to the next activity. I had a lot I wanted to pack in, but we'll have to save some of it for another day."

"Oh shoot, I have to see you again?"

"Ha ha. You better be careful or I will not follow mistletoe protocol."

"You would never," she narrowed her eyes at him.

Greg pushed his chair back, slowly walking around to her side and pulling her chair out.

"You're right, I could never resist those lips," he whispered, pulling her into another kiss.

God help me, I never want to.

GINNY

❄

Ginny was dizzy. The drinks, the food, the thoughtfulness, the kisses. Greg had her head spinning. After a very thorough mistletoe maze, they'd made it back to the car and were on their way to their next activity. The way Greg rubbed his thumb over her hand added to her dizzy spell. She had the insane urge to crawl onto his lap.

Get it together, Ginny.

She mentally slapped herself.

"So where are we headed?"

"Thought it would be fun to wander around the festival. I need to pick up some decorations for my house, get it looking like Christmas. Maybe you can help me?"

"I love our Christmas festival. The market stalls have the best decorations, too. It's all I can do to stop myself from throwing everything out each year to buy all new again."

Greg found a spot close to the Christmas tree stall.

"I also need to get a tree on our way out," he confessed.

"Man, you really are in need of decorations. Let's get to it."

Ginny pulled him toward her favorite stalls. Soon his arms were full of bags stuffed with black bear tree garland, different ornaments and bulbs, and a beautiful wood carved star for the top of his new tree.

"Ok, I'm going to drop these off at the car so I can carry more. Why don't you get us two mulled wines to keep us warm?" Greg kissed her lightly before heading towards the car.

Ginny couldn't look away from his retreating figure. The view was too good to not appreciate.

"Now, don't you look like the cat that caught the canary," her mom teased, bumping her hip.

"Mama," Ginny groaned, hugging her and Annie. "What're you two doing here?"

"Well, I told Vicky about that gorgeous creature that you and Lacey had over last night who also picked you up this evening, and then we found out you might show up here."

"You're spying on me?"

"Oh, absolutely," Annie took a bite of her funnel cake, powdered sugar flying everywhere.

"Now, Gin, don't be upset. I just had to get a look for myself at the man that could be capable of stealing my Ginny's heart."

"Mama, no one is stealing my heart."

"Oh, well, then the man you're handing it over to." Her mom had the decency to look slightly guilty as she bit into her fried Oreo.

"Ok, you two got to go," Ginny herded them away from Greg's general area as she walked towards the drink line. "This is a date, thank you. Not a time to meet the family."

"He's handsome, Gin. Annie, you were right. The way they looked at each other, too. Definitely reminds me of my Thomas."

Ginny's skin erupted in goosebumps at the mention of

her daddy. A pit formed in her stomach at the memory of losing him. At the memory of her mama's heart breaking. A reminder of what love could do to you.

"Where'd you go, Gin?" Grandma Annie snapped her powdered sugar-coated fingers in her face.

"Uh, nowhere. It's not like you and daddy, Mama," Ginny added as she took the two glasses from the cashier.

"Sure, Gin, whatever you say." Mama winked at her as she grabbed Annie's arm.

"Just because it's like them, doesn't mean the ending will be the same," Grandma Annie added quietly, squeezing Ginny's arm as her mama dragged her away.

Ginny offered her a thankful smile, no longer shocked when Annie could read her thoughts. That woman could read every look and action for what it really was.

She sipped her warm spiced wine, waiting for Greg to reappear and replaying her mama's words. She was certainly smitten with Greg but they'd just met, they were far off from anything more than 'like'.

Sure, Ginny. You were well past like, and on your way to head over heels seven months ago.

Greg emerged from the crowd and butterflies erupted in her stomach. A smile she couldn't fight stole across her face.

How do you miss someone who is gone for less than five minutes? Better question, how do you miss someone you barely know?

Ginny sighed. She knew Greg better than most of her acquaintances on the mountain. Definitely better than any man she'd dated in the last couple of years.

"Miss me?" Greg smiled at her as he took his glass of wine, sipping it slowly as he watched her. "Damn, that's good."

"Right?" Ginny cleared her throat and broke eye contact. "It's their own secret blend of spices."

"You ok?"

"Yup, we have some more shopping to do, come on." Ginny tugged him towards the next row of stalls.

Twenty minutes later, Ginny was in trouble.

"Of course." Ginny muttered to herself as she picked up the closest garland to inspect.

"Well, well, well, couldn't hack it with me so you've moved on to the next new guy in town?" Zach used a singsong voice as he walked up.

Ginny clamped her lips shut to prevent the obscenities from flying out.

"Hi there," Greg interjected, saving Ginny. "I'm Greg Hix, I don't believe I've had the pleasure of meeting you."

"Zach Smith. I should warn you about this one," Zach answered, shaking Greg's hand and motioning towards Ginny.

"Oh?" Greg hadn't released Zach's hand.

"Yes, just a few nights ago she was out with me. Practically throwing herself at me because I was the new, fresh piece of meat on this mountain…"

"Excuse me?" Ginny spun on him, unable to keep her voice within normal octaves. "You were the one who threw a tantrum because I wouldn't let you touch my boobs, you sleazeball."

"I believe douche canoe was the original term," Greg supplied with a smile, before pulling Zach in closer. "Now, listen to me Zach, we all have to work at the same place so I'd prefer we kept it civil, but if you ever speak a lie about Ginny again…" He let his voice trail off, squeezing Zach's hand tighter and pushing him back.

"Why would I waste my time talking about this hussy," Zach scoffed, straightening up.

"Hussy?" Ginny's voice hit an octave she didn't know it could. She pulled her hands from her pockets ready to break his nose like she should have the night of their date.

Greg bent quickly, picking up something that had fallen from her pocket.

"You heard me." Zach shouted as he stepped backwards. "It's not my fault if you've convinced this guy you want more than a roll in the hay, but I'm damn well going to warn him!"

"Whoa," Greg grabbed her around the waist preventing her from attacking and giving Zach time to run in the opposite direction. "He's not worth it, Gin. We all know what really happened."

Ginny took a deep breath as Greg purchased the live garland she'd been holding earlier.

"I should have used that as a weapon," she huffed as Greg grabbed her hand and pulled her towards the tree lot.

He stopped walking as they reached the first row of trees, causing Ginny to bounce back into him.

"What?" She asked confused as she turned to look up at him.

"You dropped this." He held up his hand, holding the item that had fallen from her pocket.

Ginny stared at the ball marker, Greg's signature staring back at her.

"Oh, uh, thanks," she muttered as she tried to snatch it back from him.

"You carry this often?"

Ginny shrugged, stuffing her hands into her pockets and looking around.

Greg stepped towards her, as she kept her head turned away.

"Ginny, look at me," he urged, but her face burned with embarrassment. Here she was teasing him about finding her on the mountain when she was the one who had followed him all these months, holding onto the trinkets as if they were a lifeline.

"Ok, keep looking that way then," Greg sighed as he pulled something from his pocket.

Her bear key chain dangled in front of her face a second later.

She closed her eyes. Her cheeks heated and her heart beat erratically.

"I've carried it every day," he spoke softly, undoing her.

Ginny could only nod as she turned towards him and buried her face into his jacket, hugging him tightly as the tears fell.

"Let's pick out a tree and go home, Gin." He squeezed her tightly.

Ginny let Greg pull her around the rows of trees until they found the perfect one. She watched as he secured it to the roof of the car, following him to the far side. The side facing away from the festival, towards the woods. Her mind raced, trying to get a hold of her feelings.

"Greg," she spoke his name with a smile. He turned to look at her as he finished securing the last bit of rope.

"I've carried it every day." She took a deep breath as he fully turned to face her, leaning against his car.

"I'm not sure what happened that day. Or what brought you here, to this mountain. To me. But I'm…" She shook her head, fighting to find the right words.

"Ginny…" Greg started, fear in his voice.

"I'm so fucking glad you found me," she breathed out in a rush.

There was a beat of silence between them, where Ginny could only hear her heart beating out of her chest. And then Greg was on her, pulling her into him and kissing her deeply.

He spun her around and pressed her against the car. His hands on her hips as hers worked their way into his jacket.

"More," he muttered against her lips as he lifted her legs up around his waist.

Ginny pulled him even closer to her as his arousal pressed into her.

"Greg," she broke the kiss, pulling his face back from her. His eyes dilated, his desire mirrored her own. "More, much more. Let's go."

Greg nodded as he lowered her to the ground. He leaned into her as their breathing regulated.

❄

The drive back seemed twice as long as when they'd left. Ginny used every minute to her advantage, leaning across the console to kiss Greg's neck, innocently rubbing herself against different parts of him.

She moved his hand inside her jacket, causing him to hiss out a breath between clenched teeth.

"Ginny, if you want to get back to my place you should stop. I'm five seconds away from pulling the car to the side of the road."

Ginny laughed headily, squeezing his hand as it found her breast.

Greg barely had the car in park before he was out and around to her side.

He slowed as he opened her door, his eyes darting to her car in the driveway.

"Had Lacey and Alice bring it by in case I was going to be late decorating," Ginny filled him in as she grabbed his hand and pulled him toward the house.

Greg fumbled with his keys, missing the lock twice before finally opening the door.

"God, you're sexy," he told her as she shed her jacket and worked on his.

"You're pretty hot yourself." She pushed his jacket off and fumbled with his shirt buttons.

Pushing her hands down, he pulled the shirt apart, scattering buttons.

"See, fucking hot," she smiled as her hands finally found his skin.

His eyes fluttered shut as she replaced her hands with her mouth, kissing her way up his firm stomach to his chest.

"My turn." He smiled mischievously as he pulled her shirt over her head, revealing her black sheer bra. Ginny shuddered as the cool air hit her chest, hardening her nipples even further.

"Oh my God." Greg's voice was strangled as he picked Ginny up and carried her through the living room to the bedroom, using his mouth to explore her neck as he walked.

He deposited her on the bed, climbing up, and over her till his face loomed above hers.

"I've been dreaming about this for quite some time, Gin, so it could take a while."

"Best way to sample top shelf is slowly," she challenged him.

He stared at her, breathing heavy as the tension continued to build.

"See, sexy." He whispered with a smile as he lowered his lips, finding her mouth, and then continued down.

Ginny moaned as his mouth found her breasts, his hands all over her body.

A Gin sampling had never lasted so long, or been so good.

❄

"Best Gin I've ever had," Greg spoke in between deep breaths an hour later.

"Uh huh." Ginny nodded in agreement as she laid across his stomach.

"I've been ruined for all others," he continued, sounding surprised.

"Just how many samples have you had," she teased, rolling over to stare up at his handsome face.

"Never any like this, that's for sure."

Ginny smiled. She could say the same. Greg had done more than use her body for his pleasure, he'd made love to her and she'd given it right back to him. That wasn't an experience she'd had with a lover before.

"I should get the tree off the car, it started snowing."

"Really? I love it when it snows." Ginny sat up, letting the sheet fall.

"Ok," Greg's eyes became unfocused as he stared at her breasts.

Ginny laughed, snapping her fingers in front of his face.

"OK, tree and decorations inside, round two, and then decorating." Greg wiggled his eyebrows at her as he got out of bed and dressed.

"I think you mean round four," Ginny teased as she got up and pulled on a sweatshirt he produced.

"Whichever, just more." He grinned, kissing her and squeezing her ass before heading out to get the tree.

Ginny smiled, biting her lip and reveling in her pure happiness. She wandered to the kitchen to make some hot cocoa and find snacks for their decorating party.

As she rummaged through the drawers for spoons, she pulled out a stack of papers and set them on the countertop. She forgot her search for spoons as she saw the letterhead for one piece of paper. A competing resort two states over. Dated a day earlier.

Ginny's curiosity beat out her Southern manners.

Dear Mr. Hix,

We are pleased to offer you the position of head Golf Pro at The Austen. The start date would be January 2nd with a...

Ginny's eyes blurred, preventing her from reading the rest. She dropped the letter and pulled another from the stack. A copy of his lease for the house. Ending in January.

Ginny's head spun as she dropped the lease. The Earth seemed to move underneath her.

The next piece of paper was from a university near The Austen about classes for a golf management degree.

A post-it note with a moving company's name and appointment for January.

She slid to the ground as the tears slid down her face.

He was leaving.

She'd allowed herself to fall, and now she would be as broken as her mama had been.

Shaking her head, she pushed all the papers back into the drawer and ran back to the bedroom, hurriedly pulling on her own clothes.

Her hands shook, but she managed to fasten her boots.

She heard Greg come in as she found her purse in the living room.

Taking a deep breath, she rubbed her eyes and went to the front door.

"That snow is no joke." He laughed, rubbing his now wet head. The laughter died as he saw Ginny's face and state of dress.

"What's going on?" he asked, on edge. He dropped the tree and moved to her.

"Uh, I just need to go home. Totally forgot I have to work early tomorrow."

"On Christmas Eve?"

"Yup, so uh, I'll see you."

"Ginny," Greg pleaded, grabbing her hand. "What happened? What's wrong?"

"Nothing, Greg." Ginny avoided eye contact. "Tonight was great, really. Thank you, but I should go."

"Ok." Greg dropped her hand, sounding so defeated and so much like he did all those months ago that Ginny almost stayed, but he was leaving.

So it didn't matter.

"Are you sure I can't drive you home?"

Ginny shook her head, not willing to risk a sob escaping.

"Can I call you tomorrow?"

She shrugged as she headed outside.

"Not sure how late I'll be working," she called back as she climbed into her car.

She drove home going ten miles an hour. Between the snow and her tears, it was the only way to go safely.

As she crashed into her room and allowed the sobs to come loudly, she saw the texts from him.

Gin, please, I don't understand what happened?

I'm sorry for whatever it was.

Please, Ginny.

Tonight was the best night of my life. Please talk to me. What happened?

Are you safe?

Please let me know you're safe.

She fired off a quick, *I'm safe. Talk to you soon.* Hating herself a little for being so short, but dying inside at the idea of him leaving her. At the idea of allowing herself to finally fall in love only to have him leave her like her daddy had.

The tears fell softly on her pillow. Images of her mama and daddy ran through her mind. Greg's sparkling eyes haunted her as sleep finally took her.

GREG

❄

Greg was distraught.

There was no other way to describe his feelings. He had just experienced the most perfect evening of his life, and then something had ruined it. He spent the first thirty minutes after Ginny left alternating between texting her and retracing the evening. He'd left her in a blissful and happy state, and then five minutes later everything was a disaster.

He couldn't stand being in the space that had been so magical merely an hour before. Greg dressed and headed for the bar to work things through in his head.

"Greg?"

Alice found Greg at the bar after his first round.

"Hey, Alice," Greg rubbed his face.

"Aren't you supposed to be with Ginny?"

"Yes, yes, I am. But something happened, and she fled my house in tears."

"What did you do to her?" Alice pounced on him, pulling him halfway across the bar by his collar.

"Alice, I swear to God, I did nothing to her. I have no idea what happened."

"All right, take it from the top." Alice released him and made another round of drinks, including one for herself, and settled in next to him. Her hazel eyes stared at him expectantly as she tied back her brown hair.

Greg sighed, defeated, and ready to spill his guts to yet another friend of Ginny's.

He took a full half hour explaining the entire evening to Alice, leaving out some bedroom details but ensuring she got the gist of everything that happened.

"Hm," Alice said, sipping her drink.

"What?"

"So, you're in love with her?"

Greg didn't reply. He took a moment to sip his drink and think. For the past seven months, Ginny had been a constant thought. Her kindness changed his life, saved him. He'd found her again, against all odds. She was dazzling. Her sense of humor kept him on his toes. Her smile intoxicated him. She was sexy, the most gorgeous woman he'd ever met. When they were together, he smiled nonstop.

"Shit." Greg slammed the glass down, harder than he intended. He winced as he looked at Alice, who just sat smiling at him.

"Thought so. Lacey and I both did, just so we're clear. And also, we're both pretty damn sure she's tumbled down the love hill too. Question is, what the hell happened tonight to send her running scared?" Alice didn't seem like she was asking him.

"Relationships never work out, Alice. I've never known a happy couple that's lasted."

"Well, that sucks for you. I've seen it, Greg. They do work out. When two people love and respect each other."

"My parents cheated on each other constantly."

"Well, see, that's not love or respect."

"I guess that's true." Greg picked his glass up again. It

was empty. Ironic as he realized how empty his childhood had been. Empty of love, of relationships. Empty of respect and trust. "Alice, I'm going to need another drink to wrap my brain around this."

"Coming right up," Alice said, jumping down from her stool.

"I'm broken, Alice. Like, emotionally. I've never seen love, so how do I know how to do it? I've spent most of my adult life acting like an idiot and being unhappy, so why would I get love now?"

"Not how it works, my friend. There is no earning love. There is being worthy of love, and everything I know about you indicates you're worthy. And I don't say that lightly about one of my best friends."

Greg sipped his drink, processing the idea.

I love Ginny Wellner.

The thought alone made his heart swell. Chased away his doubts about relationships.

"Alice?"

"Greg?"

"I love Ginny Wellner."

Alice's smile almost matched the one he wore.

"Who doesn't?" She asked, lifting her glass in a toast.

"Problem is," Greg's smile vanished. "I think she hates me. Why else would she leave like that?"

Alice leaned against the bar with an exasperated sigh.

"I've been thinking about that. Do you know about her parents?"

"She told me about her mom, she still lives nearby, right?"

"Yea, Vicky would never leave the mountain. But has she told you about her dad?"

"No, actually. Where's he at?"

"Hm. Let me make a call."

Greg sipped his drink as he watched Alice have a very animated conversation.

"Ok," she sighed upon her return, downing her drink. "Tomorrow, you're having lunch with me and Lacey at 1PM. Meet us here. I'm not allowed to say anything more, so don't ask and give me twenty minutes and I can drive you home."

Greg just nodded, confused as ever, staring at the shelf lined with gin. He wasn't sure how long he'd been daydreaming when his phone rang.

Hoping it was Ginny, he answered without looking. "Hello?"

"Gregory, darling! You never take my calls these days."

Greg ground his teeth together, letting his head fall onto the bar at the sound of his mother's voice.

"Hi Mom. How's it going? It's pretty late for a call."

"What do you mean, it's only 9:30?"

"Well, I live in the Eastern time zone these days."

"And, how would I know that exactly?"

Touche.

"What's up, Mom?"

"Well, Gregory, I was worried about you. It's been weeks since we spoke, and I had no idea where you were."

His mom sounded genuine, which wasn't typical. Usually her voice dripped with manipulative saccharine. She was never going to win a trophy for 'Mom of the Year' so typically her inquiries about him were to induce guilt or find out intel about his dad.

"Well, I'm safe. Found a beautiful spot in the Blue Ridge Mountains."

Greg chose his words carefully, not wanting an invasion from his mother.

"Uh huh. Well, I called to inform you that I'm getting married."

"What?" Greg was sure he'd misheard her. His parents'

divorce was contentious, but his mom had walked away with a nice chunk of monthly alimony - which would go away if she remarried.

"I'm getting married, darling. I've found the most perfect man."

"Wealthy?" Greg grimaced at how that sounded. "I mean, can he take care of you?"

"Well, not that it matters, but yes, he can. There's more to marriage than wealth, Gregory. He loves me. He treats me like a queen, and I can't imagine a second of my life without him."

Greg's eyebrows hit his hairline. He'd never heard his mom talk about a relationship as more than a meal ticket in his entire life.

"I'm guessing from this lengthy silence that you're confused. Well, me too," she chuckled. "But, it's the truth. It's completely different from anything I've ever experienced in my life. And it's not just some crazy fling. We've been together for a year, Greg. A solid year, no cheating, no breaks."

"Wow. I'm thrilled for you, Mom."

"Thanks, darling. Me too. I just didn't know it could be like this. I cannot wait for you to meet him."

"Me too. Email me the details, I'll be sure I'm available for the big day."

"You better be. I need someone to walk me down the aisle, and that's a job for my son."

"I'd be happy too. Talk to you soon, Mom." Greg hung-up, rubbing his head.

"What was that?" Alice asked, setting another drink in front of him.

"Thank you," he said, downing half of it in a gulp. "That was my mother, or maybe fate since it seems to enjoy interfering in my life lately. Either way, they were just flipping everything I've ever known about relationships on it's head."

"Love," Alice shrugged.

"Apparently. What is this?" Greg asked, holding his cocktail glass up. "Not what I've been drinking."

"Damn, you do have quite the gin palate."

Greg blushed, remembering his sampling earlier in the evening.

"Keep those thoughts to yourself," Alice said, making a face. "This is another local gin. Little distiller down the mountain."

"It's delicious. I can't believe they make it here."

"Yea, it's a small blonde's absolute favorite too." Alice winked, turning to grab her bag. "All right, let's get you home so that tomorrow comes sooner."

❄

The next morning came, but not as quickly as Greg would have liked. Ginny had sent some crap text about being home and hadn't responded to his calls or messages since. He'd called the spa, and she wasn't working.

He checked his phone for the third time as he finished walking through the second house he was viewing that day. His rental was up at the end of January and he was interested to see what was on the market. Neither property had him excited. He'd felt empty as he walked through the drab interiors. He was rethinking his requirements for buying when he walked into the Black Bear Tavern for his lunch with Alice and Lacey.

"Are you kidding me?" Alice shouted at him as he entered.

"What?" Greg ducked, looking around for whatever was about to attack.

"You're leaving?"

"Me?" Greg looked at her and Lacey in disbelief.

"Yes, you. Your lease is expiring? You're moving? You got a job offer to start in two weeks? You start classes at an out-of-state university soon?"

"Yes?"

Alice looked ready to throw a bottle at his head as Lacey stepped in.

"So, we all thought you'd be staying on the mountain?"

"I am," he said cautiously, not wanting to irk Lacey as he had Alice.

The three of them looked at each other in confused silence.

"You're staying on the mountain?" Alice asked, testing the waters.

"Yes."

"But you got a job offer from The Austen?"

"How'd you know about that?" he asked.

"Forget how we know, Greg," Lacey interjected. "You got a job offer, aren't you taking it?"

"What? No, of course not. People haven't realized I've taken a position. I get a new offer every other day. I've been shoving them in a drawer when my agent sends them to me. I've told him to politely decline each."

"What about the classes? That school is right by that resort?"

"The classes are online, it's one of the few universities in the country that offers the program. It's the only one that has online options. I just have to do a few weeks in person. It'll make me a better golf pro and help me make The Artis more successful."

Lacey and Alice looked at each other. They shook their heads and rubbed their faces.

"Wait." Lacey dropped her hands and looked at him. "Your house?"

"Yes?"

"Is it yours?" She asked tentatively.

"No, it's a short lease."

"Why? Because you're thinking of moving?"

"Yes?"

"To your new job somewhere else?" she hedged.

"Uh, no." Greg shook his head. "You guys, trying to get rid of me? Alice, is it because I told you I love Ginny?"

"You did?" Lacey looked like a little kid opening a Christmas present.

"Yes. What's going on?" Greg sighed, rubbing his temples.

"Why are you moving then?" Alice asked, crossing her arms.

"Uh, because my house is a short-term lease? I'm trying to figure out where I want to be on the mountain, so I didn't want to buy or sign anything long-term right away. In fact, I was looking at houses this morning, but I'm not really liking any of them. Maybe you guys know of some places?"

Greg picked at the bowl of nuts in front of him.

"Oh my God," Alice muttered, banging her head on the bar.

"You ok?" Greg asked, seriously concerned for her well-being.

"Let's go get a burger," Lacey offered, patting Alice on the back.

The three of them trudged around the corner to one of the few local spots open on Christmas Eve. After they ordered, Lacey leaned in.

"Ok, listen up, we're about to break some major best friend-code because we like you and think Ginny loves you."

Greg nodded eager for any help.

"Remember, I asked you if you knew anything about Ginny's dad?" Alice asked, matching Lacey's posture.

"Yea, and I don't know anything."

"Ok, so Ginny's mom and dad were legends around here back in the day," Lacey began. "The kind of love story that all the older couples go on and on about and the sort of couple that create problems for those less in love."

"Oh my God, my parents got into it once when he brought her flowers for no reason." Alice laughed.

"Not now, Alice," Lacey shushed her.

"So she knows what love looks like?" Greg asked.

"Big time," Lacey continued. "Love story for the ages. Until…"

Unshed tears filled Lacey's eyes, and Alice rubbed her back.

"I've got it," she told Lacey, turning back to Greg. "Her dad was the nicest guy. One of our favorite people."

Greg hated the way Alice spoke of him in the past tense. His heart constricted tightly at the idea of Ginny losing her dad.

"He was in the military. Trained up-and-coming kids. One day, there was an accident…" Alice trailed off, swallowing a couple of times.

"I got it." Greg patted her hand. "Her dad died when she was young."

"Right, and you'd think that's enough to sour someone on life, but the thing that broke Ginny…" Lacey's voice cracked on the word 'broke', and Greg's eyes moistened. "The thing that really did a number on her was watching her mom get the news."

Greg thought about what that would look like, for someone so in love with their partner to be told by strangers that they were gone.

"Oh," he breathed.

Lacey and Alice nodded.

"We were at the funeral, and she fell apart. I'll never

forget the sound of those sobs, or the look on Ginny's face." Lacey wiped at the tears on her face.

Alice shook her head, as if to erase the memory.

"So, she's scared?" Greg asked, hoping that it was as simple as fearing losing love.

They both nodded at him as their food arrived.

"Well, good," Greg said, picking up a fry.

Catching the looks on their faces, he quickly continued.

"I mean good because I'm not going anywhere. I love her and I'm going to show her she doesn't have to be scared to love me."

Alice and Lacey dug into their own fries and burgers.

"Wait," Greg dropped his fry. "She found those papers, didn't she? The lease? The job offer?"

Lacey and Alice grimaced.

"From what I understand, she was looking for a spoon to make hot chocolate," Lacey offered as she sipped her soda.

"Oh, for fuck's sake." Greg rubbed his forehead, silently cursing himself for not trashing the job offer right away. "All right, well, I think I have an idea but you two have officially been drafted into helping me."

Lacey and Alice smiled at him.

"I knew it," Alice smirked, grabbing another fry.

"What?" Greg asked, digging back into his food.

"That going to that golf tournament would be good for her."

Greg smiled at his new friends, as they began to plan.

GINNY

❄

Ginny heard her mama arrive. She heard Grandma Annie shuffling around, making breakfast. Christmas morning, her favorite holiday, yet she couldn't drag herself out of bed.

Lacey and Alice had tried to get her up and out the day before, but finally accepted her pleas to be left alone. She wasn't sure she'd be as lucky when her mom and Annie got together.

At last count, her phone had twenty-seven unanswered texts from Greg.

She'd thought if she'd cut off all communication and just told herself that it was over, that it didn't matter, her heart and head would get the message and the pain would be less.

Apparently, falling in love was not something to be talked out of.

Her head hurt from crying, she'd been unable to eat, and all she wanted to do was sleep.

She'd replayed the past couple of days in her head, unable to pinpoint the exact moment when she'd fallen completely in love with Greg.

Maybe it had started all those months ago, and she'd just inched closer and closer as time went by.

The evening they'd shared was the most perfect night of her life. However, the realization that he was leaving soon was too much to bear. She'd never leave the mountain where her mama lived, where her daddy was buried, where her best friends were seconds away. It would never work, so she had to let it go. Deal with the broken heart and move on.

"Ginny Mae Wellner!"

Ginny groaned, rolling over.

"Ginny Mae, are you kidding me with this?"

"I told you, Vicky. It's ridiculous."

"Well, Annie, go get the bucket, we'll get her out of this bed one way or another."

Ginny's eyes went wide.

They wouldn't.

She heard the water running in the bathtub across the hall.

Holy shit.

"Ok, ok, I'm getting up." Ginny rolled over.

"Well, that's a start. You look like hell, girlie."

Her mama, the sensitive southern belle.

"Thanks, Mama." Ginny sighed.

"What's gotten into you?" Grandma Annie demanded as she came back in holding the bucket.

"Don't you dare!" Ginny shouted. "I'm up and out of bed!"

"Oh, please, it's empty you ninny." Annie showed her the empty bucket.

"Uh huh," Ginny eyed her suspiciously.

"Now, what is going on? Last time we see you, you're in heaven staring after that fine young man's bum, and now you're laid up in bed like somebody ran over your favorite pet."

"Mama." Ginny rolled her eyes, heading for her dresser.

"Tell her, Ginny," Grandma Annie ordered.

"Well, if you know everything you tell her, Annie."

Vicky's swift intake of breath was the only reminder Ginny needed that she'd been rude to an elder.

"Sorry." She shook her head. "I'm tired and jumbled up."

"Out with it this moment, young lady." Mama's tone brokered no resistance.

"Fine. He's leaving, ok? He's gone in January. New job a couple of states over. No point in continuing to see him."

"That's it?" Grandma Annie shouted in disbelief. "Way you've been carrying on here, I figured you must have watched him go at it with another young lady or some such."

"Annie!" Vicky laughed.

"Well, she's acting like he cheated or lied or died!"

The laughter and lightness fled the room at her last comment.

"Ah." Annie sighed knowing.

"Ah, indeed," Vicky added, sitting on the bed.

"Ah, what?" Ginny swallowed hard, unable to breathe.

"Ah, your daddy died and left your mama," Grandma Annie whispered, acting as if she wasn't kicking the air out of Ginny as she did so.

Ginny's eyes filled up instantly.

"Silly girl." Mama sighed, then patted the bed next to where she sat.

Ginny sat down, all the fight fleeing her.

"Your daddy died," Vicky said. "He did not choose to leave. He loved us beyond explanation, Ginny Mae."

"I know, Mama," Ginny cried. "He didn't get a choice in the matter, and neither did you. You loved him so much it broke you in half when he died. I saw you when those men came to the door, when they lowered his casket into the Earth. It broke you, Mama. I can't let that happen to me."

Grandma Annie tsked at her. "You silly, stupid girl. Do you have any idea how many women would kill to have that kind of love in their lives? To feel like they've found their second half? To have those years to look back on and revel in?"

Ginny looked at Mama, hoping she'd chime in to defend her. That she'd explain to Annie that it wasn't worth being broken. Instead, her mama smiled and tears slid down her face as she nodded.

"Ginny Mae, your daddy would be beside himself if he knew you were scared to love with your whole heart because of him. He loved me without reserve. He loved you with every ounce of himself. That kind of love, it's like a meteor. It's so rare, the only way you know it really happened is that it leaves that kind of crater in your heart. I wouldn't trade my time with your daddy for anything. Not a damned thing. Being broken like that by the loss of your partner, it's a blessing that I pray you understand someday. That man was my heart, and I so hope that you find someone who is that for you. And if it is this young man of yours, well, I hope that this silliness hasn't ruined your chances, my love."

Annie hugged Vicky, patting her cheek lightly before they left the room hand in hand.

Ginny took a deep, cleansing breath, trying to clear her head.

As she showered and dressed for the holiday, she thought through everything Mama and Grandma Annie had said to her.

The aching in her chest might as well have been a crater in her chest. She doubted it would be any worse if she continued seeing Greg until he left. At least then she'd have the memories and smiles to look back on.

Having made up her mind, she entered the living room feeling lighter.

"There you are." Alice and Lacey shouted at her.

"Yes?" she asked. "Where else would I be?"

"Listen." Lacey pointed to the chair across from them.

Ginny sat as her mama handed her a plate with all her favorite holiday breakfast items.

"You're an idiot." Lacey said, no hint of humor on her face.

Ginny froze with a sausage link halfway to her mouth.

"Beg your pardon?"

"You're an idiot. Actually, you're a conclusion jumping idiot."

Lacey grabbed the sausage link from Ginny's fork and bit into it, wagging the other end in her face.

"He's looking at houses here. He's not taking some other job or moving for school. Never was."

Lacey and Alice crossed their arms in unison, giving her the death stare.

"What are you talking about? I saw the papers."

"Yes, you saw some papers, but did you even ask about them? No, you just fled the scene, leaving him to try to work it all out. How could you do that, Ginny?" Alice asked.

"How do you know any of this?"

"We had lunch with our friend, Greg." Lacey huffed as she took a seat.

"Your friend?" Ginny chortled.

"Yes, at least he's honest with us. At least he explains the full story of the day you met. At least he filled us in on his life the past seven months." Lacey crossed her arms again.

Ginny found her plate very interesting.

"I was embarrassed," she mumbled. "I had a silly crush on an almost complete stranger and was allowing myself to wallow in it."

"Correction, Ginny," Alice chimed in. "You had a crush on someone whose life you changed. Someone who told us both that you saved his life. That they'd been thinking of you every day for seven months."

Ginny stared, mouth agape, at Alice.

"Someone who told us very clearly that he loves you. And has no intentions of leaving this place, Ginny."

Ginny looked to her mama and Grandma Annie. They didn't appear angry, but they didn't seem thrilled with her.

"Do you love him or not?" Lacey asked. "Because our friend will probably be heartbroken if you don't."

"He's not leaving?" The ache in Ginny's chest ceased.

"Nope." Lacey shook her head.

"No." Alice smiled.

"Oh my God. Oh my God. Oh my God. What did I do? What kind of fucking stupid, idiotic person am I that I would do this?"

Ginny jumped up and ran for the bedroom.

"Someone better get in here and help me do my hair and makeup immediately!" she shrieked at her friends and family.

Alice and Lacey jogged into her room.

"Will he forgive me?" The ache in her chest has ceased but her breathing had reached hyperventilation level as the pit in her stomach grew. She laid on the bed, desperate for comfort. Hopeful that she hadn't ruined her chance at love.

"Someone that stupidly in love?" Alice asked as she sat next to her friend.

"One hundred percent," Lacey chimed in, sitting on the other side.

"But you can't run like that, Gin," Alice continued. "You should've seen him last night."

Ginny's mind flashed back to the man she'd met behind the tent. The person she'd told to be happy, to not take a second of their life for granted.

Yet, she'd gone and caused him unhappiness. Dulled the sparkle in his beautiful eyes.

"I'm the worst, he deserves better," Ginny groaned, rolling to her stomach.

"Eh maybe, but he seems to want you. Now is the time for glamour, not wallowing. When you find him and convince him to give you another chance, you can apologize and explain how stupid you are," Lacey chirped as she went to the closet.

"Right," Alice spoke up. "However, before we get to that point, we're going to need some convincing."

"Oh, you're right Alice." Lacey said turning back to Ginny, arms crossed.

"What are your intentions with our friend, Greg?" Alice asked, giving her the stink eye.

"I love him. I think I started falling for him the second I got hit in the head with that golf ball, and I tumbled over the edge when he came over for dinner."

Alice and Lacey shared a knowing smile as they both turned for the closet.

"Break out the sheer lingerie," Ginny spoke up, determined to ease any hurt and pain she'd caused the man she loved.

GREG

❄

Christmas was not going the way Greg had hoped.

He'd intended to wake up with Ginny in his arms. Call his parents and introduce her. Shower her in affection all day long.

Instead, he'd woken up alone. Lacey and Alice assured him they could help undo the disaster he found himself in. He trusted them, but sitting alone and doing nothing was not in his wheelhouse.

He hadn't bothered putting up any of the decorations he'd bought with Ginny. Everything reminded him of her, and it seemed too precarious a situation to bet on it working out. The weight on him was a familiar feeling. He felt it often when he had been on Tour. The ache in his chest was new. He didn't care for either.

Enough of this feeling sorry for yourself shit.

They had a plan in place and he just needed to see it through.

Unable to sit still and wait any longer, he threw on running clothes and hit the pavement.

An escape mechanism when he golfed professionally, he happily lapsed into the mindless action again.

Greg ran down and around the golf course, through the resort, and was making his way through the remnants of the festival when he saw a flash of blonde.

He slowed to a brisk walk, catching his breath as he waited for another flash of whatever had caught his eye.

"I'm such an idiot," the blonde said to herself. "If he's not at home and not at work, where the hell could he be on Christmas Day?"

Greg came up behind Ginny and enjoyed the view and the monologue.

His eyes drank her in greedily as she darted into one of the two churches on the block.

He found her car halfway down the block amongst the folded-up festival tents. Sitting down on one of the tents, he waited for her to come back out.

"Can't just tell the guy you freaking love him, can you? Now you're chasing him all over the fucking mountain," she muttered as she shoved her hands into her gloves.

She looked up as she pulled out her keys and froze.

"Hi." He smiled hopefully at her.

Tears filled her eyes as she let out a breath. "Hi."

"Whatcha doing out here on your favorite holiday?" he asked, as he stood up.

"Well." She took a deep breath and approached. "I made a fool out of myself, and let this perfectly amazing man that I'm head over heels in love with feel like he did something wrong, when it was actually my fault for being scared. I was worried he might have left town or given up on me because of it."

"Ginny," he breathed out her name, relieved to be saying it again.

"I'm so sorry," she said, grabbing his hoodie and pulling him close. "I was an idiot to run away like that and I know it now. Can you forgive me? I just cannot bear the thought of causing you to feel like you used to."

"Ginny, you could never be the cause of sadness or misery, when you've done nothing but bring clarity and joy to my life."

"But I left you alone that night." She looked up at him and Greg saw the pain in her eyes. "I ran away"

"I know, Gin, but I also know that you're scared. I know about your mom and dad, about the love they shared. I was scared too. I've never seen a relationship work, Ginny. My parents are about as far opposite of yours as possible. And then—" he tilted her chin up. "—my mom calls me and tells me she's getting married, and that she's happy and in love. So, I figure if it's possible for her, why am I doubting that I am beyond in love with the beautiful woman who saved me?"

"Weird how these types of conversations keep happening behind tents?" Ginny teased through her tears.

"Seems appropriate," Greg added as he kissed her.

"Let's make a deal?" she asked, breaking the kiss.

"Hm?" Greg's mouth found her neck, and he enjoyed the feeling of Ginny under his lips and hands again. The ache in his chest and the heaviness went away with Ginny in his arms.

"Greg, baby." She pulled back, breathing heavy already. "Let's make a deal."

"Right, what kind of deal?" he asked, smiling at her.

"No more being scared? We face things head on, together. If either of us has concerns, we talk to the other one about them. No more running."

"Deal. Ginny, I don't plan on leaving. I haven't taken a second of my life for granted since I met you, and I fully intend on never doing so again."

"Let's go home?" Ginny looked at him, her eyes filled with hope, her head tilted to the side, unsure.

"Well, it's only home for another week or two. I've been

shopping but could use some input. Or, you could just move in with me and we pick it out together?"

Ginny's smile bowled him over.

"Greg," she said, kissing his lips lightly. "More, home, now."

"Yes, ma'am." He laughed, sprinting for the passenger side.

❄

Greg couldn't keep his hands off of Ginny in the car. They both jumped out as soon as it was in park.

He wasted no time and scooped her up and over his shoulder.

"Greg!" she squealed, laughing as he patted her ass.

"Ginny, I gotta tell you, I like my present."

"Oh baby, you haven't even seen it yet," she teased him, wriggling in his arms.

He slid her down his body as they got inside, wanting to feel her on him.

"Wait." She pushed back from him. "Why aren't the decorations up?"

"Oh," he said, running his hand through his hair. "Well, after you left it just didn't feel right decorating and celebrating."

The look Ginny aimed at him brokered no discussion. They were decorating, immediately.

"I will make it more fun for you." She winked as she slowly stripped from her outer layers, leaving only a sheer layer of lingerie.

Greg was sure his eyes were the size of saucers as he watched her unwrap herself.

"Really like my present, Gin." He eyed her up and down.

"Uh huh, well, no more unwrapping until this place looks like Christmas."

Greg needed no further instruction as he carried the tree into the living room, adding water to the tree stand and plugging in lights.

Ginny placed live garland around the room.

They'd started hanging various ornaments and bulbs when Greg excused himself.

He'd hoped that he'd have the opportunity to give his gift to Ginny on Christmas.

"Ginny," he started, mesmerized by the view of her bent over and hanging ornaments.

"It doesn't seem fair that you're so dressed for our decorating party, Greg," she replied, hands on her hips.

"Uh huh," Greg nodded and stripped down to his boxers faster than he'd ever done before.

"Better," she commented as she eyed him up and down, licking her lips.

He groaned in response.

"Decorating is done," she confirmed.

"Time to open your present." He sat on the couch, motioning for her to join him. "Then I get to open mine."

He stared at Ginny as she walked over, drinking in every millimeter of skin like a man who'd been thirsty for decades.

Her skin was flush and her breathing heavy as she finally sat next to him.

"I didn't get you anything," she said, disappointment lacing her voice.

"Gin," he said in a no-nonsense tone. "You are the best Christmas present I could ever receive. This is a small token."

Ginny gave him a bit of side-eye as she opened the envelope.

"I don't understand?"

"I discovered a local gin distillery that I loved the other day."

"Yea, they're my favorite." She smiled at him.

"I might have heard that from a couple of birds." He winked at her. "So I went and looked around at the place, and it turns out they were interested in taking on a partner."

Ginny looked at him and back at the paper in her hands.

"You bought into a distillery?"

"No, I bought us into a distillery."

"But, why?"

"Well, not a day has gone by in the past seven months when Gin hasn't been on my mind. So what better way to prove my devotion than putting down some major roots and buying into a local organization where we can grow and make our own imprint on the best liquor out there?"

Ginny stared at him. Her mind unable to process what he said. Her heart bursting.

"All this for us?"

"For us, always, Ginny. Someone wise once told me to 'never underestimate what top shelf can do for you'. Well, it changed my whole life, and I don't want it to stop, ever."

"Ever?"

"Never. Ginny, I've never thought much of fate, but when a small ball falls out of the sky and lands directly on your head. Or you end up on the same tiny mountain where the small blonde that saved your life lives. You start to think about it. I don't know why fate gave me a mulligan in this life Ginny, but it's clear that I'm supposed to spend it loving you."

Ginny smiled, folding the paper.

"I love you too, Greg. I promise to never be scared of that again. Now," she said, standing up. "Take me to the bedroom and unwrap your damn present."

Greg lifted her into his arms, not needing to be told twice.

As he laid her down on the bed he drank in the joy spread out before him.

"Merry Christmas to me." He smiled as he crawled up and kissed her.

The End

ABOUT THE AUTHOR

STELLA BRECHT

Stella Brecht has always believed in make believe and loves all things love. Insert swoon here. Her nose can most often be found in a romance novel, and while she constantly plays sub-genre roulette, she has yet to lose. Whether it's based in reality, the paranormal, current day, or the past, Stella will gladly read it or write it. Her current jam is writing sexy sports romances.

When she's not writing, Stella is happiest in a plane, train or automobile heading to the next location on her ever-growing travel list. She currently resides in southwest Florida in the midst of her own happily ever after with her husband, and the apple of their eye, a Shiba Inu-Beagle mix.

※

To keep up with the fun that Stella is having - follow her on her website (StellaBrecht.com), Instagram, and Facebook.

facebook.com/SeeStellaBrechtWrite
instagram.com/seestellawrite

Snowmen and Shenanigans

by
Ivy Fernwood

CHAPTER 1

Fucking hell.
Emery froze as a sugary sweet voice rang through her bookstore.

Not Tina. Not right now. Emery's aching body couldn't afford the headache she'd inevitably have from dealing with Tina.

Instead of hiding like she wanted to, Emery turned to greet her least favorite person in all of Pine Forest.

"What can I do for you, Tina?" Emery asked, fighting against a grimace.

She looked Emery up and down with her beauty pageant smile. "I wasn't sure if you'd heard. They asked me to be in charge of the Jack Frost Festival this year."

"I've heard."

Oh, Emery had heard.

She heard all about Walter and the other town council members passing along the reins to Tina. Emery wasn't jealous, not of all the work Tina was doing. No way could Emery have organized the festival, finished the holiday baskets, finished her chili for the cook-off tomorrow while, somewhere in there, helping her best friend with a parade float to repay her for helping Emery later that evening with said baskets.

No, Emery definitely wasn't jealous. Just *why did it have to be Tina?*

"Well, that's not a surprise," Tina said as she moved further into the bookstore, clipboard tucked against her puffy black winter coat. The matching fuzzy snow boots cost more than Emery made in a week. Dressed up like winter Barbie. Emery's dark denim and cream knit sweater made her comfy Barbie or maybe cozy Barbie.

Emery stopped a few feet in front of Tina. Balled up holiday ribbons and more scented candles than her nose could handle, surrounded them. At the moment, she was having a love hate relationship with Christmas.

"Again, what can I do for you, Tina?" Emery asked, crossing her arms. So many other things she could do. Like hitting herself over the head with an ornament. Or walking over a shattered one barefoot.

"Were you still planning on entering the chili cook-off tomorrow?" Tina grimaced around at the Christmas mess her store had morphed into. Books were stacked on all the tables scattered around the bookshelves with a pile of baskets needing finishing touches spilling into the walkways. "You just seem rather busy is all," Tina tossed her free arm around as if Emery wasn't aware of the chaos they were currently standing in the middle of.

"I am, which is why I don't have time to chat considering you already confirmed all of this with me the other day," Emery bit out.

Why me?

Tina glanced down at her clipboard, tapping it with her bright red pen, lips pursed. "You dropped out of the pie-making contest over Thanksgiving and with the chili cook-off being the town's most popular event, after the snowman competition well, we can use every inch of space we can get."

"I had the flu!" Emery screamed, nails digging into her palms. *How was I expected to bake a pie from scratch while puking my brains out all night?*

The bell above the door chimed.

"Sorry I'm late," Lana called, head down, "I wanted to warn you I saw the wicked wit--" Her head popped up, landing on Tina. "Oh. Guess you know." She continued moving through the store, tossing the bags she'd been carrying onto the table behind Emery before joining them.

Tina's eyes squinted, then she took a deep breath and said, "You two haven't changed a bit. Why I thought today would be any different, I'll never know." She sighed.

She fucking sighed!

Slapping her hand over her heart, "Oh," Emery started, "Forgive me for still being upset about you not only ruining my first kiss by stealing Peter McHenry from me freshman year, but *Andrew*?" Her heart pounded in her chest. "He was my first love and my first, well, *first* and you fucking knew it!"

Lana squeezed her forearm in warning. Right. Keep it together. This wasn't the time or place. As a redhead Emery was more than aware of the cliches and stereotypes about her temper, and while she did her best to avoid them, she felt her face heating and her anger rising.

"Okay, Tina," Lana stepped between the two of them. *Smart*. Emery's knuckles were white, ready, and willing if Tina kept at it. "Unless you need anything else, I think it's time you go before one of you takes this too far."

"Maybe it's time to move on from high school Emery, see if you can keep a guy around for longer than a few months," she said, brow arching, begging Emery to slap it off. "It's not my fault they weren't satisfied, but maybe it just runs in the family? Your dad had to be pretty bad in bed for dear old mommy to find it somewhere else. " Tina sneered, giving both women a once over, lingering on Lana's dark sweater and oatmeal colored corduroys.

Emery's anger finally won as she snapped, "It's not my fault you're such a cunt and can't get your own men." Tina's eyes widened. Steam seconds away from coming out of her ears.

"Like that," Lana said, her entire body sagging in defeat.

"Is that so," Tina stepped forward, smiling like a shark now. Emery was more than ready. In all those years, she'd never attacked Tina. Not even a slap, no matter how tempted she had been.

"Alright, time for you to leave." Lana herded Tina to the exit. "We'll see you tomorrow bright and early at the parade. Maybe next time just give Emery a call instead of stopping by?" she shrugged as she shoved her out the door.

Emery hated to admit it, but if Tina had called, she would have ignored it, putting them in the same position they were in now.

"If I thought she would answer, I would've," Tina said, knowing Emery better than Lana did at the moment.

It was time to chill out, not make a scene in the middle of her store where anyone could walk in and see her being a bitch to Tina. And she knew she was being a bitch, but damn, Tina got under her skin.

That Emery was part Irish and had a bit of a temper didn't help the situation either. It rarely helped in any situation she was in.

Emery moved behind a table, needing distance between them in case things went south. Taking a calming breath, she closed her eyes and thought of her dad's words of advice.

Pick your battles, my little firecracker.

Okay, maybe her temper was closer too explosive, but with Tina and the list of things she did throughout their lives? Let's just say Emery wished Tina stealing her boyfriend was the worst thing she'd ever done.

"It's fine," Emery said, opening her eyes, forcing a polite smile. "You can come by if there's anything else you need from me." It took a lot more effort than she would have liked to pretend she still didn't want to punch Tina in the face, but as Frank Sinatra suggested over the sound system, *it was time to have myself a merry little Christmas.* And getting arrested for assault wasn't a part of the plan.

Tina squinted her eyes at Emery, nodding before turning on her heel and heading out the door.

As soon as it closed Lana whipped around, her long dark waves flying around her shoulders, a look of awe on her face. "That was big of you Em. I was half expecting you to throw a punch. Especially when she brought up the whole thing with your mom getting her freak on with half the town."

"Me too and it wasn't half the town," Emery corrected her, holding her temper at bay as she thought about the mess her mother had left them. "But she isn't worth it no matter how crazy she makes me." She moved back over to the supplies to finish what she was working on before Tina arrived. "Why couldn't Tina have just stayed in Chicago?"

Emery never understood why Tina left the windy city. She was always complaining about the town being too small for her. How there was so much more out there.

"No clue. You think she'd even tell anyone the truth? I'm sure it's something embarrassing or she'd be shouting it from the rooftops."

Lana was probably right. Emery needed to get Tina and all the anger that she brought on out of her system. So, she cranked up the tunes and got in touch with the holiday spirit, letting it all go.

The two of them spent the next few hours finishing up the holiday gift baskets and chatting about their upcoming plans. They decided on a post-Christmas pancake breakfast after all the chaos was over. And maybe a spa day depending on how the festivities went.

Her business, *Emery's Enchanted Used Bookstore,* had been a gift from her grandfather after he died. Two stories, all a beautiful cherry wood that her grandfather took pride in seeing as he'd built most of it himself. Emery did her best to keep as much of the original wood as she could while creating an open concept for the store.

She missed him and his stories, especially around this time of year.

With Lana's help, Emery could assist customers that came in to shop while still making progress on her 'to-do' list.

"That's it," Emery said, leaning over the back of her chair to stretch, "We are officially done." She turned to Lana, "I'm starved and craving tacos. You in? I'm buying."

Lana stood, twisting her torso around, "Oh, you know I'm down for tacos. But coffee was also a requirement, so how about I run across the street to Haro's before they close," she offered, hand to her chest, "and you run over to Katie's and grab us some fuel because the night is young."

Emery loved Lana.

She loved her even more when she suggested getting coffee for after the tacos, which may sound crazy, but after the long day she'd had, it was welcome.

"Perfect," Emery agreed, standing to stretch more. She slipped her navy puffy vest over her sweater, tugged on her grey knit cap and shoved her gloves in her pocket with Katie's Koffee only two buildings over.

Lana threw on her wool sweater she lived in even when the temperatures dropped another twenty degrees. Her red hat, scarf and gloves popped against the darkness of her black sweater and her beautiful waves that were barely a shade lighter than her sweater.

"See you in a few," Lana said and was out the door. Emery took longer, having to lock things up while they were out grabbing stuff.

As she did this, her thoughts drifted to Tina and all the crap she put Emery through over the years. She never fully understood how or why Tina had it out for her. It didn't help how the entire town loved her and praised all the 'good' she did, volunteering for any and everything.

Lana always had her back, but Tina never made her a target of the unfortunate things that *happened* to Emery. Like in high school, when *someone* spread a rumor that Emery had herpes. *Herpes!* Or the time Tina called Emery's dad, asking how Emery was doing since she failed the huge history test. After high school, it became more about beating each other in any and every competition they could. Like the chili cook-off tomorrow and the snowman building contest the day after. But that didn't mean Tina didn't cozy up to damn near any guy Emery showed an interest in.

Maybe it was time to let go of high school dramas? Or maybe it was time to do something about little Miss Tina.

The crisp air cooled Emery's skin as soon as she hit the sidewalk. She loved the fresh scent of the town.

Yanking out her cell, she wanted to set a few alarms so she wouldn't forget about prepping her chili. Head down, finishing that up, she slammed into a wall with a yelp.

A warm, wet wall smelling like sweet coffee and softness. If that was even a thing. The wall also growled.

Jumping back, she did her best to brush the liquid now coating the front of her vest off. "Shit. I- I'm so sorry. I should've been paying attention."

Emery's gaze locked with warm honey brown eyes and she froze.

I just body slammed my crush!

"No worries Emery, I wasn't paying attention either,"

he drawled, his voice smooth and damn near enchanting. Finn shot her a polite smile as he mopped up the worst of it with a napkin.

But she stopped breathing, Emery's mouth agape because, "You know my name?"

Finn gave her a strange look, "Yeah Emery, I know your name."

Her breath caught at what him knowing her name could mean.

Alright. This was news to her because one; she was rather sure they had never been formally introduced, and two; while she got Finn's name from her other bestie Katie, it was only because Emery had called her the first time she saw him across the street three months ago and three being that Finn never noticed her or had spoken to her until now.

"I'm gonna go out on a limb and say everyone in town knows your name considering the name of your bookstore."

A gust of wind sent chills down her back, taking any thoughts about Finn being interested in her right out the window.

Wetting her dry lips, she decided she should offer him some help since she was the reason he was now soaking wet, in the most nonsexual way ever.

While she was sticky and wet, it was only her outside layer, luckily missing her jeans, thank *God*. Finn's peacoat was open, exposing the flannel shirt underneath that now dripped with what smelled like a cappuccino. It wasn't near as cold as it could get this time of year, but it was still close to freezing out.

"Again, I'm sorry," Emery said, looking him over, this time lingering on his face longer than was polite. He had been clean shaven the last time she saw him. Not this time. This time he had scruff that would turn into a full beard by next week, dark like his eyebrows and his hair, which she remembered was cut almost to his scalp under that charcoal grey beanie. He reminded her of a character from a romance novel. A GQ lumberjack

"There are worse things," he said, his voice a deep rumble.

"If you come with me, I can warm you up." She turned around, then stopped. *Oh, shit-* spinning back to face Finn. "I didn't mean..." He smirked as Emery's face heated.

"What did you mean then," Finn asked, stepping closer to her.

What *did* she mean?

"Um," she swallowed. "Just, if you want to clean up or dry off, I can help." Emery turned back, feeling silly for getting nervous around him. That was something she wished she would grow out of. Talking to men she found deliciously attractive was a roll of the dice. Sometimes it worked out okay, and they ended up becoming something more, but more often than not, she made a fool of herself. Like knocking his coffee all over him the first time they ever speak.

So what if he was hot? Or the first guy I wanted to jump in months.

Moving quickly, but carefully, she did her best to avoid any slippery areas as snow fell around them. That's all she needed, to slip and fall on top of an already disastrous meeting.

By the time she twisted the lock, Finn was right behind her. The wall of heat at his closeness made her pause, absorbing as much as she could.

She pushed open the door, immediately discarding her vest and hat before heading straight to the fireplace. "There's a bathroom back in the corner," she said, pointing to the back of the store off to her right, close to where she stood.

Looking around, Finn took in her bookstore. His eyes moved over the lounge area. A small sapphire velvet couch with emerald wingback chairs on each side that faced the brick fireplace Emery was standing in front of.

"Appreciate it," Finn muttered before heading in the direction she'd pointed.

Emery released a huge breath as soon as the door clicked shut and gave herself a once over. She hung her damp vest over one of the velvet Christmas stockings hanging from the mantle above the fireplace.

While her vest dried, Emery searched behind the checkout counter for something Finn might fit into since she was sure she'd ruined everything he was wearing under his coat. Though she doubted anything she might find would even fit his six-foot frame, but it was worth a shot.

She popped up at the creaking sound the bathroom door always gave off.

Okay, just act normal and try not to make a fool of yourself.

That was always easier said than done.

"I tried to find you something to wear, but—" Emery choked on her words as soon as her eyes landed on his golden, glistening skin. And there was a lot.

Finn's attention was on hanging his flannel and white t-shirt over the stockings next to Emery's vest, so he didn't see her shocked expression. Or the drooling.

There was no doubt he worked out regularly. The fire glistened off of all his gloriously tanned chest and deliciously sculpted abs. She guessed he was eastern European or maybe had family from the Middle East.

The sporadic tattoos along his arms and chest were beautiful. His snug-fitting jeans were mouthwatering and for half a second she got lost in that skin, wanting to see if it was as soft as it looked.

Wait. Why was he half naked?

Getting her wits about her, she moved toward him, one question on her mind. "While I'm not complaining," she swallowed, "I'm confused why you're shirtless?" Emery's voice cracked a bit at the end, trying her best not to stare at those hard abs. Or his pecs. Or biceps.

Shit! Her stomach clenched. Eyes back to his, hers wide as she chewed her lower lip, awaiting his answer.

He tracked the movement, watching her a beat before he answered. "Everything got wet, including the inside of my coat," he pointed over to the couch where he'd laid it open, "And until something's dry this is going to be my outfit." That smirk from earlier appeared, and she wondered again what his lips would feel like. If they were soft, like they looked, or would they be rough and demanding?

Emery released her lip as she turned away, trying to stop herself from ogling him anymore than she already had.

She needed to get laid and soon if Finn shirtless had her ready to jump him. He probably wasn't interested in her that way. A damn travesty, but she'd live.

"So," she started, focusing on the flames. "Um, what brought you to Pine Forest?" The silence was only letting her mind drift back to a half naked Finn and all the things a very horny Emery wanted to do.

He didn't answer right away. She looked over to find him watching her. Trapped in his lion's stare. The feeling of fear and excitement coursed through her limbs as the crackling of the fire faded away.

Seconds or maybe it was minutes later he said, "I needed a change and my family once rented a cabin in the woods near here. I never forgot how much I loved the quiet or the fresh smell of pine that encompassed the entire area."

He wasn't wrong. Whenever she went somewhere for

more than a few days, she'd noticed the hint of sharpness from the pine trees growing throughout the town whenever she returned.

"I think that smell is in my bones," Emery admitted, her lips turning up at the thought. She was a part of Pine Forest, and Pine Forest was a part of her.

He inched closer. Close enough to reach out and touch the tattoo she'd been eyeing on his left shoulder. Which was exactly what she did.

Sucking in air as her nipple brushed against his chest, her fingers slid slowly along his soft skin, tracing the image.

"Why an angel?" Emery said, whispering as she got lost in the way his warm honey-colored eyes danced opposite the flames.

He hadn't moved away from her touch or asked her to stop. Instead, he leaned down, his lips a breath away. Her body tingled as she waited for an answer to a question she barely remembered.

"It's an Italian charm. All the men in my family get them when they turn 21." Finn's words were soft, the crackling the only other sound in the bubble they'd created.

How sweet.

There was something about a person who was close to their family, so close in fact that they carried on with the family tradition of getting tattooed. She would have laughed at her mom if she ever asked her to do something like that.

"It's beautiful."

"So is your smile."

Her stomach dropped. Emery couldn't breathe or think with him so close.

Shit, she had it bad for Finn.

"I think," his voice dropped an octave, "I make you nervous."

Is that how he sounded first thing in the morning

Her breath hitched as he tugged on her bottom lip with his thumb, brushing it gently where she'd been worrying it before dropping his hand back down.

"Do I?" Finn asked.

"Huh?"

His soft chuckle warmed her. "Make you nervous?"

Her entire body was overheating with the effect of whatever woodsy scent he used for soap, and her throat was like a desert.

Yeah, he made me nervous, but who cared.

"Yes." She went with the truth. Lies rarely did anyone any good.

Then it happened. His lips were on hers. His hand sliding up her neck before cupping her face.

Her hands snaked around his hips, clasping against his lower back. *Oh God, I missed this*. It was a slow, teasing kiss. Until her tongue licked along the seam of his lips. His growl hit her deep in her belly. Gasping at all the sensations, his mouth, his body, all that soft skin, he deepened the kiss.

Then the door banged open.

They leaped apart, panting as something magical flowed through her. She held his stare, somewhat wild and definitely dangerous. *That was the most amazing kiss ever.*

"Hey Em, come help me with — oh shit!" Lana froze.

Oh, shit was right.

CHAPTER 2

"So," Lana started, hands on her hips, "How long have you been making out with Finn's fine ass? And how did you not tell me about it because, hot damn!" Eyebrows raised, she waited for Emery's answer.

Finn had left right after Lana showed, saying he'd see her later. When later was going to be she couldn't say, but the gesture was still nice.

Emery crumbled up some tissue paper, launching it at Lana from her seat at the table, "I'm not."

Lana scoffed.

"At least I wasn't before a few minutes ago. We ran into each other."

Lana burst out laughing, "Yeah, that's one way to describe it." She shook her head at what she thought was an exaggeration.

I wish.

"You know I would've told you if there was something to tell. This was just," *what the hell was it?* "It was just a kiss."

Sure felt like more than just a kiss, but they didn't even know each other.

"Your face is a million shades of red right now so I'm not buying what you're selling sister."

"Stupid fair skin," Emery muttered under her breath. "Fine," she fidgeted with the end of her sweater, "It was the best kiss I've ever had and I've had a crush on him for months."

"Spill."

And so she did.

❄

Lana shot Katie a text to meet them later at the pub.

Apparently her lip lock with Finn was a big deal. *Whatever*. It hadn't been that long since she'd gotten any action. Who was she kidding? Eight months was way too long.

They inhaled their tacos, cleaned up, then headed on over to the pub to meet Katie for celebratory drinks. The place was crowded, but they found three open seats at the end of the bar. She loved the giant old-fashioned Christmas bulbs lining the mirrors behind the bar and looping around the rest of the room.

Emery hadn't drunk more than a glass of wine in months.

Katie was holding up her tequila shot, blowing her brown bangs off her face, and gave her toast. "To our girl here finally getting some!"

Emery clinked her shot glass with the other girls and threw it back. Her eyes watering as the burn settled in her stomach. "A kiss is not the same as getting some." No matter how great that kiss was.

Maybe I'll run into him soon.

"*Woo-hoo!*" Lana slapped the bar top, "Another round Duncan," she hollered in the owners direction. He was one of those hands on owners. Duncan waved back as Lana turned her glassy eyes to Emery. "You are correct unless that kiss ended in an orgasm I missed or you somehow neglected to mention."

Cheeks hot, Emery covered her ears, "Please stop," she all but begged. She didn't think of herself as a prude, but letting everyone in the bar in on the fact that she didn't have an orgasm today was a bit much for her, but not so much for her friends.

An overflowing shot of tequila was pushed in front of Emery. "You ladies better know how you're getting home. Can't be your taxi this evening. Got plans." Duncan was sweet and none of them could drive, at least not for a few hours.

If she hadn't known Duncan for so long she would have considered trying something with him. He had that whole 90s rock thing working for him. While she was aware many women liked that look, like her girl Katie who was rocking tight black Levi's with a Soundgarden concert shirt that was one size too small under a cropped leather jacket.

"I'm walking," Emery chimed in before hiccuping.

Ugh! She hated hiccups.

"And I plan on stopping after this one," Katie said, crossing her fingers over her heart as she gave Duncan her puppy dog eyes.

"Like I haven't heard that one before," Duncan said, shaking his head before leaving to help another patron.

Emery's entire body was hot and tingly. Those shots were coursing through her, making her feel lighter if not a little fuzzy in the head.

"Alright," Katie sat up straighter, "Let's talk about the fact that you snagged one of Pine Forest's most eligible bachelors during one the most romantic holidays and you are over there acting like you have a giant stick up your ass."

"I wouldn't say snagged," Emery said into her water glass, ready for a change of subject.

"Well," Katie kept going, "I say that Finn's been here for four months and from what I've seen and heard," she looked to Emery with a smile, "he hasn't gone on a single date let alone shown any interest in anyone. Trust me, all the old biddies at my shop have been gossiping about him since he arrived and confirmed single." She cocked her head to Emery, "They had their money on Tina."

Oh, I just bet they did.

Time for some lighter drinks so she didn't murder someone thinking about Tina. Katie switched to beer, while Lana and Emery went with red wine.

Not long after, someone must've lost their mind because Mariah Carey was singing about all she wanted for Christmas on an endless loop. Duncan looked too busy to bother with it, zooming around the now almost packed bar. Or maybe he hadn't noticed yet?

"Holy mother of all that is holy," Lana pushed back from the bar, "Who's got quart—Ahhh!" she screamed, toppling to the floor, taking three chairs down with her.

Oh fuck!

Emery leapt up, "Oh my god-" *Whoa, the world was spinning.* Grabbing the back of her chair, she fought the nausea starting to rise inside her. Damn all that tequila.

Throwing her head back with laughter, "Lana just—!" Katie said, hands holding her stomach.

It took effort, but Emery blinked away the dizziness, taking a deep breath. She needed to check on her best friend since Katie was pointing at poor Lana while cracking up. What a friend.

"You okay?" That familiar deep rumble sent goosebumps along her arms.

Finn.

Finn was here. Kneeling next to an injured and angry Lana. Where did he come from?

"It feels like my heart is beating inside my wrist," Lana hissed, eyes shining.

Finn hoisted her up, careful as Lana cradled her right arm against her body. Katie and some other customers righted the chairs. When Lana settled back into her chair, Emery eased back into her own with Katie taking her spot again between them.

"Well honey, you smacked it pretty hard," Emery said, swallowing as she watched Finn.

He looks good. Real good. The casual light jeans and green sweater fit him well.

"Oh shit, it's already swelling," Katie finally noticed through her drunken haze. She was dangerously close to touching Lana's wrist.

"I can see that!" Lana snapped, slapping her hand away with her other arm, leaning away from Katie's hand. "I just wanted to put a stop to Mariah's endless torture."

Looks like it's time to call it a night.

She glanced back at Finn, wishing she'd have noticed him early. She might've been able to talk with him, find out some things about who he was. What he liked.

"I already called you a cab," Duncan said, appearing out of thin air, cell phone in hand.

"Thanks," Emery tried not to slur and instead ended up hiccuping.

Finn and Duncan chuckled as she gulped down water. How did she forget how much of a lightweight she was?

"Come on La-La, let's get you taken care of," Katie said with a goofy smile. The few years Emery had on Katie reared its ugly head only twice so far in her life; when they worked out and when they drank.

Finn slid into the empty chair on her other side. "Were you planning on leaving with your friends or you wanna join me for a drink? And when I say drink, that includes things like water or coffee," he said, ending with a wink.

She spun back to her girls. Until Finn offered, she had been planning on heading home. But now? She was reconsidering. It was probably the tequila talking, but she went with it.

Turning back to her friends she asked, "If I did stay," Emery started, Katie smiling huge, Lana's mouth dropping open, "Are you two going to make it in the morning to help set up for the parade without getting into any trouble?"

Katie scoffed. "That was one time and the police officer ended up having to apologize to us eventually so," she said, crossing her arms over her chest. There had been a lot of 'one times' with those two.

Emery looked over to Lana, "You sure you're gonna be okay? Maybe you should go to the hospital?" Seemed like a reasonable thing to do considering how hard she hit her wrist, but, from what Emery could tell, it looked mild. Or she hoped it was.

"I'll go in the morning if I need to, now stop worrying about me." She leaned over, kissing Emery on the cheek. "Enjoy the rest of your night." Katie did the same and a few minutes later they were gone, leaving her alone with Finn.

Well, alone in the middle of a pub on a Friday night in a town she'd lived in most of her life.

"So," she smiled up at him, the dizziness easing a bit, but not the warmth.

He smiled back. "So."

Chewing her lip, she tried to think of something to say or ask him. *Why am I nervous? We've already kissed, and I've seen him half naked for crying out loud.*

Finn's thumb tugged her lip free, rubbing the pad where she'd bitten it. Her stomach dropped. "Why'd you open a bookstore?" he asked before returning his hand back to the bar.

"I loved the escape books gave me when I was younger. Having a place where I knew I could go to read, relax, and the rest of the world fell away." She smiled wide, "And things always worked out. Magic was real, the hero shows up and saves you or you do the saving. Either way, the journey may be hard and long, but it works out." His eyes sparkled as he listened, his gaze never leaving her. "Anyway, other than the town library, there wasn't anywhere else to go," she tilted her head. "I guess-I guess I opened it for myself or well, people like me, who love to read and needed that escape."

Her cheeks heated at her honesty, but it was the truth. And maybe a little of the tequila.

"What about you?" She asked, sick of her own voice, but mostly afraid of saying something embarrassing.

"Why did I open a bookstore?"

"Ha. Ha." She smiled despite the lameness of his joke. "Why'd you leave and- wait-," Emery sat up straighter, "What do you do for a living?"

He glanced away, taking a long drink from his draft before he answered, looking straight ahead. "I'm a carpenter." The gruffness hit her.

Why is he saying that like it's an embarrassment?

She toyed with her water glass. "And why a carpenter?"

After a few seconds he said, "I've always loved building things. Didn't matter what it was, I just liked creating things not just with my hands but my mind. It's the only time I felt like myself." He watched her, waiting for what, she wasn't sure.

It made little sense, but everyone had a past, dealing with things she'd never understand.

Wonder who made him feel this way?

Tilting her head, she asked the question rolling around in her head and, without the tequila, more than likely would've stayed there. "Why are you speaking as if," she hiccuped, "*Grrrr!*" She gulped down water then said, "as if you're something less?" No answer, but the lines around his eyes had eased. "What you do, even without having ever seen anything you've created, is more than I could ever do and that is something to be proud of, not ashamed of."

"I appreciate it, but your opinion isn't held by everyone."

"Well," she tried to think of something encouraging to say and ended up with, "Whoever they are, they suck."

Finn released a deep belly laugh, mouth wide as she again tried not to drool. His laugh was soothing, doing things to her insides.

"Hey brother, it's starting to really come down out there," Duncan interrupted as he spoke to Finn.

Were the two of them friends?

"Blizzard hit early," Finn said, his hands rubbing over his cropped head.

While she wasn't happy that the storm was cutting into her night with Finn, at least there'll be plenty of snow for the snowman building cont—.

"Oh, no." She slammed her fist down on the bar, her head following right behind it. "No, no, no!" Her chanting would not change the truth.

"What's wrong?" Finn asked, voice straining.

He was going to think she was a nut with what she was about to say, regardless she popped up and said, "The snowman building contest is in two days and Lana was my partner."

"Bad luck, Em," Duncan said, frowning her way.

"Can't you find someone else? You said you have two days, right?" Finn asked. And while his suggestion was logical, they did Emery no good.

"If it were that simple, I wouldn't be freaking out. Lana was my artsy person. I suck at the designing part. I'm only good for physical labor and adding my two cents. Without Lana, I'm only two cents," she said, finally taking a breath.

The look Finn and Duncan gave her was comical. She sounded silly, but losing to Tina wasn't an option. Not this year. Never again.

"I can do it."

Emery's heart spasmed. *Did I hear him correctly?*

"What?" she asked, needing confirmation.

"I build and create things out of wood for a living. Doing it with snow can't be that different." *Oh sweet Jesus, he wasn't kidding.*

She sat up straighter, licking her dry lips. "You get that you're agreeing to wake up early on Christmas Eve to help me build a snowman in the cold?"

"Not sure what you don't understand Em. Why don't you stop trying to talk him out of this and just take him up on his offer?" Duncan said, hands on the bar.

"I've been drinking tonight and want to make sure I didn't make it up," she told Duncan. Turning her attention back to Finn, she continued, "Are you being serious, because with the world still looking somewhat fuzzy, I can't tell."

Finn sipped his beer, making her wait. High pitch laughter drew Emery's attention over to the sports themed holiday tree Duncan refused to get rid of, even though the branches were barely holding up.

"Yes, Emery." She liked the way her name rolled off his tongue, "I'm serious, and it's not that big of a deal."

Maybe she was making it too big of a thing, but Tina had gotten under her skin earlier that day and she was having a hard time letting it go even after all the alcohol she ingested.

"You guys better get moving before the roads get slick." Duncan said, slapping the bar. A screaming woman who was apparently dying of thirst required his attention. "Be safe," then he was gone.

Finn's fingers warmed her skin as he brushed a strand of hair behind her ear. "We need to get moving, darling."

"We?"

"Yeah, I'm giving you a ride home and no arguing," he said, throwing her a wink. He grabbed cash from his wallet, tossing some bills on the bar.

She wasn't planning on arguing with him. Okay, maybe her mouth was hanging open, about to turn down his offer.

Face scrunched, she bit back the need to argue if only to prove him wrong. Finn snickered, losing his battle not to laugh at her.

"Fine, but wipe that smirk off of your face there buddy or I won't offer you one of my famous caramel pecan brownies as a thank you," she told him, face serious.

Only friends and family experienced Emery's baking. And she was good. If she hadn't opened a bookstore she would've opened a bakery, but figured avoiding the potential weight gain from being around desserts all day was the smarter move.

"Yes ma'am," he saluted. She stuck her tongue out at him.

Once coats were on, they waved to Duncan as they weaved through the crowd and out the door. She stepped outside and froze; it was a whiteout. Flakes stuck to her eyelashes as she blinked away the flurries.

Finn took her hand in his, "This way." Using his hand to block the worst of the snow from his eyes he led her to his truck, which she was thankfully an SUV.

After getting her in the passenger seat, Finn jogged around the front of the truck, jumping in the driver's seat, and they were off. The ride didn't take long, even with him creeping along with how slick the roads were already. *Fine with her.*

Emery leaped out of Finn's truck, carefully walking up her candy cane lined walkway with white lights. Those lights were the only thing guiding her. The slamming of a car door and beat of boots crunching behind her was the only reason she knew he followed.

"Come on in," she said, shaking out her hat and scarf. Everything was wet. Pointing to the hooks above the bench in her makeshift mudroom. "You can hang your things up there," she offered.

"Can't stay long or I'll end up stuck here until morning," Finn said.

Tempting. Oh, so tempting.

She stole a look over to him, trying to gage his words. *Did he want to stay all night with me? Or is he just being polite?*

After discarding his outer layers, he turned with that sweet smile again. Or maybe it'd be good if she got out of her head and stopped overthinking his every move.

"How about some coffee then before you head back on the road?" She asked, scooting into the kitchen as she talked, pulling some mugs down from the cabinet.

Finn all but purred right behind her, "Sounds wonderful."

"Jesus!" Emery spun around, coming face to face with a slightly damp, devilishly handsome man who had done more kind things for her and her friends in one day than any previous boyfriend had ever done. The warm honey eyes and close shaved head she couldn't wait to run her hands over didn't hurt either.

Not sure if that was a dig at myself or the men I date. Maybe both. It wasn't like Emery tried to find men who would treat her like crap, but more often than not, it went that direction. Or Tina would somehow get involved and ruin everything.

His laugh was light, intimate, which kept Emery from scowling at his amusement. "I believe brownies were promised," he said in the same soft voice.

"You like them hot?"

Finn's gaze darkened, hands holding her hips, tugging their bodies closer. How had she not noticed him touching her?

"Yeah," that one word was a growl, hitting her deep. "I like 'em hot."

Holy shit! Emery swallowed, her face heating as she thought of all the ways they could be hot together. It'd been a long time. Her last date ended before she even made it to dessert.

"I can take care of that for you, but you have to let me go," sucking in air as her breasts grazed his chest as he inhaled. They were so close, the body heat radiating from him was almost too much.

"What if I don't want to let you go?"

"I- I'm-"

His nose gently slid along hers and then her stomach rumbled from all the alcohol and not enough food. "Looks like you need a brownie too," Finn said, easing his body from her. A mix of fireworks and butterflies filled her as she wondered where things were headed.

Hopefully, between the sheets.

"Why don't you tell me where the brownies are while you go relax on the couch." Chewing her lip, she didn't want to be in poor form, this being her house and all.

"They're in the container by the cookie jar," Emery said, having given in to how tired her body was even if it felt electrified when Finn was near.

Her L-shaped grey couch that took up most of her open concept living room was comfy and cozy. The kitchen island was all that separated the two rooms with the dining table in front of the bay window off to the kitchen.

Sleepy, but not ready to pass out, Emery turned on one of her favorite holiday movies while he clanged around in the kitchen, making her chest feel tight.

She turned her attention back to the movie, hiding her staring. Settling in, she squashed a throw pillow in the corner of the couch and got lost in the old black and white film.

"Wasn't sure if you added anything to your coffee," Finn said, handing her a steaming mug, placing the plate with an enormous brownie on the coffee table in front of her.

"Thanks," she whispered. That brownie looked almost as yummy as Finn in her living room.

He sat right next to her. Not the other side of the couch or the two other chairs she loved almost as much as her couch.

Nervous and unsure what his plans were, Emery sipped her coffee. *"Mother Fu-"* Emery spit the scolding liquid back into her mug. "Sorry," she twisted to him, "Wasn't thinking." Setting the mug down, she leaned back, trying to get comfortable like before Finn joined her.

This was stupid. They'd already kissed for Christ's sake, and he was into her. At least she thought so. Why else would he be here or have volunteered to help her at the Jack Frost festival?

"How long have you known Lana and Katie?" Finn asked after a few minutes of quiet. Having seen the movie dozens of times, she didn't mind the interruption.

"Katie since high school, but we didn't really become close until after college. In middle school Ricky Weaver rubbed mud all over my bookbag after school and Lana stopped him. Made him apologize. Been friends ever since."

Emery was smiling at the memory as Finn said, "It's good to have people like that still in your life. People who know who you really are. Know your hopes and dreams."

His words sounded wistful, and her heart broke at the bit of sadness around his eyes as he spoke. *Why was he so sad?*

"What about you?" She asked, a little unsure. "You and Duncan appeared to know one another." At least Emery hoped so. She didn't want Finn to be all alone in Pine Forest.

"Yeah, Duncan's a good guy. We get together from time to time, but anyone from, well, from before," he cleared his throat, "I don't keep in touch with any longer."

That sounded ominous. And something she wanted to ask about another time.

After that, he became extremely interested in his coffee. *Alright. New subject.*

She glanced out the windows to the backyard opposite the dining room and said, "Oh Lordy Finn, it's really coming down. It can't be safe to drive anywhere for awhile."

Finn propped his feet on the coffee table as he slid further down into the couch. "Long as you don't mind, I'll just hang here and watch movies until it's safe enough to leave."

She didn't mind. Not at all.

"Stay as long as you like."

He shot her a toothy smile and slid his arm along her calf that was curled underneath her, giving it a pull until her leg was straight. Her foot resting against his thigh. "This better?"

With a quick nod, he repeated the same movement with the other leg. Emery stretched out on the couch, half lounging on Finn's lap as he lazily massaged her foot, her calf, her shin.

She did her best to fight the pull of sleep, but with how relaxed and warm she was in Finn's hands, she lost that battle.

CHAPTER 3

"Stop whining and take an aspirin." Lana said, waiting for her to move the enormous crate into the back of the pickup truck she'd borrowed for the holiday parade.

"Don't you have dance moms or dads that could help you with all this who aren't nursing a hangover?" Emery was squatting down to lift the crate. Nope. Didn't even budge, but the throbbing behind her eyes was coming back with a vengeance.

"I do, but none of them asked me to spend hours packing and decorating baskets the day before a holiday parade my dance girls are in." Lana looked up from her notebook that held her to-do list, brow arched. "You did and the parents are dealing with cranky kids who are cold and tired at this ungodly hour. They've got enough on their plates, trust me."

Emery didn't think 9 a.m. was that early, but she got her point. But Emery wasn't Superwoman, and no way was she going to move this thing without help.

"How do you expect me to lift this all by myself," Emery huffed, kicking the damn crate. "Ouch, ouch, ouch!" Her toe throbbing took the pain off the throbbing in her head at least.

Waving her air cast clad wrist at her. "I'd help if I could." *Yeah, that sucked.*

"At least it wasn't broken," Emery threw out, crossing her arms as she tried to figure out how in the hell she was going to get the stupid thing in the truck.

Having no other choice but to drag it, Emery pushed and pulled it until it was propping open the front door of the studio.

Wiping the beads of sweat from her temples, she decided to pull it the rest of the way. So, sticking her butt out, she bent down and tugged her little heart out, "*Ughhhh-*" It barely moved.

"You tryin' to throw your back out. Or maybe you just get your kicks trying to hurt yourself?"

Turning too fast, Emery's foot slid out from under her on a patch of ice. She flung her arms out, praying she didn't break her wrist or bruise her tailbone when she slammed into the sidewalk.

She never hit the ground. Strong arms surrounded her, pulling her into the delicious sandalwood scent that clung to Finn like a second skin.

Candles. Emery would be buying lots of sandalwood scented candles in her future. Damn, but he smelled good.

She shivered as his lips slid along the shell of her ear. "If you wanted to be in my arms, all you had to do was ask darlin'."

"*Em!*" Lana hollered from the doorway.

Emery jumped, making Finn chuckle.

"You can't leave the door wide open with the heat blasting in the studio. I'm not made of money?" Lana clocked Finn, an enormous smile spreading across her face. "Perfect timing, Finn! Em needs some help lifting that crate that I might've over packed. You think you could give us a hand for a few minutes?"

Finn still held Emery in his arms, in the middle of the sidewalk, downtown during the start of the holiday festivities where anyone could see them. She looked around, noticing a few onlookers watching them, their curiosity peaked. *By the time the chili cookoff started people will think Finn proposed to her right there on the street.*

Gossip in a small town could be a bit much, but Emery was used to it and did her best not to believe every rumor she heard. That could sometimes be difficult with Katie as her bestie.

"Sure. Just gotta tell Walter I'll be a few minutes." Finn gave her a quick squeeze, then let her go. He jogged down the block to Walter's Furniture Store and disappeared. Anxiety crept up, taking Emery's mind to places it didn't need to go, but she let it anyway. "What if this is a mistake? I think Finn has secrets."

"Everyone has secrets, Em."

"Yeah, and the last guy who had secrets ended up with a police raid at my house."

"Yeah," Lana's lips flattened. "That did suck balls."

"Exactly! And yet you ask him to help without even knowing how things went last night." She huffed, as thoughts of her mother's betrayal seeped in. *Could Finn be a good guy?* "What if it was shit?"

"Look, I'm your best friend, so don't pull this crap on me. You were all over him when I came out here and that, along with Finn being big and strong, was why I asked for his help. And stop being a bitch because you're hungover."

She hated when Lana was right. Emery was being a huge asshole to her injured friend.

"Sorry for being a bitch. I just don't know what's going on with me and Finn. I passed out last night before anything really happened. When I woke up in the middle of the night, I was warm and toasty under a blanket. Then this morning I found a note on the kitchen island that he'd left." Those butterflies made another appearance as she remembered finding it earlier.

Lana did a little happy dance, including trying to clap, "Fucking hell," she cursed before getting back to their conversation. "So…What'd it say?"

She checked the sidewalk for any potential eavesdroppers before she told Lana. "He said my brownies taste better than Christmas and that I looked like an angel when I was sleeping." Emery's heart pounded in her chest and she wasn't even done.

"Well, that's hot as hell Em. You need to jump on that and fast." "Is there more?" She stared at Lana, looking around for Finn, who could pop back up at any second.

Emery's voice dropped. "He said he would've stayed, but had to make sure Mrs. Greenly's place got shoveled before she went for her walk." She closed her eyes as she let the warmth of Finn's kindness wash over her. "You know, her grandson had to move back to Ann Arbor for his job. She's all by herself again."

Emery was a little swept away with Finn and all that his letter had revealed. He was kind and caring. Selfless and thoughtful. All the things she was hoping for in a partner.

"Damn that guy is the real deal huh?" Lana said awed. Emery knew the feeling.

"*Shhhh*. He's coming this way," she warned Lana before she said anything embarrassing, like finding his shoveling snow for a little old lady sexy as hell.

"Put me to work ladies," Finn said as he joined them. Emery shivered, and it had nothing to do with being cold.

Lana gave orders, and they hopped to it, packing up supplies and stashing the bigger pieces for the float in the bed of the truck.

Things had been going smoothly, and they finished up

just as Walter called Finn back to help him with something at his store.

He waved goodbye and asked Emery to save him a seat at the chili cook-off. Hopefully, they'd be able to celebrate afterward when she won. If she beat Tina, that is.

❄

The sunshine made the town square sparkle with all the snow.

Beautiful.

"If you've already signed in, please find your number and place your dish behind it and be careful of the other wires." Tina's voice grated on Emery's ears. But there were plenty of other people there to act as a buffer. Or so she hoped.

"Good luck Emery and Merry Christmas," Walter's dark weathered and wrinkled face smiled up at her as he handed her a number.

He had always been so sweet to her and her father, especially when things got tough for dad in her late teens. Walter was a good friend of her grandpa but Emery had spent little time with him since she got things up and running at her bookstore.

"Thanks, Walter." She turned away, then thought better of it. "You should come by after the holidays for some coffee and treats. It's been too long since we've talked."

The old man's dark chocolate eyes sparkled at the invite. "That sounds wonderful. Thank you, honey."

With a nod, Emery turned to get her hopefully first prize chili to its proper place under the heated tent. Scanning the crowd, she noticed Lana and Katie at one of the many circular tables near a heater.

Why every festival was outdoors was something she'd always questioned, but no one ever had an answer. The tent stayed up and somehow didn't collapse after all the snow the night before, which was a miracle.

"Hey ladies," she called once she was close enough for them to hear. They each had a steaming cup in their hands, heads bent together.

"Hey girly, where have you been? Tina was about to get her panties in a twist. Though I think she secretly hoped you wouldn't show." Katie looked past Emery, pursing her lips. Emery turned around to see for herself. "She sure seems to like your boy Finn, huh Em," Katie said. Tina hooked her arm through Finn's, leading him over to the opposite side of the tent.

Emery sighed. "Of course she does." She had a feeling the headache she finally got rid of might creep back in if Tina pushed her. It wouldn't take much.

Emery had passed on the parade, instead hustling back to her store for some early basket pickups so she could fit in a nap before she had to be there at 5 p.m. That and the enormous bacon cheeseburger she'd eaten had kicked most of her hangover, but none of that would matter if she had to do battle with Tina.

"Don't act like you aren't aware he's into you, Em," Lana said as if it were that simple. "He had plenty of time to ask her out since he moved here and he never did." This was true and eased the stabbing pain the sight of them together caused.

"He hasn't asked me out either," Emery countered, plopping down in an open seat at their table. Glasses and random personal items were scattered around, so she knew they weren't alone. Most likely Duncan and one of his buddies he somehow dragged with him.

"Oh boohoo," Katie said, reapplying her bubble gum pink lip gloss even though it was fine before she touched it. "It's not his fault you spend all your time at the bookstore instead of out living your life like you know you should be." Katie was focused on the compact, so she missed the hurt her words caused by hitting home.

Lana poked Katie in the forehead, "Harsh."

"Hey," Katie swatted Lana's hand away. "All I'm saying is, it might do you some good to get out and shake your ass a little. Loosen up girly."

Luckily, their conversation was interrupted by Duncan and his friend. His friend who just so happened to be Finn.

"How much longer until we eat?" Duncan asked, taking a seat where Emery assumed he'd left his things. Glancing around the table, she saw a set of keys and sunglasses in front of the chair on her right. Exactly where Finn was heading. She suppressed a giggle of excitement at her luck.

"No clue, but I'm sure you'll survive until then," Lana chimed in, Duncan groaning. "Em, you know when things are supposed to get going?" she asked her.

"Yeah," Emery bit her lip as Finn's jean clad thigh pressed against hers. "In about ten minutes, I think. I was cutting it pretty close." She tried to keep her focus on her girl friends across the table, but then Finn gave her knee a quick squeeze. She stole a glance to find him watching her playfully.

"Alright, I can wait ten minutes," Duncan leaned back, taking a pull from his bottled beer.

Emery sure hoped the grown man could wait that long.

A gentle tug on her hair had her turning. "You sleep okay?" Finn asked only loud enough for Emery to hear. His fingers continued to toy with the ends of her hair.

Locking eyes and sprouting a secret smile, she nodded. His eyes and mouth softened, as he leaned closer.

"I didn't get a chance last night, but I wanted to ask if you were free--"

"Everyone, can I have your attention," Tina rang through the speakers, pulling Emery out of her Finn bubble. Tina always loved being behind the mic. "Our fifty-forth annual Jack Frost Festival Chili Cook Off is about to begin, and I just wanted to thank everyone for coming out and supporting all our participants."

Emery stared down at her hands in her lap, wishing she wasn't battling a hangover all day and that Finn had finished his sentence. The nervous sweating had started along with butterflies that were borderline painful. She could use a drink.

"Any reason you won't look at me darlin'?" he asked again, only loud enough for her. "You didn't have a problem with me being close to you this morning. Or last night," Finn said a bit louder. Duncan's eyebrows shot up into his hairline.

Son of a bitch.

Duncan pointed his beer at them, a smirk spreading. "So are you two..."

The bastard thought this was amusing?

"No-"

"Yes," Finn countered, talking over her. Eyes wide she threw a look at Finn.

"So what are you guys then?" Katie was putting him on the spot. It was an asshole move, she was aware, but she was wondering the same thing.

Her eyes landed on the soft scruff she wanted to rub. Her fingers twitched at the thought.

"Two people exploring an attraction while getting to know one another." His answer surprised her. Tilting her head, she spoke without thinking, "Is that what you're doing with Tina?"

"Whoa," Lana said as Katie squeaked.

Shit, she should have kept her mouth shut. *Too late to take it back.*

Finn's face pinched, his eyes searching Emery's face. If he was playing her she had every right to know. The last thing she wanted to do was be the laughingstock of the town if she ended up the last to find out, like her dad when mom cheated.

The look Finn gave her unsettled her, but she couldn't place it. Disappointment? Annoyance? He blinked a few times, and the look disappeared, replaced with a bit of warmth. "I'm not interested in exploring anything with Tina."

While he said the exact words she wanted to hear, it wasn't as reassuring as she hoped.

"Alrighty folks, it's time. Make sure to sample them all!" Tina interrupted.

It was time to eat. Conversations turned to chili and seasonings and what hot peppers were used in the spicy ones or how much grape jam went into the sweet ones. Emery always likes hers with a kick, and her secret recipe was the mix of Indian spices she added along with a mix of peppers.

Eating twenty-five different chilis was a feat, but winning this thing was big time in Pine Forest. The winner's chili would be served all winter at Rosie's Diner, and the winner got to name it. She only won once, but Tina never won.

With only numbers, Emery had no clue if Tina had made something worth worrying about.

"Yours is fantastic, Em," Lana cheered, doing a little dance with her plastic spoon. She'd told her which one was hers when they were waiting in line. The only other person who knew was Katie, which wasn't technically cheating as telling voters your number was frowned upon.

"Agreed," Finn said, head bent, devouring what was left in his bowl. Face scrunched, she wondered if he knew which one was hers. "Saw the crock pot on the counter last night."

Whoa, now he was reading her mind.

"You think it's good enough to beat all the others up there?" She asked with a wave of her hand.

"For sure," Katie winked.

"Absolutely." Duncan was scraping the sides of his bowl with a piece of bread.

"Isn't it enough that we all think it's the best?" Finn asked. The question seemed a little strange to her. The whole point was for her to win the chili cookoff.

"I mean, yeah, I guess. But it's not as much fun as being better than everyone else in the competition." Again, Finn gave her that look, making her chest tight. "It's not the end-all be-all. There are plenty of other reasons I do these things."

Face now blank he asked, "Like?"

"Like," Emery tapped her finger on her chin, "well, getting to spend time with my friends. And seeing people in the town come out who rarely have a reason to. Plus, I can check up on all the ones who promised to come visit me at the store and haven't." That look vanished from Finn's face.

Thank God.

She didn't like whatever he was thinking when he looked at her like that.

"Right back at ya' Em."

"Thanks Lana," she returned with a smile.

"Okay, everyone," Tina chimed over the Christmas music that was always playing whenever people were under the tent. "Let's get to it! First, though, how amazing were our contestants this year? I'm glad I wore my stretchy pants!" Emery wanted to gag as the crowd laughed while Tina yanked on her thick leggings. "Here we go, our Jack Frost Chili Cook Off champion is," she ripped open the envelope, "Oh my goodness! Number seventeen, that's me!"

Emery dropped her head on her forearm.

Ugh, this sucks. Now the rest of the night it's going to be all about Tina. How great everything she-

Heat hit her lower back. A light caress on the skin exposed above her jeans.

"We still on for the snowman thing tomorrow morning?"

"Huh?"

Right, yes, the snowman thing.

She nodded, sitting up, "Yeah, and if you want to come early for breakfast, it starts an hour before." She looked back to Tina, watching as people fawned over her.

"Em, don't let it get to you." Lana gave her a hard look. She didn't understand. Anyone else and she would have gotten over it.

"Tina's was good," Finn said, tugging on Emery's hair playfully, "But yours was better, darlin'." His sweet smile eased the tightness in her chest, just a little, but she'd take it.

"Thanks."

"Seriously, girl, don't give her a second thought." Katie smiled.

Katie was right and the things Finn and her friends were saying were sweet, but deep down she knew the truth. Tina's was better. She'd always been better than Emery. Why else did she win all the time?

It wasn't like Emery didn't get better but, despite what Katie said, she was busy living her life. Okay, so sometimes that busy was being curled up on the couch with an excellent book, but whatever.

Emery's insides cringed at Tina's praise, like watching a car crash. She couldn't look away.

Between the hangover and the tragic news of Tina's win, Emery felt nauseous and ready to go home.

Go home and drown herself in hot chocolate and brownies.

"Hey" Finn called, "You want to take a quick walk with me?"

Emery didn't have to think about her answer, "Of course," she said, standing. "But I'll probably head out after. Going to be an early night for me."

She said her goodbyes to everyone at the table then followed Finn to the outskirts of the tent close to a heater since the sun had set a few hours ago. If the wind picked up, it was going to drop below freezing.

He found a spot near a tree with a little hiding spot created by the hollowed out trunk. Emery tucked herself into the hollowed space, Finn standing directly in front of her, hiding her even more from the crowd mingling around and keeping her warm.

"I thought you said we were going for a walk?" Emery asked, a sly smile spreading across her lips.

"We did." His smile was megawatt compared to hers. "We walked all the way over here."

I don't think I'll ever tire of seeing him smile like that at me.

She wasn't sure why he wanted to pull her aside, but whatever the reason, she was glad. He looked at her like she was someone special. Someone he wanted to spend his time with. At least that was what she was hoping his smile said.

"Well you got me here, so what is it you wanted to talk about?"

Finn leaned closer, their coats brushing one anothers. "I got cut off earlier." His gloved thumb rubbed against her chin as he said, "I wanted to see if you were free after the holidays. I know we'll be seeing each other tomorrow, but that's not a date. Not really."

Sucking in a shocked breath, Emery tried to collect her thoughts. "You're asking me out?" She sounded like a teenager, asking if they were going steady or something, but for her, this was big.

"I'm um," she thought through the next few days, "Well, I won't be free until at least the twenty-seventh, but if you don't mind chilling out, you could come over tonight and we can watch a movie, again" she asked, feeling bold.

His smile fell a bit, "Wish I could darlin' though I'm glad to hear you're interested." His deep rumble had her shivering.

Without warning his head descended down on hers, his warm, gentle lips pressing against hers. Pulling back, his eyes were so close, she was shocked to see flecks of gold ringing his pupil that she never noticed. *That's why they looked like honey.*

"Why would you think I wasn't interested?" she asked, his lips merely an inch from hers. She wanted to keep kissing him, but someone might see and she wasn't sure he was ready for the town to know about, well, whatever was happening between them. And something was absolutely happening.

His mouth tightened before he said, "Sometimes, it's like you aren't sure whether or not you like me. So then I wasn't sure, even after our kiss. Figured it was worth a shot though. That you were worth a shot." His whispered words floated straight to Emery's heart, thawing it in a way that she didn't know she needed.

"So why do I have to wait to see you until the morning?" She really wanted to kiss him again.

It's never felt like this when I've kissed other guys. Like falling, but knowing he'll catch me when I do. God I hope he catches me.

"Got to finish up some work before Christmas so I have time to take my girl out," he answered with a wink. "Just the two of us. And hopefully without any spills."

Laughing she pondered out loud, "But without that spill, would we be standing here? Would we have kissed?"

Her voice was hushed as she focused on said lips, still only inches from her own.

"Glad that isn't something I have to worry about." He kissed her long and deep this time, her arms snaking around his shoulders, his circling her waist. Yes. This was what she wanted. Not long after he started, he released her, both of them panting, the fog of their breath mixing in the air. "Wish I wasn't busy tonight darlin'."

I love when he calls me darlin'. Hits me right between the thighs.

"I have to tell you though," she started saying but then regretted bringing it up. "You know what, nevermind."

"No, tell me." His words rushed out.

Okay, here goes. "It's just that, well, I haven't had the best of luck with men in my life and," Looking him in the eyes she admitted, "I don't trust easy, so all I ask is be careful with me."

"That's not a problem darlin'."

I sure hoped it wasn't because, with Finn, I think he might do more than just hurt me. He might break me.

Let's hope not.

CHAPTER 4

The blaring alarm woke Emery from a random dream of her and one of her favorite childhood crushes heading to a circus. She slept terribly, tossing and turning with anxiety over the competition and her loss at yesterday's cook-off.

Why did Tina have to take everything from her? Why couldn't women like Tina or like her mom just keep their hands to themselves?

Snagging her phone on the way to the shower, needing it nice and toasty before she hopped in, she noticed she had two missed calls and three text messages from Katie.

No voicemail and the messages said to get a hold of her as soon as she woke up. Until Emery had coffee in her system, she didn't consider herself to be awake so her phone call had to wait.

After gulping down some caffeine, Emery jumped in the shower. Taking too long under the hot stream, she ended up rushing around and forgot about calling Katie. The road was way too slick from the flurries last night, and didn't want to risk calling until she was no longer behind the wheel.

Before Emery turned off the car Katie was on her, "What the hell! I told you to call me ASAP. Did you lose your phone?" Emery shrugged off Katie's concern as she climbed out of the car.

"No. I was running behind and if it was something important, you'd have left a voicemail or tried to call me this morning, none of which you did." Emery said, leaping out of the car, excited about spending the next few hours with Finn and hopefully beating Tina.

"I called you five times! *Jesus*," she tugged her over to the side of the parking lot away from where people gathered under the tents. "Look who I saw out on a date last night at Rosie's diner." Katie pushed her phone in front of Emery's face. It was Finn and some blonde woman.

What the shit...

Emery snatched the phone out of Katie's gloved hand. Using her teeth to pull off her thick wool mittens, Emery enlarged the image with her fingers.

"Fucking Tina."

Her entire body felt feverish with the hurt overshadowing her disappointment.

"I'm sorry, but I thought it was better for you to find out now and not down the road. We both know how that ends." Katie was a good friend, and she was only looking out for Emery, but that saying about not killing the messenger existed for a reason.

"Why the hell didn't you tell me this before I showed up to build snowmen with that cheating prick?" Emery was fuming.

"Okay," Katie stepped back, hands raised as she continued, "I get you're pissed, but direct that shit to the people who deserve it. And for the record, I was trying to do it last night but you go to bed before my grandma so here we are."

Damn it. Katie had a point.

Emery needed to get out of there before she saw anyone. It would kill her to let Tina win again, but if she stayed Emery was afraid she'd end up stabbing her with one of Frosty's arms.

"Hey Emery" Finn called from between the parked cars, "Wait up." He joined their small group.

"I have to go."

Real mature Emery.

"Go?" He grabbed her hand, halting her. "What the hell are you talking about?" That look was back. Furrowed brows, straight mouth.

"I-"

"Em, come on!" Lana appeared out of nowhere with a bag slung over her shoulder. "Tina's been here for half an hour. I swear the bitch paid someone off to let her in early. Hey Finn. You ready to kick some snowman ass? Wait-," she scratched her chin, "that doesn't make sense. You know what I meant," she shrugged, giving up her motivational speech.

"What's it gonna be girly?" Katie asked.

All eyes on her, she swallowed the scream trying to escape. Katie wouldn't think Emery was a bitch if she ditched. Lana would be there to support her and this was her town. Finn shacking up with Tina would not stop her, even if it meant having to work with him when she'd rather be hurling snowballs at his head.

Maybe later, when he isn't looking.

"I- I thought I forgot something in my car," she said, gnawing on her lip as she slipped by Finn.

Doing her best to avoid talking with him, Emery chatted with every person she'd met in Pine Forest she could find. Was this an excellent strategy for winning? Nope, but it was better than her freaking out on Finn or slugging Tina if she so much as even mentioned her new man.

"Hey." Lana gave her arm a squeeze, "You gonna tell me what the hell is going on and why you won't even look at Finn, let alone speak to him?" Lana asked, sounding confused.

"Katie didn't send you the photo last night?" Lana shook her head, so Emery showed her the evidence. "He lied, but I refuse to let Tina beat me at anything else. I can't say I didn't expect it. Everyone breaks your trust eventually."

"Em-" Lana's voice filled with sadness.

"We can talk about it later. Right now I have to focus on winning this damn thing." It was dangerously close to starting time.

Time to bite the bullet.

Finn watched her approach. His body coiled tight as he waited in their designated area.

"Hey sorry I-" Emery noticed his clenched jaw and seething eyes. "What?"

"You really plan on acting like you didn't just spend the last 45 minutes hiding from me?" His tone grated over her, bringing up the anger at how easily she believed he liked her.

"I wasn't," she lied. "Let's just get this over with-" Emery slammed into a warm wall.

Not again.

This time she kept more than an arm's length between them. No need to tempt herself.

"That's it, tell me what's going on," his voice strained, sounding almost hurt.

Man, his eyes looked beautiful in the bright morning sun.

Shaking that thought she figured it would be better to get through this without making a scene with Finn. Or Tina, who Emery had spotted a few spaces over as she took in the surrounding area.

Gritting her teeth, she growled then turned and

marched away, needing some space. He smelled too good up close.

"Girly, I got you a coffee and snagged you some donuts in case you get hungry later." Moving closer, Katie asked, "Did he say anything about what you saw in the pic?"

Oh thank god for Katie.

"No, I haven't said a word and I don't plan to. Once this thing's done, no more Finn. I swear, if I didn't want to beat Tina so bad I could taste it, I'd have quit this thing in a heartbeat." She rushed as Lana joined them.

Lana had a look of determination Emery only saw when she was coaching her dance students. "You two better tell me what the hell is going on," she snapped at them.

"Our girl here thinks she can go the whole two hours without getting into it with Finn or Tina. Fifty bucks says Tina and Emery are rolling around in the snow before this shindig ends," Katie said with a huge grin on her face as she looked at Lana.

Lana eyed Emery, then looked over her shoulder toward Finn. "You're on, but I say it happens closer to the one hour mark."

"Are you two serious right now?" Emery stomped her foot before giving up on her useless friends and marched away, tossing over her shoulder, "You keep this up and I'm going to find new besties."

"So it looks like you're just angry at everyone today, huh?"

Finn's words stopped her just as the announcement for the snowman competition came over the loudspeakers: "Two hours on the clock."

"Why do you think I'm angry at you?" Emery asked, hands on her hips. So much for not getting into it. But if she kept her mouth shut, she couldn't live with herself.

"Honestly," he shrugged, exasperated, "I have no clue.

We've had an awesome couple of days, at least I thought so." The softness around his eyes made her waver.

"So what you're telling me is that you don't feel you've done anything that might've upset me?" Out of the corner of her eye, she noticed Lana and Emery setting up their folding chairs right next to their space. Lovely. Now she had an audience.

"That's what I'm telling you, so stop playing whatever game it is you're playing and explain to me where the sweet and funny woman I ran into a few days ago went because you aren't her."

Ouch. That hurt.

Blinking fast, she went back to her original plan of ignoring Finn and started working on building their damn snowman, rethinking her whole 'not making a scene with Finn' thing.

"You going to help me build this thing or what?" she said instead of answering him.

He was quiet for so long Emery had to turn around to see if maybe he left. Well, not leave, more like go over and visit with his new girlfriend. Sharp pain stabbed her chest at the thought, but she didn't let it sway her. Pain reminded her she was still alive. Or at least that's what they say.

"Yeah Emery, I'll help."

Tears formed at the coldness of his tone, and the anger attached to her name.

"You haven't called me Emery since I spilled your coffee." Softly, so softly she said the words that it wouldn't have surprised her if he hadn't heard her.

"You guys need to start building if you have any chance of winning today," Lana called out to them. Neither Finn nor Emery acknowledged her.

"What?" Finn asked, again too close for her to think.

"Emery." She kicked at the snow, "You don't usually call me that."

"I don't get you," he said, throwing her a bit. "You act one way the last few days and I can't say I didn't see glimpses of this version of you at the cook off, but this? How you've been since I showed up is unacceptable." This time he turned away from her.

"Stop acting like this is all on me when you're the one whose not really who they said they were," she said, dangerously close to laying into him. But she would not do that here. Not in front of the town, and especially not in front of Tina.

"Oh, really?" He laughed. He fucking laughed!

"Really," she kicked the ball of snow she'd attempted to form for all of ten seconds.

"Oh, this is getting good," Katie said, as Emery watched her shoulder bumping Lana.

She tossed a handful of snow at them. "Will you two shut up!" Emery snapped.

Mouth wide, Lana just blinked at her while Katie yelled back, "Girl, just rip that damn band aid off and get on with it. Damn," she turned to Lana, "I should have brought popcorn."

"You guys know the contest started, right?"

Oh, hell no.

"Yeah Tina we know, now run back to wherever the hell you just came from and mind your business." Tina scoffed but by the grace of God did as Emery asked, but not before shooting Finn a smile and a wink over her shoulder.

Finn moved in front of her, blocking her view of Tina. "Why are you acting like a bitch to her when she was only trying to help?"

"You're defending Tina to me? Are you kidding me?" She spun away, "Wouldn't want her to think anything was going on here and ruin things."

A hand on her shoulder spun her back to face him.

"What in the hell are you talking about?" He asked, jaw working as his nostrils flared.

"How'd your date go with her last night?" Emery hissed. "You know, after you spent days pretending that you were interested in me."

"Pretending…?" Now he just looked confused.

Nice try, buddy.

"Katie saw you last night at the diner with Tina so you can drop the act. You thought you could play the field while stringing me along, but that isn't going to happen. At least not with me!" She shouted, drawing attention from the other contestants and the few people who came to support them this early.

"Ohhh yeah, here we go!" Katie cheered.

"What in the fuck are you talking about? The only person I've been trying to date is you. Though that is up for debate after seeing who you really are." She let the hurt of his words wash over her. This wasn't the first time a guy hurt her, but if she could help it, it would be the last.

Searching her pockets for her cell, she found it and pulled up the image Katie had sent. "You care to explain how this shows you tw*o* on a date, yet you're standing here telling me that was a lie." Her voice wavered at the end, but she pushed through.

He stared at the image for almost a full minute before he said, "So your crazy friend sees me at the diner and instead of saying hello, or anything for that matter, she snaps a picture of me and uses that as evidence that I was on a date. Then, instead of calling me or attempting to speak with me about it, you come here having already written me off."

The way he said it didn't make her sound good.

"A picture is worth a thousand words." She was holding her ground, and she didn't miss that he still hadn't explained.

Looking deep into her eyes he said, "It is and what this picture says is that while I was having a late dinner after spending a few hours working in the shop, Tina asked if she could have a seat while she waited for her to-go order. Drink in hand when she sat down, she chatted while I listened then when her food was ready, she left."

Her heart pounded so loud in her ears she thought he could hear it as she took in his words. Swallowing, she asked, "Is that really what happened or did you make that up in case anyone told me?"

It was shitty to ask, but the lies she let herself believe before couldn't happen again.

"You guys, it's been more than a half hour and you've done nothing!" Lana bellowed in their direction, damn near throwing a fit.

Whatever. She would get to it. They had plenty of time.

"Told you what? That I had dinner with another human being, which isn't even the case. But, if it was, it wouldn't matter because you and I aren't together," Finn said, arms flailing around as his temper showed.

Face heated, his words like a slap in the face, "Oh I am very aware that we are not together," she said, now pacing, her arms all over the place. "I thought you'd be worth the effort, but oh boy was I wrong."

Finn blocked her path, "Oh darling," his words were arctic, chilling her to the bone, "I am worth it but it looks like you weren't."

"Are you guys sure you don't need any help?"

"Beat it, Tina!" This was not the time.

"Oh, I see you heard about me and Finn," Tina said with a grin that would give the Grinch a run for his money. Ever the winter Barbie, looking stunning and put together, while Emery looked like she wrestled a bear.

"Tina," Finn warned.

"Yes, yes, yes! Here we go." Katie would be the death of

Emery. Or at least the reason for the prison sentence when she murdered Tina.

Shooting her best friend a death glare, she returned her focus to her real enemy. "Tina, if you know what's good for you," she said facing off with her, "You'll leave now before I do something I can't take back." Emery's words were a threat she didn't want to have to follow through on, but her fist clenched, ready for whatever happened.

"How's it feel? Maybe you should ask your dad how he got over the enormously embarrassing betrayal your mom caused. Maybe daddy wasn't man enough for her." Tina's eyes sparkled, her glittery pink glossed lips shining.

"Em…" Lana said, overhearing Tina's words. Finn was just out of earshot as he started packing some snow, which was strategic of Tina. She'd give her that.

"Walk away," Emery said, closing her eyes as she took a deep, calming breath.

"Oh Emery, you're just a walking disappoint to so many." With that Tina marched back over to her family of snowmen that her partner, someone Emery had never seen before, built that reminded her of A Christmas Carol with the top hat and gown.

Clever.

She wasn't sure how long she was staring off, but her mind was all over the place.

"Don't you think it's about time you stopped whatever childish war you have with Tina?" Finn startled her out of her head.

"You just don't understand."

"Alrighty folks," the announcer rang over the speakers, "only a half hour left. Keep it up!"

"Trade me spots!" Lana was jumping up and down, gaining Emery's attention. "You guys have done nothing but argue and the contest is almost over."

Funny how Emery hadn't thought about the contest or beating Tina since she and Finn started going at it.

What does that mean?

"Maybe you should switch her. She'd be better company," he mumbled under his breath while he continued packing snow to build, well, something. The square shape didn't look like the start of a snowman, but who was she kidding. They weren't going to have anything worth beating Tina, let alone winning.

"So, you think I'm being ridiculous?" Emery snapped, her inner bitch here to stay.

Popping up Finn's anger radiated off of him. This time steam would come out for sure. "No, I think you're being an immature girl who never left the drama of high school behind. Grow up and get over whatever the hell is keeping you there. Because," his body closer now, that soft sandalwood scent hitting her, "I have no interest in dealing with that shit again."

She sucked in a breath, catching Tina watching them over Finn's shoulder.

"Damn," Katie's voice chimed in, "that was harsh."

Emery agreed, and it was so unnecessary that Emery lost it.

"Oh, don't worry, you won't need to be dealing with my shit after this fucking snowman contest. I thought I could trust you," she yelled, kicking the start of whatever snow thing he had been working on.

Everyone near them stopped, all eyes on them. Fine, whatever.

"And I thought you weren't a bitch!" Finn threw the little shovel he was using off to the side.

"Emery," Tina stepped into the ring way too close to her. "Why don't you take a five-minute break."

"Why don't you get out of my face!"

"Finn," Tina turned to him, "I tried to tell you last night how awful she could be."

Pain exploded in Emery's hand as she cracked Tina in the jaw.

Then chaos ensued.

"Jesus Christ," Finn said, yanking Emery away from Tina.

"Hell yeah!" Katie cheered.

"Oh shit, ohhhh shit," Lana swore, running over to her.

Everyone else around them hurried over to Tina, who you'd have thought got by a car the way she was wailing.

"Emery McCormick! What is the meaning of this?" Walter made his way over, shaking his head as he stared her down.

"I- Well Tina said-"

"Unless she was attempting to cause you physical harm, nothing you say can justify what you did. Your grandpa is rolling over in his grave."

Walter's word gutted her, and the stinging along her knuckles brought her out of her head and into reality.

She just punched Tina in the face in front of the whole town during a snowman building contest. And tomorrow was Christmas.

Who knew that she could get this low? Not Emery.

"I'm sorry," she said, voice cracking as she fought the well of tears that wanted to spill over. Crying was the only thing that could make this worse.

"Gonna have to ask you to leave Em," Walter said, face hanging as he looked at her.

"I got your stuff, honey," Lana said, lifting their bags.

"Okay, give me just a sec," Emery said, searching for Finn, who'd moved over to check on Tina.

Might as well knock out two birds.

Tina tensed at her approach, hooking her arms through Finn's. Swallowing down the shame and hurt she said, "I'm so sorry Tina, you didn't deserve what I did." No matter how it felt to shut her up. It wasn't worth all this.

"I'm honestly surprised you've never swung at me before this," Tina spat.

"So am I," she agreed with a shrug.

Now on to bird number two.

"Finn, you were right. I, it's just," fuck this was hard. "Seeing you with her hurt. Hurt more than I was prepared for, and I thought the worst of you. I'm sorry," she said, throat tight from keeping the tears at bay.

He slid out of Tina's grasp, walking just out of earshot of the crowd. Emery followed.

"You asked me why I left my life behind and moved here." The emotion was gone. "I was engaged and even though I loved her and had for years, I couldn't take her constant need for drama and love of fighting as time went on. She never left that high school mentality behind, and I'm not willing to make the same mistake again."

That made sense, and Emery understood that she may never come back from this moment. With a slight nod, and the tears finally escaping, she let Lana and Katie walk her to her car, no longer welcome.

"It'll be okay, girly."

This time, she wasn't so sure.

CHAPTER 5

A bottle of wine and too many red and green stuffed Oreos to count, Emery was finally ready. Picking up her cell, she hit Finn's name on her screen and waited as she held the last family photo her mom was in before her life exploded.

It only rang twice before he sent her to voicemail. Harsh, but not unexpected.

At the sound of the beep, Emery let it all out.

"My mom started cheating on my dad when I was eight. It wasn't until after I turned thirteen that he found out. She never apologized for breaking my trust in people. My mom was perfect to so many, but at her core, she was heartless and cold. I haven't spoken to her since the day she left. But in my mind, that's how all relationships end up. With someone cheating or lying or just leaving. What I said to you today and how I acted was beyond atrocious, and no amount of 'I'm sorry' can fix this. My problems with Tina are the same problems I have with my mom. It's easier to blame things on them than it is to look in the mirror and admit that I'm at fault. You did nothing to make me think you'd lie to me, but I still thought the worst of you. I'm rambling, I know, but I think the wine has finally taken over my brain. You are the most delicious smelling and tasting guy who has only ever shown me and those around you kindness. The way I feel around you scares me, but that's kind of the fun part," Emery breathed deep into the phone, "please forgive me. I was too afraid to let you have my heart, but from how much it hurts I'd guess you've had it since we kissed in front of the fireplace."

Emery hung up and turned off the power, not being in any condition to talk to anyone that might call her, anyway. She doubted Finn would call her back. It'd be so much easier if he was to blame for how she felt, but alas, it was all on her and her stupid mouth.

Dropping like a log onto her couch, she snagged one of the throw pillows and closed her eyes. She'd had enough of today. Hopefully, if her hangover didn't kill her, tomorrow would be better.

❄

Why is the thunder so loud? And yelling her name.

Blinking away the dreamless sleep, Emery tried to gain her bearings. That wasn't thunder. Unless it was now thundering while it also snowed.

"Open the hell up Emery!"

Oh shit! The voicemail. She drunk dialed Finn.

"No, no, no..." Why had she let herself drink so much?

Boom! Boom! Boom!

The door rattled against Finn's onslaught. Shuffling over to save her door from any permanent damage, she unlocked it, flinging it open.

"Why aren't you answering your phone!" Finn shouted, stomping in and soaking her with snow flurries.

"What the hell Finn?" She asked instead of answering.

"It's the middle of the night and" she stopped, seeing how hard it was snowing, "Did you just drive here through that?" She pointed outside, but he was like a bull ready to run right through her.

"Yeah considering I tried to call you ten minutes after I got your voicemail but you never picked up. Then I got worried because you mentioned you'd been drinking and I couldn't fall asleep until I knew you were okay. So why the hell didn't you answer?"

He was shouting, and it made Emery shrink back a little, but his words were also sweet. She was also pretty sure she was still drunk.

"You called me back?"

"Yeah, because we had a fight and fighting doesn't mean we walk out of one another's life."

See, that's exactly what she thought until it came to her own relationships. However, if she was being honest, they seemed like they had more than a fight. That was a blowout if she ever saw one.

"I can't say I'm happy with you, but I get it. I get people who feel like they are in your life only to drag you down."

That was one way to describe Tina. No, she would not think about her right now.

"So what? Does that mean you forgive me?" All night she was telling herself that it didn't matter if Finn never wanted to see her again, but she knew it was a lie.

"It means I'm willing to give us a shot as long as you promise to let this thing with Tina go. For good."

That was the thing, wasn't it? So much of my time ended up tied to Tina's. And for what?

"I think that would be best," she said with a smile and a yawn that overtook her entire face. "I also think I should get back to sleep soon since I think I'm still a bit drunk." She looked out her windows, "And there is no way you're leaving with all that snow."

"Works for me." Finn smiled big as she removed all of his outside layers.

Emery was still wearing black yoga pants and an oversized sweatshirt with a cat on the front. Finn's jeans and black thermal wouldn't be comfy enough to sleep in.

"Why are you not in pjs? What were you doing awake?" Emery moved through the living room, Finn right behind her. When she hit her bedroom, lifting her up, flying, landing softly in the center of her king sized bed.

"Finn!"

He laughed, joining her in bed, still fully clothed. "You good with me sleeping in here with you tonight?" His fingers slid along her jaw, then up into her hair. *That felt wonderful.*

"Yeah, but there is no way you're going to be comfortable in what you're wearing."

She heard a growl before his lips crushed hers. His body tangling with hers as they devoured one another.

How is this kiss even better than the last one?

After some time he pulled back, both of them breathing hard. She looked up into his heated stare as he said, "Don't pull that shit with Tina or anyone and I think we'll be just fine because darlin', kissing you felt like I've found my home. Not gonna lie," the deep timber of his voice was beyond sexy. "Part of why I was so mad was because you were taking the best kiss I'd ever had with you if you turned out to be just like my ex."

"I will promise to do my best not to punch people," she whispered back again in their bubble. "I would like to add that there may come a time when I am justified in throwing a punch and when that day comes, you aren't allowed to get mad."

His laugh took over his whole body, shaking hers.

"Sure darlin'." He kissed her on the forehead before rolling to his back, laying next to her.

Catching a look at the old digital clock on her nightstand, she noted the time. 12:14am.

She rolled onto her side, facing him. "Merry Christmas, Finn."

Hand raised, his fingers brushed against her cheek. "Merry Christmas, darlin'." His lips found hers and she explored, taking her time until she wanted more.

"How about this? Since it's Christmas and all, do I get to unwrap a present?"

Finn's eyebrow shot up. "I didn't bring it with me since I practically ran out of the house."

I would be speaking to him about running out into a snowstorm later. She was just glad he got here safe and sound.

"Oh Finn, don't you get it," she said, hand slipping down to the front of his jeans, finding his hardness, "You're my present tonight." She popped the button and before she made it to the zipper, he was on her.

"You can unwrap me as soon as we wake up. Our first time will not be when you're drunk."

Emery protested until he continued, "Want to make sure my girl remembers every minute."

Oh yes, this was going to be a very merry Christmas indeed.

ABOUT THE AUTHOR

IVY FERNWOOD

Ivy Fernwood loves the adventures and unpredictability of growing up in the Midwest. Spending most of her time with her daughter and two cats, she takes every chance she gets to read or even more to write.

Reading romance novels has become an addiction Ivy's fine with keeping though her overflowing bookshelves beg to differ. Whether it's vampires or witches, hockey teams or football players, detectives or special agents, or good ole' fashion present day, as long as she gets her happily ever after, Ivy's in. Same goes for her writing.

Books have and always will hold a special place in Ivy's heart and now, being on the other end of she loves them even more. She hopes you do too.

If you want to stay up to date on all things Ivy Fernwood you can find her on her Facebook page and her Instagram page.

❋

facebook.com/IvyFernwoodAuthor
instagram.com/ivyfernwoodauthor

That Big Romantic Moment

by
Celia Mulder

CHAPTER 1

*D*ecember 26th

Agnes dug through the remnants of the popcorn to find the crispy, slightly burnt kernels. These she ate in loud, teeth grinding crunches. "What's the plan for New Year's?"

Mio cringed at the sound and glared at her but she didn't look at him to see it. He leaned back against his lumpy futon, pulling his festive red blanket up to his chin. "You. Me. A bottle of cheap champagne and *Sleepless in Seattle?*"

"You don't have a party or something to go to?"

Mio sighed. "Working until 10pm remember? And then, by the time I get home and changed, it'll be eleven. Then I show up and less than an hour later am reminded of how horribly single I am. Again. So, no. No party."

Agnes stopped crunching on kernels. "Mio. It's literally your favorite holiday."

New Year's was Mio's favorite holiday, normally. He'd loved it ever since he first saw *When Harry Met Sally* and pictured himself as Sally, waiting for Harry to get over his hang ups and confess his feelings. He loved the parties—the build to the fever pitch of midnight and the wind down into endless, drunken renditions of "Auld Lang Syne."

He loved the promise of a new start, the celebration of the exhausted year passing and the young, fresh year arriving. There was hope in the air and it was impossible not to get high on it. For one night, anything could happen. Anything might happen.

New Year's was the time of beginnings and resolutions and wishes. Before everyone stumbled home and woke up on January 1st regretting their promise to start going to the gym, before reality set in and the new year blended in with the dull gray of the last one, there was a night when wishes could come true. And there was a wish Mio made every year without fail. It may not have come true yet, although he'd been close a few times, but he knew, someday, some year, it would. Just maybe not this year.

Because this year, everything seemed intent on being miserable and terrible, even his favorite holiday.

He told Agnes this.

"Cheap champagne and Tom Hanks it is," she said and went back to eating the popcorn dregs.

The movie credits were still rolling. Mio turned them off. They sat in the glow of his sad little strand of Christmas lights, the only strand he could stretch to the single outlet in the room.

Just as he was about to tell Agnes he was taking the popcorn away from her, she set it down on the stained, wobbly coffee table. She touched her green mud mask and then turned and peered at Mio.

"These are ready to come off," she announced.

Mio touched his, feeling the dry bits of the mask flake off under his fingers. "Thank God."

Agnes hopped up and headed toward the bathroom. Mio, his skin suddenly itchy and uncomfortable, headed for the kitchen sink. He moved the dirty dishes out of the way and proceeded to splash at his face until most of the green gunk was gone. At which point he discovered the lack of a towel not covered in suspicious food stains and stumbled to the bathroom.

Agnes handed him a cleanish one.

He scrubbed at the mud, wondering how it had gotten into his short brown hair and on his ear lobes. Then there were the bits which stubbornly refused to leave his five o'clock shadow. He imagined his already oblong face stretching out more with his efforts to remove the damn cleansing mask.

"As long as I can hang out here while you're at work, I'm good with whatever."

It took Mio a second to catch up. New Year's. "Obviously you can hang out here. Spend the night on the thirtieth if you want to."

"I might have to. Mom is getting ice sculptures this year."

"Yikes."

Their parents' New Year's parties, which had been blissfully absent when they decided to spend last year on a cruise, were as wild as a teen party movie. Only with adults in their fifties, top shelf liquors, and rumors of swinging. God knows they didn't care what their long-suffering children thought of said parties.

Could his life suck anymore? Wasn't it enough that he was barely making rent working at his crappy cafe job, trying desperately to finish applications for jobs he would undoubtedly wouldn't get, and hanging out with his little sister almost every night because all of his former friends were off doing more glamorous things? And he'd had to break up with his boyfriend for being a truly terrible person? No, the final icing on the stale Christmas cookie would be that, once again, on his favorite night of the year, the thing he wanted most in the world would still be out of reach.

"Oh my God, I almost forgot to tell you!" Agnes's exclamation bulldozed through his mental chastisement not a moment too soon.

"What?" he said without enthusiasm as he applied moisturizer to his tender skin. He loved Agnes more than any person in the world but usually the things she stored up to tell him were nothing to write home about.

"You'll never guess who I saw today."

Mio was in no mood to guess and told her that.

Agnes rolled her eyes at him in the mirror. They had identical light caramel colored eyes, which he often thought of as their only discernible family resemblance. "Elliot," she said and left the bathroom.

"Elliot?" Mio repeated slowly, blinking and following her back to the futon.

"Yeah. Elliot." Agnes grabbed the remote and scrolled through the streaming options, presumably looking for the next movie.

Elliot.

At the mere mention of the name, his stomach had done a flip. Elliot, his friend from seventh grade to twelfth. The nerdy, awkward, quiet guy who Mio had had intensely not-just-friends feelings for. Feelings that could never be acted on because Elliot was, by all accounts, straight. He'd never said so, but he hadn't said no when their friend Fern had asked him to a dance and had even dated her for a few months after that. No, there had been nothing to indicate Elliot thought of Mio as anything more than a friend and he'd been stupid to hope there might be. He'd been utterly foolish about Elliot—the desperate naiveté of a first crush. Yet, even now, four and a half years after making a complete ass of himself in front of the guy, Mio was still not completely over him.

He tried to cover up his reaction. "Cool. So, Elliot's in town. Cool."

They hadn't kept in touch after high school. He checked in Elliot's social media accounts more often than he'd admit, but the guy's last post had been from September. And that had been a close-up of a latte.

Agnes stopped scrolling and narrowed her eyes at him. "Why does your voice sound so weird?"

"What are you talking about? It's my normal voice."

"No, it's all high pitched and strangled sounding."

Mio said what any well-adjusted older brother would say, "Your voice is weird."

"Your face is weird."

"Your Mom... oh wait, no that doesn't work for us."

Agnes laughed one of her great honking laughs, complete with snorts. The laugh they both could do, and both reserved exclusively for sibling time where there was no chance of anyone else hearing. It was an unattractive laugh. A giant, snorting guffaw.

"Jesus, it wasn't that funny," Mio frowned at her. He couldn't help smiling. That damn laugh was contagious. But he wasn't sure where it'd come from.

Agnes finally got a hold of herself. She'd had her own short brown hair clipped back with some pastel barrettes she'd found in her old room. They were constantly falling out and the laughing attack had exacerbated the ongoing struggle. She deftly began redoing her hair, pulling and smoothing with seamless expertise. "You want to ask me about Elliot so badly. You're just sitting over there dying to ask me what he said. It's hilarious."

Mio curled in on himself, drawing his legs up against his chest. His face was red. "Don't you have someone else to annoy?"

Agnes sighed dramatically. "I wish. Mom and Dad are

having date night. I swear they don't remember I'm at the house half the time."

Mio snorted. "Exactly why I moved out. You could stay here for the rest of break, you know that, right?"

Agnes looked aghast, purposefully so. "What and give up my beautiful room for your futon? No thank you. Besides, I much prefer coming over and eating all of your food instead."

It was Mio's turn to roll his eyes at her. "Fine. Just tell me about Elliot."

For a minute it looked like Agnes was going to keep teasing him. Then she cleared her throat. "Well," she said with an authoritative air, "he's home to see his parents."

She paused like she was waiting for Mio to react. He wasn't about to give her the satisfaction.

"He was doing a grad program at State in something. I don't remember. Anyway, he's in town, I don't know for how long, and yes, he did ask about you."

Mio's heart did cartwheels that his brain was not at all pleased about. *Nothing happened between you*, he reminded his celebrating organs. *Nothing will happen. He's probably straight. A lot of people are, I've heard.*

"What did you say?" he said, unfortunately having to clear his throat before he could speak.

"I said you were bumming around here and you two should hang out and catch up. I told him to come to the cafe and find you."

If Mio had been drinking something, he would have sprayed it across the entire room. He still managed to splutter and gulp a lot. "What? I mean, why? Why did you tell him that?"

Agnes raised an eyebrow. With her new large frames, she looked especially wise and all-knowing. It was terrifying. "Because, idiot, he said he wanted to see you. Did you want him showing up at the parents' house?"

Mio shook his head. "But I'd also rather he didn't show up at my place of work."

Agnes huffed. "Well it's done. I told him and it's done. You'll just have to bear it."

Sisters. He scowled at her but she didn't notice. Not ready to let it go yet, he dug around behind his back until he got a good hold on the pillow behind him. He lobbed it at Agnes, hitting her in the head at a short distance, causing her hair to stick up in a staticky mess.

"God Mio, you're so immature," she said in one of her pretending-to-be-older voices. She took the pillow and added it to the stack behind her back, leaving Mio to lean against the hard futon as penance for his behavior. "What's the deal with you anyway? Don't you want to catch up with Elliot? I like him."

Mio had more than liked him. "I don't know, I just don't want to see him. And you didn't have to tell him where I worked. Now I have to worry about him stopping by."

He knew exactly why he didn't want to see Elliot. For one thing, there was the whole him having had a crush on the guy. His stupid, unrequited crush. There was no point explaining that to Agnes. She didn't get crushes.

Then there was the feeling he should be doing something cool and interesting by this point in his life. Elliot had gone to grad school. Mio worked a shitty job, lived in a dung heap of an apartment, and generally failed miserably.

Yeah, he knew exactly why he didn't want to see Elliot. There was nothing to be done but hope Elliot wouldn't follow up. Maybe he'd only asked about Mio to keep the conversation with Agnes going. Mio knew better than anyone how awkward talking to Agnes for long periods of time could be. She had a terrible habit of forgetting she was talking and drifting off in the middle of her sentences when she started thinking about something else.

"Don't get your panties in a bunch. It's just Elliot. Now, will you give me a ride home?"

Just Elliot. Yeah right. Aloud he said, "How'd you get here?"

"I walked. But it's dark and cold and you don't want to make me walk home in the snow, do you?" Agnes blinked rapidly behind her thick framed glasses.

Mio sighed and got up to get his coat.

CHAPTER 2

❄

*D*ecember 27th

The twenty-seventh started out busy and didn't let up. Mio arrived at work two minutes before his shift was due to start, clocked in at lightning speed, and was immediately handed a tray of baked goods and told to get stocking. Then he was stuck on drinks and there he stayed, serving the endless line of customers desperate for an eggnog lattes and peppermint mochas. The cute little café, with its checkered floors and punny names, filled with the smells of espresso and sugar. Christmas music played relentlessly in the background. Groups of weary shoppers and exhausted snow frolickers crowded around the tables, talking loudly to be heard over the carols and the constant roar of the steam wand. Holiday chaos at its peak.

When Agnes came in, Mio gave her a dramatic look to show how little he was enjoying this particular day. She laughed and headed towards her usual table in the corner, shaking the fresh snow from her coat as she settled in. She'd been off school for a week and spent almost as much time at the cafe as Mio did, working on her graphic novels.

Always at the same table in the corner, which was never taken, even when the rest of the cafe was packed. Possibly because it was weirdly ten degrees colder in that spot. Not a big selling point during the winter.

The cashier, a high schooler named Jenny, threw a desperate look at Mio to indicate that she was about two seconds from peeing her pants. Mio called another high schooler out to the front to cover the register. But the kid was taking forever so Mio paused his drink making and hopped on the register. Which was how he ended up being front and center when Elliot stepped up to the counter.

Mio was punching in his employee code and didn't look up right away. "Welcome to Like a Latte, what can I get for you?"

"Oh, hey Mio," said a voice. A terribly familiar voice. A terribly familiar and incredibly deep and sexy voice.

Mio's eyes shot up and met the face that had haunted his dreams all these years. *Ok, stop being dramatic*, he told himself sternly, *not even*.

Still. In front of him stood Elliot and he looked incredible. He'd been tall and lanky as a teenager. The type of kid coaches tried to get to try out for basketball even though he was clumsy and completely uninterested in sports. He'd filled out since Mio had last seen him—his shoulders were a little broader and his body more solid than it used to be. His face had gotten more angular, his jaw prominent and free of facial hair. He wore a peacoat over jeans and a button down like he was auditioning to be a sexy young professor with black framed glasses. His gray eyes were watching Mio and his mouth was split into a grin. He looked happy and relaxed, comfortable in his skin.

Mio stifled a groan. His heart flip flopped around, partly out of delight at seeing the guy and partly out of embarrassment that their meeting was taking place while

Mio was dressed in an old t-shirt and an unflattering green apron.

And could Elliot be any straighter looking? He would probably announce his engagement to some beautiful, smart scientist at any moment. That haircut... Sure Mio wore his hair styled to a T and he wouldn't expect every gay guy to do that, but Elliot's short, crisp, no-nonsense cut screamed heterosexuality.

A hard jab in his side made him jerk back into the moment. He shot a look over his shoulder in time to see the high schooler he'd called take his spot at the espresso machine. *Great. No escape there. Also did the kid just jab him? What the hell?*

"Um, Mio?"

Mio looked back at Elliot. Elliot was looking uncertain, his grin gone.

"Hey Elliot," said Mio, snapping back into his ludicrously outgoing work persona. "What a surprise to see you here!"

Elliot's smile was back.

A smile that did things to Mio's insides. Jello-y things.

"Didn't Agnes tell you I was back?"

"Oh yeah, that's right. She did mention something about you maybe stopping by to say hi. I can't really chat, we're swamped," Mio was talking a mile a minute. He could hear it but was helpless to stop.

"Oh. Yeah, you are busy."

Elliot looked...disappointed?

Mio's heart clenched. "I might be able to take a break soon. And Agnes is here, right over there in that corner. Why don't I bring you guys out some coffee and snickerdoodles while you wait for me?"

"How'd you remember I like snickerdoodles?"

I remember everything. He didn't say it out loud because they hadn't seen each other in years, and he was determined to not be a creeper. He also didn't remark on how Elliot had always smelled like the cinnamon sugar cookie and when they'd kissed, that one time they'd kissed, he'd tasted like them too. Instead Mio laughed a little too loudly. Someone tapped his shoulder. It was Jenny, back from the bathroom. "Better get back to my station. I'll be over soon with the goods. No charge."

This last part he said to Jenny. She gave him a look that he chose not to pay any attention to. He booted the other kid out of his spot and set about brewing a fresh pot of coffee while prepping an order of four peppermint mochas, each with a different type of milk.

In no way was he watching Elliot out of the corner of his eye. He wasn't watching Elliot as he put some money in the tip jar. Or while he strolled over to Agnes. He definitely wasn't watching when he greeted Agnes and she pushed aside her notebooks to make room for him at the table. Nor when Elliot half turned his chair so his back wasn't to the counter. Mio definitely wasn't watching that happen.

❄

Mio's break came and went without a chance for him to step away from the counter. He'd had to give the coffees and cookies to another coworker to deliver, drowning as he was in drink tickets. He watched Elliot and Agnes chatting in his periphery, trying, and failing, not to stew with jealousy. When Elliot got up to leave, he said something, but Mio couldn't hear anything over the espresso machine. Mio waved goodbye and smiled and hoped it made sense with whatever Elliot told him.

Then Mio watched him go, his long peacoat snug on his body, his neck wrapped in a steel gray handknit scarf that matched his eyes, his skinny jeans protected by snow boots. Elliot could easily be a model for hipster men's outerwear. The nerdy man's guide to staying warm in harsh climates.

Even though he was busy, his mind was free and it was now impossible for him not to think about Elliot.

He'd met Elliot the same year he'd realized he was gay. He'd discovered this new aspect of his sexuality while reading a book at the library about a prince who falls in love with a knight instead of the princess everyone thinks he'll fall in love with. He was so excited, he told his mom right away and she was so excited about it, he told Agnes. Agnes was less excited, but more because she still didn't know she was asexual and because she was kind of a pill of a ten-year-old than because she was mad about him being gay. In fact, she got mad when she found out she couldn't also be a gay boy because she didn't identify as a boy. The whole family ended up on an exploration of sexuality and identity that transformed their Christmas plans in the most magical way possible. Certainly one of their most memorable bonding moments as a family.

Then it was New Year's and he and Agnes convinced an older cousin to let them watch *When Harry Met Sally* for the first time. As the movie reached its romantic climax and the clock edged towards midnight, Mio wished for his own romantic moment. He wished for a boyfriend to start the New Year with—someone to kiss at midnight, someone who he loved and who loved him.

No boyfriend magically appeared that year.

When school started up again, Mio told his friends he was gay. They, being somewhere between eleven and thirteen years old, had mixed reactions. Some thought they knew that already, a few were a-holes who thought Mio would have a crush on them now, and a lot of dumb questions were asked.

It also happened to be the day Elliot showed up at his school. His parents had moved to the area over the holidays and Elliot was the lone new kid, forced to start school in the middle of the year. He'd walked into the classroom wearing a *Star Wars* t-shirt and baggy jeans, his hair wet from the snow outside and his expression a mask under which the fear peaked through. He sat down in the only available spot, which happened to be next to Mio.

Mio looked over at Elliot and Elliot slowly looked back at him. He still remembered the first words he said. "Hi, I'm Mio. This is an ok school, but you'd better stick with my group. Also, I'm gay so you'd better be cool with that."

At first Elliot blinked, clearly not sure what to make of Mio's declarations. Then Mio grinned and Elliot smiled back, his whole face lighting up and making Mio's heart pound faster. "Yeah, that's cool," he'd said and that was that. The next five years were the Mio and Elliot show, with a back-up chorus.

Mio smiled as he remembered the hours spent just hanging out. His parents were the ones who were away the most so his house was the unofficial group headquarters. Most days after school they sat down in the basement, watching *Grease*, battling at Guitar Hero, and playing endless games of Never Have I Ever. Mio usually won those games. He might be out, but he had trouble finding other guys who were also out, especially in high school. Plus, he was kind of desperately in love with Elliot and didn't want to jeopardize the potential for something to happen with his crush. Even though Elliot went out with girls and took girls to the dances and generally seemed *very* straight most of the time.

Because there were times when it was just the two of them, away from all the pressures of their friends and family, away from high school and society, that Mio wondered if Elliot might be bi curious. Elliot would ask him questions about attraction and what he liked about guys. He'd ask what was involved in gay sex and Mio, desperate to talk to anyone about this, would spout off the stuff he'd learned from the internet. Fan fiction mostly, with a few forays into more medical descriptions and frequent sidetracks to porn sites. Elliot wasn't weirded out or anything by what Mio told him. He did what Elliot usually did—he listened carefully and asked well thought out questions, like it was the most fascinating thing he'd ever heard about and he wanted to know everything. That was Elliot's way.

And then there was the moment when they were leaving for college, the moment that changed them. It was the end of their post-graduation summer. The past week had been filled with goodbyes that felt like forever. Now Mio was adding the last of his stuff to cardboard boxes and trying to keep everything in some semblance of order.

A light knock on the open door startled him and he looked up to see Elliot standing in his room, wearing a serious expression.

"Hey," said Mio, straightening up, a box popping open as he did so. "I thought you were packing today?"

Elliot shook his head. He went right to Mio's bed and threw himself back on it, despite the fact Mio had carefully sorted piles of clothes sitting on top of said bed. "I got everything at Mom's but then my dad decided to go on some work trip without telling us and I can't get my stuff from his house until tomorrow, literally the day I'm moving in. Which sucks."

Mio frowned, both at the situation and at Elliot lying on his folded clean clothes. Elliot's parents had undergone a nasty divorce shortly after moving and Elliot had been dealing with the fall out ever since. "Yeah, that sucks. What're you gonna do?"

"I guess I'm going to be extra busy all day tomorrow. What else can I do?"

They were supposed to meet up the next day to have

one final mid-afternoon breakfast at their favorite diner, Grungies. Mio had been looking forward to it and dreading it in equal measure. He'd planned to tell Elliot how he felt about him, that he liked him as more than a friend and totally understood if Elliot didn't feel the same way. Mio needed to know if they had any chance. He needed a clean start at college. He needed to know for certain a relationship with Elliot wasn't going to happen so he didn't spend another four years wanting and wondering. He broached the subject as casually as he could. "So, I take it, breakfast is off?"

Elliot sat up. "Yeah, sorry man. I can't swing it with everything else I have to do."

"No problem," said Mio, turning back to his closet. He pulled the next shirt off the hanger with more force than necessary.

He didn't know how they ended up so close. One moment Elliot was on his bed and the next he was standing behind him, reaching out a hand to gently turn him around. Mio turned, even though he didn't want Elliot to see how pained his expression was. He was going to miss Elliot so much, more than he could say aloud, and it was all welling up inside. He missed him now while he was still here, standing in front of him.

"Hey," said Elliot, and his voice was soft.

Mio looked up at him and knew he was doing a terrible job of controlling his emotions. His entire being was screaming he loved Elliot and he couldn't imagine Elliot didn't see it. It was right there, right on the surface.

Whatever else Elliot might have been about to say to him, whatever else might have happened in that moment, didn't. What did happen was Mio leaned in and kissed him. He closed the gap, closed his eyes, bumped his mouth against Elliot's and stayed there.

It wasn't an elegant kiss. It wasn't the desperate,

devouring kissing Mio had always imagined. In fact, the instant their lips touched, Mio froze, wondering what the hell he was doing.

Elliot seemed frozen too. Then, for a moment, a moment so brief Mio knew he imagined it, Elliot kissed him back.

The moment was gone, and Mio's mom was calling to him up the stairs.

Mio would have been happy to tell his mom he was busy, to close the door and get it on with Elliot right on top of his piles of clothing. But, at the sound, Elliot jumped back, literally jumped and then backed away from Mio until he ran into the dresser by the door.

The look on Elliot's face was so confused, so alarmed, Mio could only describe it as stricken. He thought his heart would break. And then Elliot said, in a desperate voice, "I can't do this. I have to go. Bye Mio."

And he was gone. Mio didn't see him again before he left for college. He didn't see him when they were home for Christmas break. He heard from other friends Elliot went with his mom to visit family out of state and wouldn't be back before Mio's school started up again. Then, over the following summer, Elliot had an internship that required him to stay on campus. After that, Mio stopped asking, stopped wondering why Elliot wasn't around, and tried to get himself to stop caring. As his own classes and general life busyness amped up, it became easier to forget his friend of five years had freaked out and ghosted him completely. That was, until today, two days after Christmas, when he'd suddenly strolled back into Mio's life, looking like nerdy sex on a stick.

Hours, possibly years, later, Mio's shift was over. The rush of customers had slowed down substantially and the closers were cleaning up. He punched out and took off his apron with a heavy sigh. It needed to be washed again.

He'd spilled hot coffee all over it and then wiped coffee grounds covered hands on it and the result was a rather smelly, crunchy mess.

He shook out what he could over the trash and balled it up before going in search of Agnes. She was still in her corner seat, wrapped in a wool poncho and staring intently at her computer screen.

"You ready?" he asked her.

She blinked up at him. "What's that? Oh. Yeah."

Mio contained himself until they'd traipsed through the snow to his car. Usually he'd put up a brotherly stink about having to give her a ride home, but today he needed information from her and he needed it soon.

"So," he started, after he'd cleared enough of the windshield to see where he was going, "What did you and Elliot talk about?"

He could feel Agnes' stare. He turned his head and met that stare. "What? I can't ask about your conversation?"

Agnes snorted. "I thought you didn't want to see him."

"I didn't. I don't. I don't care what Elliot's up to. Just making conversation," Mio protested immediately and too quickly to believe himself, let alone get past Agnes' shrewd intelligence.

Silence. Mio grew more anxious. He didn't rush Agnes, knowing she was likely to shut down and not tell him anything. But he wanted to know and he wanted to know badly. Maybe she'd decided not to tell him at all.

Then she spoke. "He's out, you know."

Mio blinked and then frowned. He thought he knew what she meant but it didn't add up. "What?"

"He's out. He's openly bisexual. And single, because I know you'll want to know that."

"I don't care," said Mio slowly, still not convincing anyone. He wanted to not care. Although, he did want to be angry that *now* Elliot was open about his sexuality, not when Mio was throwing himself at him. Oh no, it was only after being away from Mio for four years that Elliot was now admitting his bisexuality.

He knew he wasn't being fair. After all, he'd met Elliot's parents and various members of his extended family over the years. He knew what they were like and knew what Elliot faced in the journey to self-discovery. Elliot would not have been able to run home, full of excitement, and tell his mom all about his queerness and have her be happy for him. Still, if he couldn't be petty and hurt at the holidays, when could he be?

Agnes didn't respond to Mio's protest. She fiddled with the controls in a futile effort to get more heat out of the temperamental vents. "And actually, he's not just back to see his folks. He's moving back to town. He just graduated with his teaching degree. One of the high schools had someone quit suddenly and is desperate for a new chemistry teacher. So, he has a job lined up to start in January. Seems like he's sticking around for a while."

Agnes didn't tell him this in a way to suggest Mio should use the opportunity to try something with Elliot. She simply told him about it in her Agnes way, clearly and simply. He knew Agnes wanted him to be happy but she didn't want to know anything about Mio's love life, especially where the physical parts were involved. It was the same line she gave to all her friends when they got into relationships. She would support them and be happy for them but under no circumstances were they to share details of their sex lives with her.

"Does he have his own place?" asked Mio, not in any way imagining Elliot moving in with him and sharing his bed. He stopped at the light in the middle of town, pumping the brakes in case of ice.

"No. I think he's staying with his mom and her new husband for a while."

"That's rough," said Mio. Elliot's mom was fine but not too accepting of people's identities and differences.

"Elliot says she's changed. She met this guy from Korea, found out what it was like to be on the receiving end of parental disapproval from his mother, and has changed her whole outlook on life. Elliot said he told her about his ex-boyfriend and everything," Agnes said as she searched through her bag for something, talking over the sound of her rustling papers.

"Huh," Mio didn't know what to say to that. Mostly he was stuck on the Elliot's ex-boyfriend part of it. Sure, he'd seen Elliot with other girls before but another guy? Someone he'd probably done all the things with that high school Mio was dying to try out?

He pulled up to their parents' house and put the car in park. Agnes didn't look up from her bag.

"Uh, we're here?"

"Hold your horses," said Agnes. She pulled out a clump of wadded paper, peeled off a sheet and handed it to him.

"What's this?"

"Elliot's phone number. He didn't say to give it to you but I am a master of human interactions and I knew that's what he meant. Also, he was looking at you when he gave it to me. Anyway, call him. I'm not going to be in the middle of this love mess any longer than I have to be."

Agnes pulled her hat firmly over her ears and bounced out of the car. Mio watched her go, wondering what the hell he was going to do.

CHAPTER 3

❄

December 30th

A few days passed before he saw Elliot again. Not that Mio was counting or anything. Not that he was painfully aware of each passage of each minute since he'd last seen the guy. Oh no, Mio was determined to be calm and casual and not obsess over Elliot being bi and single.

It was in this state of elaborate denial he showed up to his morning shift at the cafe. He spent the whole eight hours annoyed with people for ordering stupid holiday drinks with stupid elaborate whipped cream toppings that took forever to remember, let alone execute. He tried to keep it all inside but he could tell his coworkers were feeding off his bad energy and then he felt bad about that.

All in all, it was a relief when he reached the end of his shift and clocked out. Agnes wasn't in. According to their mother, she was out ice skating or sledding or doing something equally un-Agnes like with her friends from high school. All Mio had to return to was a cold, lonely apartment and an empty fridge. He'd left his Christmas lights plugged into an outlet that was unpredictable at best and downright dangerous at worst. There was a good chance they'd shorted out during the day, taking the rest of his electricity with them. He had a sinking suspicion his afternoon plans would involve sitting in the dark, wrapped in every blanket he owned, eating a moderately thawed burrito.

Mio knew he was being dramatic. It wasn't like he didn't have friends or couldn't raid his parents' house for food. It was the whole crappy apartment and being alone and working on New Year's Eve situation that made him cranky. His bad mood had nothing to do with not seeing Elliot. Nothing.

He kept telling himself that while he walked outside to get in his shitty car and engage in a hard-core mope session. He wasn't even halfway through the haphazardly plowed parking lot when Elliot pulled up in a black jeep. Mio stopped, even though he wasn't wearing boots and the snow would soak through his work shoes in a second.

Elliot turned the car off and hopped out, jogging over to Mio. Since when did Elliot jog? The heaviness of his breathing after those few strides answered the question — never. "Mio," Elliot began, gasping slightly.

"Hey Elliot," said Mio, not sure what was going on. Rationally, he knew what was happening. Elliot was coming to get coffee and they were running into each other by chance. He couldn't stop his heart from wanting Elliot to be there to see him. "Sorry, I can't get your coffee and snickerdoodle today. I'm just leaving work but I'm sure someone else can help you."

Elliot shook his head. "I know you're leaving work. That's why I'm here."

Mio blinked up at him, not sure what to make of this statement.

Elliot shook his head again. "That came out weird. I mean I came in yesterday and you weren't there, so I asked when you'd be around today. Your coworker Jenny asked me if I was a stalker and I had to prove I wasn't before she'd tell me. I came to see if you want to grab an early bird special at Grungies."

Mio's heart fluttered and his throat constricted. He knew his feet were frozen into his shoes but he couldn't feel them with all the heat flooding through his body. He knew it was probably just an invitation to hang out and catch up but his heart didn't seem to get the message. All these years when Elliot hadn't sent him so much as a text. If Mio was going to do this, he had to tread very carefully and not expect anything. He knew Elliot couldn't give him what he wanted.

He nodded. "Just like old times?" he said, his voice light.

A frown crossed Elliot's face and then was gone. "Yeah, I guess. Like old times."

❄

It was like a scene in a small-town Christmas movie. Grungies, the favorite haunt of teenagers and senior citizens, was an old-style diner that served American classics and all-day breakfast. Located in the heart of downtown, a few blocks from the cafe, it overlooked the bustle of post-holiday activity. Inside the place was done to the nine—evergreen boughs adorned the counter, lights wrapped around the barstools and along the backs of the booths, and special holiday versions of everything dominated the menu. Despite being four in the afternoon, the place was hopping and it took a few minutes for them to get a table.

They sat in the booth where they'd sat so many times in high school. The waiter, who'd been there forever, remembered Elliot, winked at Mio, and asked if they wanted their usual. Elliot laughed saying he didn't even remember his usual, so sure. Soon the table in front of them was piled with pancakes, bacon, scrambled eggs, and tall glasses of orange juice.

"Huh," said Elliot as he stared at the abundance of dishes. "I forgot how much we loved breakfast food when we were in high school."

"We were obsessed. I mean, I still am. Give me breakfast any time of day and I'll be a happy camper," said Mio as he dug into the scrambled eggs.

Elliot smiled and set to work coating a pancake in maple syrup.

They ate in silence for a few minutes, serenaded by a jazz remix of "Jingle Bells."

Mio felt like he needed to say something, the need growing as his hunger receded. He'd always been the more talkative of the two of them. Elliot could hold a silence for hours. He went for something he thought would be simple and casual. Friends catching up. "So, how was college?"

Elliot looked at him and then back down at the pancake piece he was cutting. "Um, it was good. You know the usual classes and stuff. Late nights, too much pizza and beer, trying to get my roommates to clean the bathroom once in a while."

Mio nodded. "Oh," he said and looked down at his own plate, wondering if this whole conversation was going to be awkward as shit.

"And then less good this last year, when I found out my boyfriend had never thought we were official and literally had a rotating schedule of hook-ups. Which I was a part of."

Mio never thought he'd hear those words come out of Elliot's mouth. He'd imagined it, of course. That Elliot would be calling *him* boyfriend. But to hear him talk about his ex so casually? Or maybe not so casually? Of all the things he could have told him about the years since they'd seen each other, he'd opted to start with the guy he'd dated. Nope, Mio was not reading anything into it.

"Well, shit," he said.

"I was Wednesday and every other Saturday."

"Whoa."

"I think the weirdest part was, I didn't notice I only saw him Wednesday and every other Saturday, you know? I was so busy with everything else that, until one of my roommates pointed it out, I honestly didn't know," Elliot said. His voice was calm with a little edge of humor. Evidently, he'd been through this a few times and might be on the upswing of the heartbreak.

"That sucks," said Mio and then was out of platitudes. Maybe he should threaten to go beat up the cheating ex? No, the Elliot he'd known wouldn't have appreciated it. But then, why was he telling him this?

"Yeah, it did for a while. But then I realized I didn't love him. Most of the time I hadn't even liked him all that much." Elliot took a bite of the syrup-soaked pancake. He chewed carefully and Mio watched him while also trying to look totally engrossed in his own meal.

"What about you?" asked Elliot.

Mio raised his eyebrows. "Did I date someone with a rotating schedule of boyfriends? Or did I have a rotating schedule of boyfriends?"

Elliot frowned at him.

Mio couldn't help it. He was on a roll and he really, desperately, wanted to make Elliot laugh. He wanted to see if that easy friendship of theirs was still available. "Can't say I did either," he said with a forlorn shake of his head. "Although, I did date Danny Engleman for a hot second."

That caught Elliot off guard. "What? Danny Engleman?"

Mio nodded solemnly. "Yes. I even went to his frat's formal with him. Awkward as fuck, let me tell you."

"Because you were the only gay couple there?"

"Because Danny doesn't really talk about things. He just kind of grunts."

"Oh. I thought that was only when he played football."

Mio shook his head and sighed dramatically. "I'm afraid not."

"So, what happened?"

"Between me and Danny? Well. There we were dancing the night away when the frat president gets up on stage, takes the DJ's mic, and confesses his undying love. To Danny. And, you know when this happens in movies? Yeah, they never show you what happens to the date. Like I'm just standing there, in a freaking spotlight, mind you, while my date literally gets publicly proposed to by another guy."

Elliot's shoulders had started to shake at the beginning of the story and by the end he didn't seem able to stifle the laugh any longer. It burst out of him, loud and full of delight.

Mio couldn't help joining in.

Elliot suddenly stopped and looked stricken. "I'm sorry, Mio. It's probably not funny for you."

"Oh no, it's funny. Like it wasn't at the time, sure. But it makes a great story."

Elliot grinned and frowned simultaneously. "Huh. I never would have guessed Danny's gay."

"It's always the ones you don't expect," said Mio, waggling his eyebrows. He meant it to be light, but Elliot's grin slipped away.

"I guess Agnes told you I'm bi?"

Mio had a horrible thought. "Did you not want her to tell me?"

"No, no nothing like that," said Elliot quickly. He seemed to retreat back into the booth.

Mio guessed he was right about Elliot's coming out and

it hadn't been all loving acceptance and family discussions about identity. "I wish I could say Danny was my biggest mistake. But then I met Ryan."

"Oh? And who was Ryan?" Elliot's smile slowly returned.

"Ryan was my boyfriend for all of two hours."

"What?"

Mio nodded, keeping a straight face. "True story. We met at the beginning of a party and hit it off immediately. Two hours later we had a messy public break up and I couldn't tell you why. Only that, over the course of those two hours we went through all the relationship stages. I think I asked him to move in with me."

Elliot laughed again. "Let me guess, it was a New Year's party?"

Mio picked up his glass of orange juice like it was a shot he was about to down. "Yep. It was a New Year's party."

"And you broke up before midnight?"

Mio nodded as he drained his juice. He set the glass down with a gratifying thud. "Sure did. At 11:57pm."

Elliot knew all about his New Year's wish. His whole friend group had known but it was something he and Elliot talked about when it was just them. While he'd joke about it with the rest of the group, Mio had confessed to Elliot how serious he was. How he wished for just this one little piece of holiday magic year after year and it never came.

"So, you've never…" Elliot began.

"Been kissed at midnight? Not yet."

Silence descended. Mio fiddled with his fork and contemplated eating another piece of toast. He glanced up and met Elliot's gaze, his eyes filled with consternation and pain.

"Mio," said Elliot as he set down his knife and fork.

"Yeah?" said Mio slowly, putting down his own utensils.

Mio would have said he was prepared for anything Elliot could say to him. He'd thought he'd been through the full ringer already with the guy and there couldn't possibly be anything else. But Elliot caught him off guard.

"Mio, I am so sorry," Elliot began, not breaking eye contact, "I freaked out. I was confused and I shouldn't have run away. You were my best friend and I so desperately didn't want to lose our friendship that I screwed up and lost you. I've wanted to text you or email you so many times over the last four years but nothing seemed like it was enough to make up for what I did. And then I was too paralyzed to do anything at all. I…I'm sorry."

Mio heard and felt that there were some words unsaid in the apology. There was more Elliot wanted to share but he held back and Mio felt the soreness of the subject so acutely he didn't want to poke at it. Still, it was what he'd been waiting for, if he were to be truly honest with himself. He knew, if Elliot had asked him out for real, he'd have said ok. He'd hook up with Elliot, if he asked, but there would always be that something missing, something wrong. The apology, the acknowledgment of Mio's pain was what he needed. He swallowed hard to push down the lump in his throat. "You hurt me," he said, his voice small.

Elliot blinked rapidly. "I know. I wish I could go back and not do it because, not having you as a friend these past four years… I don't ever want to go through that again."

Mio wiped at his eyes, cursing himself for crying so damn easily. "Me neither. I missed you."

"I missed you." Elliot leaned toward him across the table, his elbow dangerously close to the butter dish, a piece of his dark hair falling over his forehead.

Mio had reached a state beyond confusion. He could feel the moment, the whole momentousness of the moment. If there was ever a time when he could confess his real feelings—that he wanted them to be more than friends—this was it. But Elliot had said he missed Mio as a friend. He'd said Mio's kiss had confused him, confused him enough to not talk to him for years. What if all Elliot was offering now was the friendship they'd had before the kiss? If Mio said he wanted more and Elliot didn't, they'd be right back where they were. It was better having him as a friend than not having him at all, right?

He didn't know. All he did know was he couldn't put himself out there and risk the hurt again. "Friends?" he said with a smile he hoped looked more real than it felt.

"Sure…" Elliot dragged out the word, clearly preparing to follow it up.

"Good because Agnes told me you're going to be sticking around town. And you got a job as a chem teacher? How'd that happen?" Mio could hear himself rambling. He still sensed Elliot wanted to tell him something else, something about them being friends. He didn't know what it was but he highly doubted Elliot was about to express his undying love so whatever it was, it was better left unsaid.

Elliot frowned and blinked at him a few times. He must have come to the same conclusion because when he spoke, it was about how he ended up studying chemistry and getting his teaching degree. This led to a recount of high school classes and adventures. Soon they were laughing and throwing digs back and forth like no time at all had passed. The moment was gone and with it the awkwardness of unspoken words and repressed emotions. At least for Mio. He didn't know what Elliot was thinking and had not only missed but had deliberately shied away from his chance to find out.

After they'd cleared away most of the food and outstayed many of the other diners, Elliot picked up the check, despite Mio's many protests.

"You'll just have to buy me afternoon breakfast the next

time we hang out," said Elliot, winding his hand knit scarf around his neck.

Hang out. Friends.

Mio didn't know why his brain was having such a hard time wrapping itself around this concept. They were friends.

On the walk back to the cafe, Elliot asked, "What was going on with you earlier today? When I pulled up you looked like you'd just kicked a puppy."

"Like I'd what? How do you know what someone who's just kicked a puppy looks like? Is this a new habit of yours? Because if it is, I'm going to have to rethink the whole friendship bit."

Elliot laughed. "It's an expression. You looked upset, ok?"

"I know. Just messing with you," said Mio. Then he let out a deep, genuine sigh. "I have to work tomorrow night."

Elliot stopped walking.

Mio took a few more steps, realized Elliot was not going to resume walking, and turned to him. They were right in the middle of the sidewalk, causing other people to swerve around them.

"But it's New Year's," said Elliot, looking down at him.

"I know." They were attracting dirty looks from passersby. Mio grabbed the sleeve of Elliot's coat and pulled him towards the stores and out of the way. "And everyone wanted it off. I took off Christmas Eve so we could go to my grandma's. Then I figured, what did it matter if I worked New Year's or not. It's not like I have any plans besides hanging out with Agnes, watching movies, and getting drunk."

"Then why'd you look like the world was ending?"

"Now see, that's a better metaphor."

"Simile."

"Whatever." Mio looked around at the other people

strolling through the snow in cheery groups. The sun was fading and the trees were lit up with hundreds of tiny clear Christmas lights. A crisp, chilly evening awaited, laced with holiday magic and spiced wine. And here he stood with someone who, up until three days ago, he'd thought he would never see again. Something about it all, the ambiance of it all, made him not deflect and joke but to say the truth, the vulnerable truth. "Every year I think it will be different. This is my year. It's not even about having a boyfriend to kiss at midnight…well, it is, but it's more than that. I always think, when midnight hits, things will be different, my life will be different. I'll know what to do, what to be. But then it comes and goes and on January 1st it's still just confused old me. It's stupid."

"It's not stupid," said Elliot, his voice firm.

Mio met Elliot's gaze, his warm gray eyes, his concern, the set determination of his jaw. "Yeah, it is. And this year I'm giving up on the whole thing. That's why I agreed to work tomorrow night. Because I'm done wishing."

Saying it aloud felt final. His eyes pricked with tears as he turned and continued walking. Elliot caught up with him and they walked in silence. When they reached the cafe, Mio said a quick goodbye. Elliot looked again like he wanted to say something more but Mio didn't wait. He got into his car and drove off. In the rear view mirror he watched Elliot get into his jeep and leave, heading in the opposite direction.

Mio tried to decide if this unexpected interlude had made him feel better or worse. It had certainly wrung him out emotionally, confused him, made him hope, and reminded him, in no uncertain terms, that he was still very into Elliot.

CHAPTER 4

❄

*D*ecember 31st

If Mio had thought December 30th was miserable, it was nothing compared to the 31st. It was 9pm, one hour before he could go home, lie miserably on his futon, and gripe to Agnes about all the happy people and their stupid midnight kisses. The cafe was full of customers who'd started their alcohol-based celebrations early and the friends of those people who were trying to reign them back so they could keep partying. It wasn't that Mio didn't like the customers. Everyone was in good spirits—celebrating and tipsy and overly enthusiastic in their praise of his latte art and whipped cream masterpieces. On any other day, the mood in the place would have perked him up and made the time fly by, reminding him that he actually did kind of like working there. Not tonight. Tonight was New Year's Eve. Tonight was the night he was supposed to meet his true love, to celebrate the start of something new, to have a boyfriend to kiss at midnight.

"So, are you going to glare at the clock all night or what?"

Mio jumped, spilling coffee beans everywhere, and turned to stare at Jenny, his fellow New Year's Eve hostage. She was leaning against the counter, her back to the register.

"Maybe?" he said honestly. They were the only two staff left, everyone else having skipped out when the orders slowed down.

"Yeah, this wasn't my first choice for New Year's either," said Jenny, crossing her arms over her chest.

Mio, in all his personal angst, could still recognize a cry for conversation when he heard one. "Oh no, did your plans fall through?"

"Yeah, but I don't want to talk about it."

"Oh." *Never mind then.*

Awkward silence punctuated by the laughter and drunken giggles of the customers. The snow had started falling again—big fluffy flakes that were beautiful to watch and a pain in the ass to drive in. Mio's mind drifted to Elliot. What was he up to tonight? He hadn't said anything about his New Year's plans, which probably meant he was going to a party or had a date or something he couldn't, or wouldn't, invite Mio to. His chest hurt.

"My parents always throw the most ridiculous, out of control New Year's party," he blurted out, desperate for something to kill the silence and his painful imagination. "They invite all their friends, coworkers, and some family members and then get plastered and destroy the house like frat boys."

"Ew," Jenny said. "How embarrassing."

"It really is," Mio agreed.

"You don't have to go to that, do you?" she asked, her eyes wide and her face full of dramatic horror.

Mio shook his head emphatically. "No. My sister and I went one year and we were scarred for life. Now we do our own thing on New Year's Eve and then bring coffee and breakfast to the hungover adults in the morning."

"Wow, that's nice of you."

It was nice of them. Especially after the year when they were in high school and arrived home to find half their teachers passed out on the living room furniture. Most of them were fully clothed, thankfully.

Jenny burst through his reminiscences of New Year's past. "Ok, fine, I'll tell you about it. Just promise you won't tell anyone, ok?"

Mio frowned. He had no idea what she was talking about or who he was going to tell. There were still coffee beans on the floor. "Um."

Jenny was already telling her tale of woe.

Mio half listened as he cleaned up the coffee. It had something to do with a boyfriend who may or may not be an ex, a couple of evil parents who'd confiscated her phone, a sister who wouldn't drive her places, and friends who were being truly heinous at the moment. He found himself standing and listening more intently, drawn into the wild narrative. Jenny was a great storyteller and her life drama rivaled some of the *Real Housewives*. The rest of the hour passed in relative ease.

"Oh shit," said Jenny, "It's time to close."

Mio blinked at the clock, whose presence he'd briefly forgotten about. It was, indeed, time to close.

"Thanks for listening, Mio. And please don't tell anyone, ok?"

"Jenny, I mean this from the bottom of my heart, that shit belongs on a reality show," Mio said, feeling better than he had all day.

Jenny's face split into a huge smile. "Aw, that's sweet of you to say."

"But I won't tell anyone," Mio promised solemnly.

They set to work letting the last few groups know they

were closing, scrubbing every coffee stained surface, and setting the espresso machine to clean. Finally, everything was sparkling and they were free to go. Mio followed Jenny across the freshly mopped floor, thinking maybe this wasn't such a bad night after all.

Then a thought, one he'd been stubbornly ignoring all day, bullied its way into his mind. What if Elliot was waiting for him in the parking lot? What if he was standing by his black jeep, the way he had been the day before, Mariah Carey blasting out of the speakers, waiting to whisk Mio away to a magical New Year's night?

Mio's heart pounded. He didn't dare look around until he'd secured the locks on the cafe doors, not wanting to ruin the magic that was already making a home in his imagination. His throat constricted; his bare hands shook on the lock. He wanted so badly for Elliot to be there, even while his realistic brain told him it wouldn't happen. He and Elliot were friends again and that was good but he shouldn't go wishing for more. Just because they were both attracted to guys didn't mean anything would ever happen between them. So what if Elliot was back in town for good? It simply meant they had more time to renew their friendship.

When he did turn around, Mio's emotions were all over the place. The whole episode lasted about fifteen seconds and an eon in his head.

The snow blanketed parking lot still had a few cars in it. One started its engine and turned on its lights. For a moment he imagined it to be Elliot's jeep. But it was a red suburban and, as it peeled out of the parking lot, Jenny yelled "Happy New Year" at him from the open window.

Elliot was nowhere to be seen. No jeep, no figure standing in the snow, waiting for him. No Mariah Carey. No midnight kiss for Mio.

He got in his car, persuaded it to turn on, and blinked

back the hot tears. Why had he been so stupid as to keep this foolish wish going? And to think Elliot showing up a few days before New Year's had been what, a sign? He'd known him for years and there'd never been any indication before that it was Elliot who would make his New Year's wish come true. Why did he think this year was any different?

He wasn't a kid anymore. He needed to grow up and move on.

The cold air blasting out of the vents had a tinge of warmth to it now. He needed to get over his sad sack self and go home. After all, Agnes was waiting for him and he couldn't let her down.

He peeled out of the parking lot, too fast for the amount of snow on the ground, and his car fishtailed wildly. Heart pounding, he pumped the brakes and took a few deep breaths before creeping forward into the busy downtown street.

Once the car was under control, he navigated to his contacts and called Agnes. It took her longer than he thought necessary to answer the phone. She was probably in the bathroom.

"Yo," she said. There was some noise in the background. Music and the distinct clink of cutlery against porcelain.

"Did you start without me?" Mio asked, coming across more stricken than he intended. He honestly didn't know how this night could get any worse.

"Just a snack," said Agnes and he could hear the eye roll in her voice. "It's after ten, you know."

Mio shook his head to clear it. "Yeah, right, sorry. Look, I'm on my way home but I'm going to stop and get some booze."

Agnes made a sound like a choked hiccup. "You don't need to do that."

Mio paused. "Uh, yes I do. In case you haven't noticed,

all I have in the apartment is half a bottle of ok white wine and a forty of Bud Light Lime. That's not going to get us far."

"We're good. You don't need to stop," Agnes said in a very un-Agnes way. She was all about the cocktails and should have had a comment about the forty of terrible beer.

"Ok," Mio said slowly, not sure what to make of his sister's reaction. Maybe she wasn't at his apartment at all but had gone out with friends. Maybe he'd arrive back to a cold, dark, cheerless place, there to spend the night in misery. No. He wasn't going to think that of Agnes. She wouldn't do that to him. Then he remembered. "Oh right, you swiped some of the booze from the parents' party."

"Yeah, right," Agnes said in a distracted tone. "Well, see you soon."

She hung up.

Mio was too filled with self-pity and despair to dwell on Agnes' weirdness. He turned on the radio and tried not to cry along to "Let It Snow."

One harrowing trip through the snow and downtown revelers later, Mio pulled up to his dark, silent apartment building. In recognition of the holiday, the complex management had put up a sign warning anyone who hung outdoor decorations or lights that these would immediately get taken down and disposed of. Usually, he gave the sign the middle finger. Tonight, it rather fit with his mood.

Mio, when he graduated, had briefly lived with his parents. But his parents had taken to the empty nester life in a big way and were not prepared to have an adult offspring around all the time. Even having Agnes with them for the holidays seemed to be cramping their style, her assessment, but an astute one. So, Mio had found the only place in town he could afford with his meager barista salary. It was an apartment complex a little out of town with yellow vinyl siding and landlords who spent more on outdoor appearance than on fixing things in the interior. Like most of the residents, Mio wasn't in any position to complain. Still, it wasn't the cute little house he imagined having some day when he became a successful... and that was where he got stuck. A successful what? What the hell did he want to do with his life?

No. He wasn't going to dwell on his lack of aspirations on top of everything else.

He entered the building, the front door slamming behind him. He checked his mail and deposited the three-day old coupons in the recycling bin. He trudged up the two flights of poorly carpeted stairs and stopped outside his door. He could hear music coming from inside. Another of Agnes' holiday mixes which meant, unlike him, she was bound and determined not to have a shitty New Year's. He was going to have to rally, dammit. Agnes may very well be the only person who loved him, and he couldn't alienate her.

Mio opened the door, preparing to cringe at the junk mail strewn card table, the dirty sweatpants he knew he'd left on the floor, the sink full of dishes, and the general smell of garbage that hadn't been taken out recently.

Instead he was greeted by soft lighting, music, and the delicious smell of a pine scented candle. His apartment hadn't been transformed, exactly, but it had been enhanced and cleaned. His string of holiday lights was turned on and connected, he noted, to an extension cord he certainly hadn't had before. The sweatpants were gone from the floor, the dishes were washed and stacked on the counter, the mail had all been piled neatly in a corner of the folding table, and a huge candle burned on the coffee table by the futon. The futon where Agnes lay, her face in a book. That explained her distracted tone from earlier. When Agnes was engaged in a book she was not easily, or willingly, interrupted.

"Holy shit, Agnes, did you do all this?"

Agnes set her book down and blinked at him. "Finally. I thought you were never going to get here."

Mio took off his coat. "It's barely after ten." Or so he guessed. He couldn't have spent that long being a sad sack in the car, could he?

Agnes rolled off the couch and onto her feet. "I've been waiting for forever. Now where are your keys?"

Mio laid his coat sort of neatly over the back of a chair and frowned at his sister. "Why do you need my keys?"

"So, I can drive your car?" said Agnes as though it was the most normal request in the world. She held out her hand.

Mio was having a hard time catching up. But before he could protest Agnes' sudden change in plans, the door to his tiny bathroom opened and out stepped Elliot, looking festive and delicious in a tight black t-shirt and skinny jeans with strands of gold Mardi Gras beads around his neck.

He was saying, "Hey Agnes, do you know where—"

His eyes met Mio's and he paused. He grinned and Mio could swear his heart had stopped beating.

"Mio, you're back," said Elliot and his voice was warm and excited.

Mio gripped the back of the chair harder. Elliot was there. Elliot was standing in his apartment and it was New Year's and holy shit. Elliot.

His face must have looked stunned because Elliot's expression grew somber and he shoved his hands into his pockets, causing his tight jeans to get even tighter. "I hope it's ok I'm crashing your hang out with Agnes."

Agnes, who Mio just now realized was going through

his coat pockets, snorted. "As I've told you ten thousand times, it's totally fine. Besides, I'm off."

Mio blinked and focused on her. "Where are you going? And why are you taking my car?"

"Party. And because the parents wouldn't lend me one of theirs. Don't worry, I'll take good care of it."

Mio noticed she was wearing a penguin sweatshirt and leggings, and her hair was gelled into little pink spikes. She even had on sparkly eyeshadow. For Agnes, that was as dressy as it got. "Um ok. You're going to a party?"

"Yes. Don't look so surprised."

Agnes hated most parties, so he guessed this was her way of giving him and Elliot some time alone. "Did you know you're the best sister ever?"

"Sure did," Agnes said as she triumphantly jingled the keys she'd found. "See you Elliot. Don't let my big brother get too maudlin, ok?"

"I won't," he said.

Then she was gone and Mio was left alone with Elliot.

❄

Mio went into his bedroom to change out of his work clothes, leaving Elliot to use whatever he could find in the kitchen to mix the sangria he'd brought. Mio offered to help but Elliot shooed him away.

He looked down at his stained shirt. He smelled like coffee, not unpleasant on its own, but not great when combined with dried sweat and souring milk. Time or not, he needed a shower. Luckily, the bathroom was off his bedroom. Unluckily, Agnes hadn't thought to clean up his room. That made sense for Agnes. In her mind, romantic scenes led to kissing and that was about it. In Mio's, he couldn't help looking at his bed without seeing Elliot on it, naked and writhing in desire. He pushed the thought away and hurried to tidy up the room. Meaning he shoved all the clothes in his tiny closet and forced the door shut. He tried to remember if he had condoms somewhere and then told himself to stop making assumptions. But did he?

He stood in the shower, scrubbing the cafe out of his skin and trying to get control over his runaway imagination. A few minutes ago, he'd been nearly in tears in his car and now Elliot was in his apartment and Mio was back to jumping to unfounded conclusions. Just because Elliot had shown up as a New Year's Eve surprise, it didn't mean he wanted to be anything more than friends.

What if Elliot did want something to happen between them? Maybe he wanted to move slowly. After all, the last guy who he'd dated had fucked with his head and maybe he wasn't ready for anything to happen so soon. Mio wasn't sure he himself was ready for anything to happen, not when he was finally starting to heal from the pain of Elliot's four-year avoidance of him.

His skin was turning red and his fingers were getting pruney. He got out of the shower, slathered himself with body lotion, and hurried back into his room. He forced open the closet and stared at the pile of clothes inside, wondering what the hell he should wear.

Elliot was wearing skinny jeans and a t-shirt. Is that what Mio should wear too or would it look too weird if he were mirroring Elliot's look? But how did he change it up? Overalls with nothing underneath? A snarky t-shirt and shorts? Or full on ugly Christmas sweater and sweats?

If they were going to be hanging out, he wanted to be comfortable. But he didn't want to be a slob, not when Elliot looked so cute and put together.

Finally, he decided on a cute pair of skinny jeans and a sweater tight enough to give him some shape but not uncomfortably tight. He took a deep breath by the door of his room and went back out into the living area, painfully aware of how long he'd taken to get ready.

At first, he didn't see Elliot in the kitchen and wondered frantically if he had left. But then he noticed him sitting on the futon, one leg crossed over his other knee, skimming through a book. Two large glasses of sangria sat on coasters on the coffee table, a plate of appetizers between them. Mio's stomach grumbled, reminding him he hadn't eaten since his break at four.

"You brought snacks," exclaimed Mio as he walked over to the futon.

Elliot jerked up guilty and closed the book. He set it down on the other side of himself, away from Mio. They were going to come back to that for sure.

First, though, he needed drinks and snacks. He sat down next to Elliot and dug into the appetizers.

"This looks amazing, thanks Elliot," he said.

He stuffed a cracker liberally loaded with spinach dip in his mouth before he realized Elliot was holding his glass, waiting for Mio to toast him. Mio did, laughing at himself. He swallowed and took a sip of his drink. It was light and fruity, not too sweet and not too dry, the taste of orange hitting him first, followed by the gentler cranberry. "Yum," he said.

"Glad you like it. Happy New Year's Mio," Elliot said, smiling at him.

"It certainly is getting to be that," Mio said and grabbed another snack. After he'd eaten enough to hold off starvation, he gave Elliot a smirk. "What were you reading?"

Elliot's face turned red. Goodness the man could blush. "Nothing," he said in a rush.

"Oh really? Is that why you put it on the other side of you so I wouldn't see it? Because it's nothing?"

"No... what?" Elliot was flustered and Mio loved it. He

set his drink down and leaned over him, catching him off guard and grabbing the book.

There was a moment where he was laying on top of Elliot. A moment where they were touching and he could feel Elliot's heat and feel his own heartbeat going wild. A moment where he was keenly aware of just how close he was to Elliot's dick. Then he scrambled back to his own side of the couch, paperback grasped in his hand.

He only had to glance at the cover to recognize it. It was, after all, one of his books. A rather lurid erotic romance about two men in Regency England who go to a country house party, which is really an orgy, and are having sex by chapter two. He started laughing and turned to Elliot, who looked slightly mortified. "You really are bi, aren't you?" Mio asked, trying to keep his voice light and teasing.

Elliot nodded and then started to laugh too.

When they'd calmed down, Elliot said, "I don't know why I hid the book from you. I mean, it's your book so you're bound to know what it's about. Habit I guess," he frowned. "I'm sort of out to my parents but not the rest of the family. My extended family have been around for the past week and a half and I kind of fell back into the hiding thing again. It's a hard habit to break."

He sighed and took a long drink of his sangria.

Mio's heart hurt for his friend. He wanted to storm over to Elliot's house and punch all the homophobes in their stupid faces but that wouldn't help make Elliot's family life any easier. He could say he was sorry about his situation but he didn't think Elliot wanted sympathy. Mio knew he was lucky to have a family who hadn't been anything but happy and accepting. Who were wildly dysfunctional in other ways but who didn't question him on his sexual identity or force him to hide it.

Instead he looked down at the book. The cover had two

men in regency clothing, their shirts open in long V-necks, their eyes glued to each other as they leaned in for a hot, searing kiss. "I blushed when I read this book," he said.

That drew another laugh out of Elliot. "Really? I didn't think you blushed."

Mio raised his eyebrows. "You must not have read the stable scene."

"I definitely did not." Elliot reached for the book. "Let me rectify that right now."

Mio held the book out and away from his reach. "Oh no. You are definitely not ready for that level of kink."

"Oh, I'm not, am I?"

Elliot was taller than him and had longer arms. He was about to snatch the book back when they ended up pressed together again. And once again, Mio hurried to extract himself and moved back to his end of the futon. He wasn't going to make the mistake of kissing Elliot in a moment of teasing rough housing and then lose his friend all over again.

Elliot moved back as well, slower. He set the book down on the coffee table and cleared his throat.

"Should we watch a movie?"

Mio tried to get his breathing under control. "Sure. What do you have in mind?" Not that he'd be watching much of whatever was playing. Not with Elliot this close to him. Not when they'd almost kissed. Twice.

"Agnes said you usually watch *Holiday* on New Year's," Elliot said, looking at Mio, his gray eyes running over Mio's face in a way which did nothing to calm the flames.

Mio swallowed and took a deep breath. "Yeah, she and I love that movie. Have you ever seen it?"

Elliot shook his head. "At first when Agnes suggested it, I confused it for *The Holiday* but Agnes corrected me quite adamantly on that point."

Mio laughed. "Definitely not the same movie."

"Great. I'm excited to see Agnes and Mio's favorite New Year's movie."

Mio was right. As much as he loved this movie, especially Katharine Hepburn with all her biting quips and snarky remarks, he couldn't focus on the screen. Elliot seemed absorbed it and every time he laughed or gasped, every time he so much as twitched, Mio noticed. This tension between them, this potent energy, couldn't be something only he felt, could it?

He tried to act normal. He ate the appetizers and made popcorn. He drank more sangria, savoring the taste. Normal stuff that normal people did.

Then Katharine was declaring she was running away with Cary Grant and before he knew it, the credits were rolling. *Now what?*

He switched to coverage of the Times Square ball drop where the announcers were chatting with cheering revelers. It didn't matter what was happening or who was playing their new hit single next. He barely took note of the countdown clock, moving relentlessly toward midnight. He wanted to, needed to, say something. Now.

Elliot picked up the remote and muted the TV. Mio looked over at him curiously.

Elliot turned his whole body to face him on the old futon. "Mio, there's something I have to tell you."

His heart throbbed. His brain was flashing between fantasies of their wedding and Elliot telling him he was in love with someone else. He nodded and stared down at the coffee table. He couldn't handle those gray eyes, even in the dimness of the twinkle lights.

"Do you know what I wanted to do that day at your house?" said Elliot softly.

Mio didn't need to ask which day. He knew Elliot meant the day they'd said goodbye, the day they'd kissed. He shook his head.

"I wanted to kiss you back. And when I saw you at the café, I wanted to do it again. I wanted to tell you everything. That you gave me the courage to come out when I got to college. That every guy I thought was cute I compared to you and they never quite measured up. That I was so scared you wouldn't talk to me or that you'd want to be just friends, I couldn't bring myself to see you. I don't want to be only friends with you, Mio, but I've come to realize, if that's what we are, it's better than not having you in my life at all. I've been such a coward and I've wanted to tell you how cute you are and how much I love your smile and your openness and your sense of humor—"

Mio really wanted to hear the entirety of this speech, this wonderful, unexpected, unreal, magical speech. But he was coming out of his skin and couldn't handle the tension of not touching him any longer. So he launched himself into Elliot's lap, trying to gracefully straddle him with one leg on either side of his. But, in his enthusiasm, he overshot his left leg and smacked into the wooden arm of the futon, hard. "Ow," he said, biting his lip against the pain.

"Oh my God, Mio, are you ok?" asked Elliot, his hand rubbing over Mio's leg, feeling for a bump.

Mio looked down at Elliot's hand and then up at him. "Keep doing that and I will be."

Elliot met his gaze and their faces were inches apart. Mio wrapped his arms around Elliot's neck and shifted so he was straddling him better. The shifting brought their bodies closer together and Mio heard Elliot's voice catch. If he'd had any doubts, any doubts at all, they disappeared with that little catch of Elliot's voice.

Mio leaned forward, closed his eyes, and kissed him on the lips.

They tasted like cranberry and were warm and soft, just like he remembered. His mouth opened and Elliot leaned forward, his hand that wasn't rubbing Mio's leg, coming up to cup his head and deepen the kiss. Mio felt Elliot's fingers start to tentatively explore and returned the caress, turning the gentle kiss into a deeper, desperate make out.

Then Elliot broke the kiss and Mio sat back hard on his legs.

"What time is it?" Elliot asked.

It was not the response Mio had expected to an excellent make out session. Something more along the lines of "holy fuck, that was the best kiss I've ever had," was more what he wanted to hear.

"What?" was the best response he had.

Elliot leaned to one side, jostling Mio and reminding him that he was very turned on. He wondered if he should move to the other side of the couch. If this was the sign their moment was over and checking the time was Elliot's way of telling him to slow the hell down.

But instead of pushing him away, Elliot frowned at the TV. "Damn."

Mio felt stupid and exposed. "What?" he said again, indignantly.

Elliot gestured to the screen.

Mio twisted around to see the cheering crowd, covered in confetti. The Times Square clock read 12:01am.

CHAPTER 5

❄

January 1st

"I wanted to make a big deal of kissing you right at midnight and making your New Year's wish come true but it looks like we missed it," Elliot explained, his expression sheepish, his eyes bright, and his mouth red from kisses.

"We *were* kissing at midnight."

"Yeah, but we didn't do the countdown and kiss thing. I thought I timed it right but...I guess I got nervous."

Mio shook his head slowly. He leaned forward and kissed Elliot gently. "I have no idea when you became so cheesy but I kind of love it."

"I could say it's the result of crushing on you since the 7th grade, but that would be even cheesier," said Elliot. His hand stilled on Mio's leg, like he just realized what he'd confessed.

"You've had a crush on me since 7th grade?" asked Mio, his voice a squeak.

It looked like Elliot was trying to decide if he should deny it or not. Then he said, "Yeah. Kind of since the moment I sat down next to you and you announced you were gay and told me I'd better be ok with it. It took me forever to realize it, but it was there."

"Oh my God, Elliot. I've been into you for like forever," said Mio, the words pouring out of him.

Then Elliot was kissing him again, gripping Mio's hip and pulling him closer. Mio let his hands slide down the front of Elliot's shirt and then played around with the hem, giving him time to stop if it was too much too fast. He broke the kiss enough to whisper, "Is this ok?"

After all, he didn't know Elliot's history of the last four years. He didn't know if he was someone who hopped right into bed with guys or if he was the cautious, thoughtful person Mio had known in high school.

"More than ok. I want you so much Mio," said Elliot, his voice gruff and so incredibly hot Mio thought his clothes would catch fire.

His hands slipped beneath Elliot's t-shirt and up the side of his bare chest, taking time to feel all the grooves of his skin, still not quite believing he was touching the body he'd dreamed about for so long. They were so close he could feel Elliot's erection, his hips jerking up as Mio reached his nipples and gave them an experimental flick. God, he could do this all night.

But Elliot's mouth was growing urgent against his own and his hands practically clawed at Mio's jeans, clearly desperate to get them off. "Mio," said Elliot with a gasp, breaking their kiss.

Mio moved down his jaw and began kissing his neck.

"Mio," Elliot gasped out again. "If we don't have sex right now, I'm pretty sure I'm going to explode."

Mio didn't stop his caressing and neck kissing. "We can't have that."

"No, we can't," said Elliot and, with seemingly little effort, set Mio down on the futon next to him and stood up.

Mio was about to protest when Elliot began stripping out of his clothes. The black shirt and gold beads came off, followed by the jeans and socks and then, finally, the boxer briefs. Elliot stood before him, naked, and it was better than anything Mio's fantasy had ever come up with. He gaped, he wanted, he yearned to reach out and touch.

"Mio?" asked Elliot, his fingers twitching like he was a second away from covering himself up again. "Do you need help getting your clothes off?"

Mio didn't need to be told twice. As quickly as he could, he wriggled out of his own jeans and sweater, sliding his underwear off and letting his eager erection spring free. Elliot's eyes were feasting on him and Mio had never felt so hot, so sexy, so excited in his life. Until he remembered. "Um, I don't have any condoms."

If Elliot was disappointed, he didn't show it. "I'm clean."

"I mean, me too but—"

"We can do that another time. Right now, I don't think I'd last long enough for either of us to get prepped."

Mio quite agreed and reached out to take Elliot's hand and pulled him down on top of him. For one hesitant second, Elliot hovered over him, looking like he wanted to say something else.

"No more talking," Mio mumbled, drawing Elliot closer until they were pressed completely together. Mio spread his legs, feeling slightly awkward on the narrow futon but not wanting to disentangle himself long enough to make it to the bedroom. Elliot leaned in and moved his hips, dragging his erection against Mio's. Mio groaned, it felt so good. When Elliot spit into his palm, slicked the top of both of their dicks, and then started thrusting up into his hand, Mio lost his mind.

They were both good sized and certainly more than a handful together. Mio reached down and his grip joined Elliot's as his hips grinding in counterpoint to Elliot's thrusts. They were both so worked up, so on edge already, that it didn't take long before they were both shouting their orgasms.

Mio opened his eyes. The weight of Elliot pressing into him felt so nice he didn't want to move. He wrapped his arm that wasn't a mess around him and rubbed his back clumsily. Elliot raised his head.

"I'm sorry I was too blind to realize I liked you back in high school and missed out on so many years of that," Elliot said, his voice tinged with regret.

Mio chuckled as much as he could. "Trust me, I was not at all good at sex in high school."

"Neither was I, but we'd have had fun fumbling around together," said Elliot, seeming determined to dig himself deeper into the hole of shame and regret.

"Fair enough. But now we get to skip all the fumbling and just have amazing sex together," said Mio, trying to soothe away Elliot's worry with his hand. "Enough apologies for one night. This was perfect and I want nothing more than to lie here with you forever but, um, we kind of made a mess and I'm gonna need another shower."

Elliot laughed and Mio felt his tired body try to respond to the vibrations it sent through him.

Then Elliot rolled off him and Mio followed him into the bathroom where they decided the best thing to do was jump in the shower together. Which led to more touching and kissing. The water had turned cold by the time they got out. Elliot borrowed some of Mio's sweats, which were too short on him in the most adorable way.

A short while later, they were snuggled together on the futon, full glasses of sangria in hand, and watching *Sleepless in Seattle*. The movie was reaching its climax when the door of the apartment opened and Agnes tiptoed in. Mio hit pause and noticed Elliot had fallen asleep, his head resting on Mio's shoulder. He looked so cute sleeping, his breathing even, his body relaxed and tucked up against Mio's side.

Agnes tiptoed over to him.

"How was the party?" Mio asked in a whisper.

"It was good." She looked down at sleeping Elliot. "Congratulations, Mio."

"What? For finding someone to kiss at midnight on New Year's?"

"Not just someone, Elliot."

"What do you mean?" They'd had only reconnected a few days ago.

"Mio, I love you but sometimes you're so dense. You made that wish when you were thirteen right?"

"Yes."

"And then a few days later you met Elliot?"

"Agnes, are you saying my wish came true when I was thirteen and I didn't realize it?" said Mio so loudly it woke Elliot up. He sat up blinking and looking blearily at the two of them.

"Oh, hey Agnes."

Mio grabbed Elliot's cute face in both hands. "Babe, you were always my New Year's wish," he said and gave Elliot a huge smacking kiss on the lips.

"Glad to hear it" Elliot mumbled and promptly fell back to sleep.

Agnes laughed. "You two are sickenly cute."

"We are, aren't we," said Mio, adjusting their position so he was lying down with Elliot curled up on top of him. He snagged the red blanket off the back of the futon and draped it over them. Elliot responded by snuggling in closer, his head on Mio's chest.

Agnes grimaced. "Alright. I'm going to go crash in your bed." She paused at the doorway to his bedroom and looked back at him. "Happy New Year, Mio."

"Happy New Year," said Mio and meant it.

ABOUT THE AUTHOR

CELIA MULDER

Celia Mulder hails from the lovely, yet unpredictable northern Michigan. She is a librarian, a former wedding planner, and an avid appreciator of all things campy and ridiculous. Friends-to-lovers plots are her catnip. She believes in three things-- the importance of representation, the awesomeness of Aquaman, and Buffy the Vampire Slayer. Her first novel *Celebrity Spin Doctor* was a double RITA award nominee.

Check out her website at www.celiamulder.com or join her newsletter.

❄

facebook.com/celia.mulder7
instagram.com/celiamulder

ALSO BY CELIA MULDER

THE CELEBRITY SPIN DOCTOR SERIES

Celebrity Spin Doctor

The Issue with Antons

Made in the USA
Middletown, DE
25 October 2020